DEADWATER

Books by Sarah Stegall

Farside
Chimera

The Phantom Partner Series

Deadfall

Research

The Truth is Out There: The Official Guide to The X-Files
Trust No One: The Official Third Season Guide to
The X-Files
I Want to Believe: The Official Fourth Season Guide to
The X-Files

DEADWATER

by

Sarah Stegall

Wavelength Books
2013

Deadwater
by Sarah Stegall

Printed in the United States of America.
First printing April 2013.

ISBN:978-0-9847738-6-2
Also available as an e-book:
eISBN: 978-0-9847738-7-9

To William M. Stegall, who introduced me
to San Francisco and taught me that a story
does not have to be true to be good.

Thank you, Daddy.

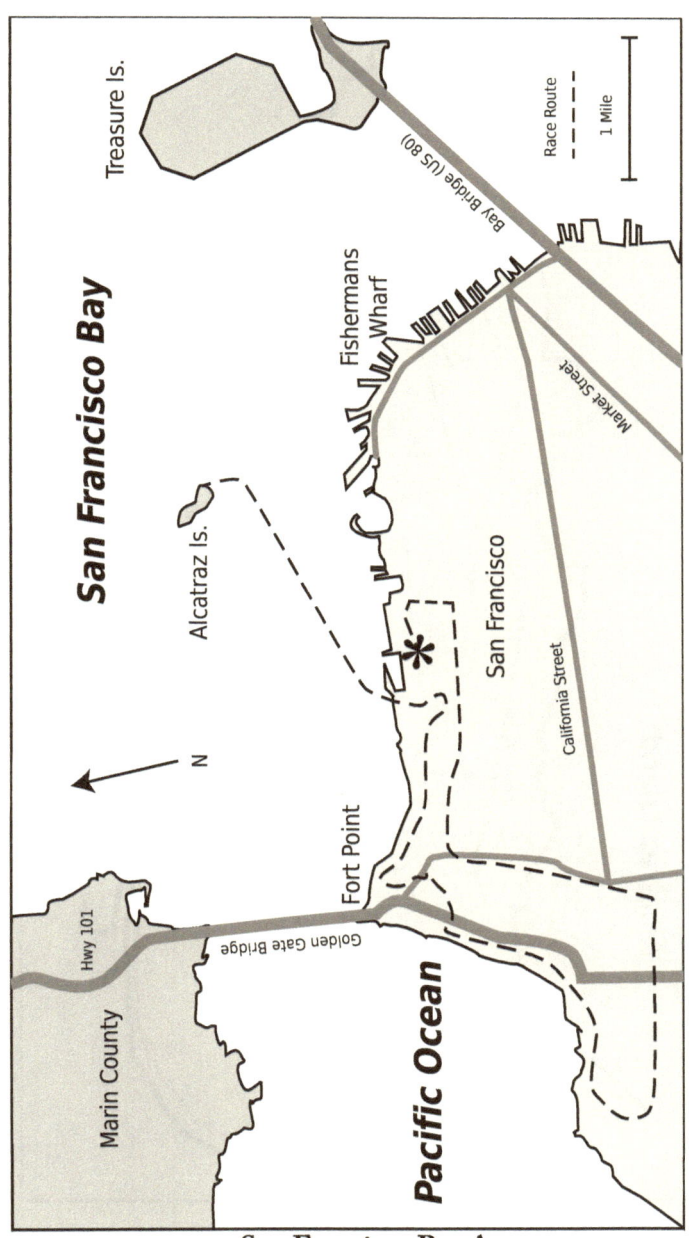

San Francisco Bay Area

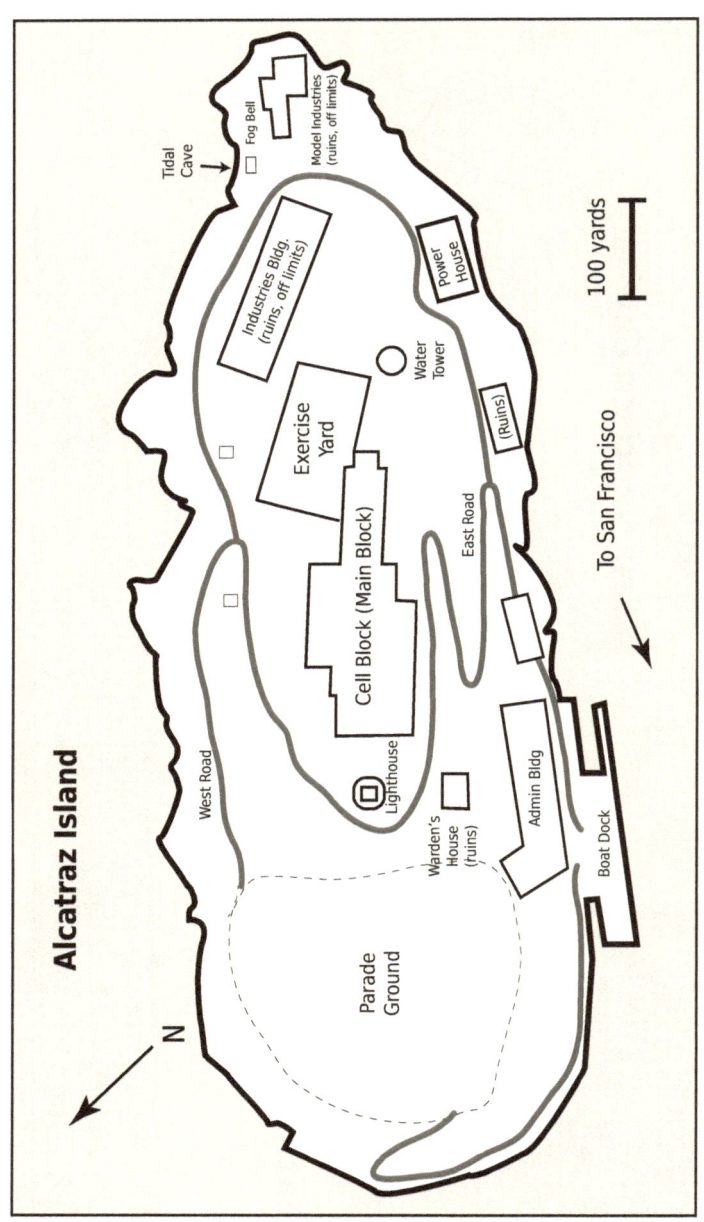

Alcatraz Island

CHAPTER 1

I was sitting in my office on a late summer afternoon in San Francisco, making out a bill to a client in an insurance scam. It had been two weeks of hard work, long hours of boring stakeouts, interviews with reluctant witnesses, and finally a nasty confrontation in the client's offices between me, the insurance adjustors, and the perpetrator. I came out on top and looked forward to both a hefty fee and a few days off.

The door opened and an excessively handsome man walked in. I wish that happened more often. He stopped a couple of feet inside the door, looked around, and asked, "Claire Turnbull?"

"Like it says on the door," I said, closing my computer file. "What can I do for you?"

He looked around the office again, like he was memorizing it. He was in his mid-twenties, extremely fit, with wide shoulders and slim hips and a shock of thick brown hair cut fairly short, not styled. He wore an open-necked yellow shirt whose short sleeves showed off well defined arms; his khakis were clean but didn't really go well with his athletic shoes. When he moved, his movements were compact, elegant, powerful. He stared around at the file cabinets, the pale olive walls, the open windows over Market Street.

"I'll grant you, it's not a flattering color. I'm planning on redecorating next month," I told him. "Something I can do for you, Mister—"

"Hancock. Marty Hancock. Just call me Marty."

"Have a seat, Marty. I'm going to have some coffee. Can I get you some?"

He shook his head, bit his lip, and sat down in the client's chair. Then when I stood up to get the coffee, he stood, as if it was an automatic response. Closer, I could see his eyes were brown, clear and very worried. Otherwise, it was a very nice face: wide brow, full mouth, high cheekbones, fine skin with a healthy tan. Movie-star good looks. I poured coffee in my cup from my little coffee machine, added various modifiers, and sat down again. He sat down at the same time. We were a well synchronized pair.

Marty's right knee bounced up and down rapidly. He didn't look as if he knew he was doing it. "A cop I talked to said you were good."

I sipped coffee. "I'll have to buy him a donut."

"Her, not him. Her name was Melton."

I nodded. "Inspector Suzette Melton and I go way back." All the way, in fact, to my days as a cop on the San Francisco force. But he didn't need to know that. "Why do you need a good private investigator?"

He looked at me then, his gaze unfocused. "I don't think my girlfriend is dead," he said abruptly.

"Why would anybody think that?"

"Nobody believes me. Even Inspector Melton."

"Got her reasons, I suppose," I said. "Maybe you can tell me who your girlfriend was. Is."

"Allison Farley," he said. He cleared his throat. "She was in the Alcatraz Triathlon."

I nodded again. "I read about it. Drowned during the swim part of the race last Saturday, or so they said." I set the cup down. "You don't think that's what happened?"

He shook his head violently. "No. I can't believe it. She was a great swimmer. Never panicked. She'd placed high in three races last year, finished in the top ten percent in the Oregon Coast Annual this spring. And she swam the beaches here all the time. No way she would have gone under in the Bay."

"If I recall, no body was found."

"Right." He clenched his jaw. "Which means she's not dead, as far as I'm concerned."

"But Suzette—Inspector Melton—clearly doesn't agree."

"She said it's happened before. People drown in the Bay, are never found."

I stole a look out my window; the blue sky was already hazing over as the marine layer off the coast gathered itself together. I knew that soon I would have to close the window against the late-August chill. "She's right," I said. "There are strong currents, unpredictable riptides. And of course, the big ships going in and out. Lots of bays and inlets. Lots of ways to get lost or swept out of the Golden Gate into the open sea." I could have mentioned sharks, crabs and other scavengers, but I'd made my point and there was no reason to creep him out.

"So you won't do it?" His tone was challenging.

"I didn't say that. Just want you to know what the odds are. They're not good."

"I can pay."

"That's a plus," I said. "But you need to know I can't guarantee results." I quoted him my hourly rate. "And I get expenses. You'll get a fully itemized bill."

He drummed fingers on his knee. "I can pay," he said again. "Do you need something up front?"

I hadn't yet said I'd take the case. I leaned back in my chair, wincing at the squeak. Gotta get that fixed. "First, why don't you tell me what happened."

"It was on the news."

"Yeah, and I'll make sure to check that out. But reporters don't get everything, and they don't get everything right."

He clasped his hands, jigged his knee a little more. I figured he was overcaffeinated and underslept, a common condition in my clients' cases. "She and I signed up for the Alcatraz—"

I held up a hand. "Start a little farther back. How long have you known each other?"

"Oh. Well, we met at a race, actually. The Monterey Bay Classic, year before last. We sort of clicked, and we dated awhile. She moved in a few months later. We often trained together."

"Got a picture?"

He pulled out a smart phone, tapped. He turned it around so I could see the image. Allison Farley had a merry smile, with good teeth. She had brown hair and brown eyes in a good face, a solid face somewhere between pretty and beautiful. "She's five foot nine, one-fifty but sometimes diets down to one-thirty-five if she's training," Marty said. He tapped again. "I'm sending this pic to you. Oh, and she has a dolphin tattoo on her left ankle."

"What's she like?"

His mouth quirked up a little, and I decided his smile must be something off the charts. He sat back in the chair, his eyes distant. "Smart. Sexy. Hot. We were terrific together. She's got this total focus, you know? When she's training, or competing, she is completely there. Nothing distracts her. I used to worry about it when she was doing road work; I was always afraid she might not pay enough attention to traffic."

"You two think about a future together?"

The half-smile vanished. He looked away. "No."

"Commitment issues?"

"Career issues," he said. He looked straight at me. "My career issues, really. I travel a lot. The more races I'm in, the more chances I have to win, the better the bonuses are. I'm sponsored by Tri-Right shoes and AllSportz ReHydrate. I'm supposed to fly to Canada tomorrow to start training for the Nonpareil Cup. It's one of the biggest purses in the world. And I should have been there last week."

I thought about my fee being dependent on this guy winning a race. In Canada. "Is this what you do? For a living?"

He shifted uncomfortably. "Mostly. Endorsements, purses. Also I do a lot of coaching, private training, that kind of thing."

"And how's the money in the racing biz?"

"Top winner in something like the Nonpareil can bring home twenty thousand."

I turned the coffee cup around on my desk. I should probably get some fancier cups. "Twenty large doesn't go far in San Francisco. You win a lot of races?"

He flushed. "Not as many as I'd like. Look, I've got your fee covered. Don't worry about it. I can write you out a check right now if you want."

Marty was facing me, with the door of my office behind him. Wyatt Earp stepped through the door. I don't mean he opened it and walked through, like Marty had. I mean he walked through the solid door, which is the kind of thing he does a lot. Wyatt died in 1929, so mortal obstacles like walls and doors mean nothing to him. We'd partnered up not long ago when it turned out I was the only living human who could see or hear him. I was still getting used to his sudden appearances out of nowhere. Wyatt wore his usual outfit—three piece black suit, white shirt, black tie, polished black boots. He was carrying his wide-brimmed hat in his hand, so his golden hair and walrus mustache dominated his lean face. The shoulder rig carried a Colt Peacemaker six shooter under his left arm. He looked about 35 years old, but he'd been born in 1848 and died in 1929; I'd quit trying to figure out what age that made him now.

"So you and Allison signed up for the Alcatraz triathlon," I said, for Wyatt's benefit.

"Yeah. No prize money, but it's a qualifier for other events, and it's local, so we both signed up. You do any competitive work?" He looked at my body skeptically. I didn't object, knowing it was not a sexual assessment.

"Who is this fellow?" Wyatt boomed. His voice was deep and gravelly. I ignored him. Marty, of course, couldn't hear him at all.

"I work out and I do a little aikido," I said to Marty. "Professional necessity in my line of work. I know a triathlon is three events, right?"

"Swim, bike, run," Marty said. "The Alcatraz race starts with a two and a half kilometer swim from Alcatraz Island to the shore, then twenty-five kilometers on bike, and finally a fifteen-kilometer run to the finish line."

"And Allison?"

"We rode out to the island on the same boat, but I lost sight of her after that."

"Before or after you went into the water?"

"Before. But you gotta remember, there were two thousand people starting that race."

I blinked. "Two thousand?"

"Are you talking about that race last week?" Wyatt said. He leaned against a wall and crossed his arms. I haven't figured out yet how he does that leaning bit, since he routinely walks through walls. Seems to me it would be like leaning against a fog bank, but I've never asked. Not sure I want to know.

"There are thousands of applicants to the race," Marty explained. "The contestants are selected by a panel of judges, on the basis of earlier qualifications. Then there are some amateurs who make it in, like Allison."

"She wasn't a professional? I thought you said she finished high."

He shrugged; the movement was graceful. Great shoulders, I thought, but then he's a swimmer. "She was good, no question, but not world class."

"And you are?"

"Yeah, I am," he said. "I'm not saying anything bad about Allison, she was a great athlete. But she was never going to be top dog. She didn't—doesn't have the drive."

I wondered if that was true. I wondered if there wasn't a bit of male ego in this mix. I decided it didn't matter much. "So you last saw Allison on the boat? You never saw her on the shore?"

"Dock. There's no shore at Alcatraz; the cliffs come pretty much right down to the waterline. The dock was so crowded one guy actually fell overboard and got disqualified for jumping the gun. It was a real mess."

"And that's the last you saw of her?"

"Yeah."

"Anyone else see her?"

"I dunno. Inspector Melton says no. I don't know if she asked everyone."

"No contact since the day of the race?"

"'Course not," he said.

"No one saw her come out."

He put one foot on the opposite knee. "That's what they say."

I leaned back in my chair. Outside, the fog had moved in, and the building across Market Street had enshrouded itself in a gray mist. "Here's how I see it, Marty, bottom line. No one saw her come out of the water. She has not been seen since the day of the race. No body has been found. Do you have any reason, other than hope, to imagine your girlfriend is still alive?"

The knee jigged up and down again. "No. Just my gut. But I trust it. I just can't believe she drowned. She could swim like a fish."

I didn't say that sharks ate fish. "So if she didn't drown, then your options are murder, amnesia or runaway." I ticked the possibilities off on my fingers. He stared at my hand, a tiny frown line forming between his eyebrows. "Does any of those sound more or less likely to you?"

"I … I don't know."

"Why ain't he more sure about her?" Wyatt strolled over to my side of the room, folded his arms across his chest, and stared at Marty.

I pressed my would-be client. "Okay. How about this: what does she do for a living? Did she make enemies?"

"Enemies? No, no, nothing like that. She sells commercial real estate. Even in this economy, she was making good money. Never had trouble with her half of the rent, that's for sure."

"He's hiding something," Wyatt said.

Marty had gone still, no more bouncing knees. I pressed him. "She cut anyone out of a deal? Leave a buyer or seller holding the bag, or think they were?"

He scowled. "No, I'm telling you."

"Okay, how about the two of you? Any fights lately? Problems in bed, or the rent, or who got the TV remote? Any outside liaisons?"

Wyatt chuckled. "Liaisons? Fancy word for it."

Marty stared at me. Then he stood up. "I guess I came to the wrong place."

"Don't get prickly," I said mildly. "If Inspector Melton had thought Allison was still alive, she'd be asking the same questions, but not nearly as politely."

He settled back in the chair, but stayed on the edge of his seat. "I didn't do anything to Allison," he said defiantly.

I sat back in my chair, saying nothing. Wyatt's eyes met mine, and I perfectly understood what he didn't say.

"Who's the other guy?"

He opened his mouth to reply, caught himself, and suddenly sagged. "I didn't think you'd take the case if you knew she'd moved out."

"When did she leave?"

"Five months and three days ago."

I drank coffee. "You two have a fight?"

He shook his head. "She just … left."

"She give you any reason?"

He put his face in his hands. "There was another guy."

Wyatt and I exchanged another glance. He looked disgusted.

"I … I followed her one night. She works out of the Spear Tower on Market. I waited until she came out after work, and then followed her. She met a guy at a bar and went home with him. I could tell they weren't strangers. I waited until three in the morning. All the lights went off. She didn't come out."

"Where was this place?"

He gave me an address on Washington Street. I raised my eyebrows. Pacific Heights was one of the most affluent neighborhoods in the City, with blocks of Queen Anne Victorian homes that sold for seven figures. "You didn't get his name? Or look him up in a street directory?"

"Rafferty. His name was on his mailbox."

"Have you called her? Threatened her? Did you follow her again?"

He shook his head vigorously. "No. Nothing like that. I stayed away. It … it made me a little sick to see her with that other guy." He twisted his hands together, hunched his shoulders. "Look. I know this looks … bad. But I love Allison. I just want to make sure she's okay. Where is she? What happened to her? I tell you, I know her. And she wouldn't have panicked, or gone under." He swallowed, scowled, swallowed again. "Just let me know where she is, if you find her."

"Kick him out," Wyatt said. "She done run off, and he just needs to learn to live with it."

I wanted to agree, but something in Marty's woebegone face stopped me. He might have lied to save his pride, but his concern for Allison looked genuine. And no one had found her body. "I won't take on a client who lies to me." I looked at him hard. Sometimes people broke into tears when I looked at them that hard. Mostly not. "I don't do interventions or abductions or anything like that. She's an adult, and if she has decided to drop out and start over, that's her privilege."

He was silent a long moment. "Okay," he said. "I guess I shouldn't worry about all that as long as she's alive. If you find her—" He swallowed again. "If you find her, all I'll ask is that you let me know she's okay, and tell her I love her and would like her back. As long as she's alive…" He slumped suddenly, and put both hands over his face. "I just need to know. I just need to know."

"Okay, just so we're clear. I'll look into this, if you want. My rates as stated. But if I decide there's nothing to investigate, or if you lie to me again, I'll cut an invoice and that will be it. Are we agreed?"

He looked like he wanted to argue, and opened his mouth to do so. Then he shut it, glared at his hands a moment, and nodded. "Sure. You want a check right now?"

"Yes. And your Social Security Number, two credit references, and your contact information. I'll also need you to sign an agreement."

He hesitated, flushing. "I didn't know there would be so much paperwork."

"Unlike Inspector Melton, my paycheck is not guaranteed by the taxpayers," I said. I opened a desk drawer for my standard packet. "I run a credit check on all clients, and the results go in the shredder as soon as the case is over. One of the things you're signing is a confidentiality agreement that I sign, too."

"Okay," he said with ill grace. "How long do you think this will take?"

"Depends on what there is to find," I said. "Sign here. And here. And fill this in."

He took the pen I offered and bent over my desk to read the forms. Over his head, I caught Wyatt's eye and raised an eyebrow. "I got the gist of that," he rumbled. "No reason to think that woman didn't drown. You're just taking this fellow's money."

I bore up under the brunt of his disapproval. Marty Hancock wrote me a check, shook my hand with a firm, manly grip and walked out, right through Wyatt Earp. Neither of them so much as blinked.

When the door shut, I shook my head. "Sometimes I wish I could do that."

"Please don't try it," Wyatt said solemnly. "I don't want to have to break in a new partner." We both remembered the time when he had accidentally touched me and I had wound up in the emergency room, with doctors restarting my heart. Apparently I'm not just the only person in the world who can see and hear Wyatt, I'm also the only one he can touch—and that touch could kill me. Now he shifted to his other foot and drawled, "You really think she's alive?"

"I don't know what I think until I do some looking," I said.

"Gonna get mighty wet looking for her," he said. "You any good at diving?"

"I don't plan to rent SCUBA gear, no," I said. "But the Bay's not that deep. Average depth is about twelve, fifteen feet. No more than a swimming pool at the Y."

"'Cept the Channel," he said. The Army Corps of Engineers had been dredging the ship channel from the Golden Gate up to the Sacramento and San Joaquin Rivers since shortly after the Gold Rush. "And the Gate itself. If I recollect, it's three hundred feet deep under the Bridge. Fast enough and deep enough to sweep a body out to the Pacific with nobody the wiser."

"But if she didn't get caught in a current," I said. "And didn't get eaten by sharks, and didn't hang up on some rock somewhere, I might find her."

He squinted at me. "You're looking for a corpse, then."

I shrugged. "Most likely explanation. The key, I think, is to find out where she was last seen in the water, and see if we can match that to any currents or underwater features."

"Like tracking a fugitive," he said. He swiped his forefinger across his mustache, right then left, absently. "That really what that fellow wants?"

"No," I admitted. "But people don't always get what they want."

He nodded thoughtfully. "Or what they deserve. Start with the police?"

"Of course. I'll talk to Suzette."

He put on his hat. He looked like an Amish undertaker. "Meet you at her office."

"Bring donuts," I said.

"That's not funny," he said, and walked through my wall into the thin air over Market Street.

Show-off.

CHAPTER 2

Inspector Suzette Melton worked out of a gray cubicle, one of many surrounding the bullpen at the Bryant Street headquarters of the San Francisco Police Department. I went through Security, giving up my gun and signing a waiver in case aliens stole it. I didn't know the officer manning the gate, so I got as far as the bullpen itself before running into the customary glare my presence inspired. Halfway down the hallway, Vic Delorey stepped out of a door.

"Hi, Vic," I said.

"What the fuck are you doing here?" he snarled. Vic Delorey was tall and thin and had a squinched-up face and didn't like me. The feeling was mutual.

Most SFPD cops didn't like me. It wasn't because I was a PI, it was because when I'd been a cop I'd been responsible—or irresponsible, depending on how you saw it—for the death of a fellow officer because I was too exhausted from lack of sleep to function. No matter that half the force suffered from chronic insomnia; the ingrained machismo of the Blue Code didn't allow for an excuse like that. So I resigned and became persona non grata to most of the force. Except Suzette. We'd been friends before my downfall and were friends still, for reasons too complicated for analysis.

"I'm on a goodwill tour," I told Vic, and walked down the hall past benches on which assorted miscreants sat or squirmed or slept or, in one case, urinated. I turned left through the door marked PERSONAL CRIMES DIVISION. I always wondered if there were impersonal crimes. Suzette's cube was across the maze of desks, which I threaded expertly. A balding black man in a tan shirt, loosened brown tie and shoulder rig looked up from his keyboard as I passed, stared at me stonily. I smiled. He continued with the drop-dead stare all the way to Suzette's cubicle. I paused at the entrance and tapped on the frame.

"Hey."

She looked up. Suzette Melton would have been a model in another life, had she had fewer choices. Her cheekbones were high, her carriage straight, and she was nearly six feet tall. Her eyes might have been a little close together, but they were large and intelligent. Her brown hair was cut short, managing to look both businesslike and fashionable. Today she wore navy pants and a navy linen blouse, and a short blue-gray jacket that reached her hips.

"That's new," I said. When Wyatt Earp stepped through the wall behind her, I did not blink. I'm proud of that. He nodded to me, did the leaning thing again, folded his arms and watched Suzette silently.

She stared into her computer screen, nodding. "The jacket? It's a Cavalli. It was on sale. How've you been, Claire?"

"Nice big buttons on it," I said.

"Better target for the bad guys," she said.

"Assuming they're sober enough to aim. You okay to talk about the Farley case?"

"Yeah," she swung around, crossed her legs, and steepled her fingers. Her eyes were gray-blue, focused. "What makes you think Allison Farley is alive?"

"I don't, really. But her boyfriend does, and he's paying me to make sure."

"Golly," she said, with no inflection. "What would we dumb cops do without you checking up on us? Probably shoot ourselves in the foot."

"And load up again," I agreed. "C'mon, Suze. The guy's just buying himself some peace of mind. Or at least as much as I can give him."

"If you can sell him peace of mind, let me know what the going rate is. I could use some myself."

"Are you going to give me a hard time on this, Suzette?"

She took in a deep breath, let it out. "Nah. It's just been a bitch of a case. First the media is roasting our ass, then the mayor's office, then the ITU—that's the International Triathlete's Union—and an insurance company or two, and oh yeah, her ex-boyfriend."

"In other words, same old, same old."

"Yup."

"So will the SFPD have a problem with me poking around in the case?"

"Case?" She uncrossed her legs, set her feet flat on the floor. "Claire, honey, there is no case. The poor woman drowned in the middle of a crowd of two thousand swimmers. The more of these events there are, the more people die in them."

"This happens a lot?"

"I looked into it a little, doing some background. Eleven people died in triathlons last year, most of them from drowning after or during a panic attack. There's even a term for it, 'swim freak'. It's not unusual."

"Is it unusual not to find the bodies?"

She was silent a moment. Her gaze slid past my shoulder to the wall behind me, where I knew she hung some of the stunning photographs she took on her vacations. One of them, of Yosemite Falls, had won a national contest. "Yeah," she finally said. "They've always found a body, as far as I know. Nobody really keeps tabs on these accidents."

"So you're being scrutinized."

She half smiled at me. "That's another reason I like you," she said. "You use words like 'scrutinize', right out in public and everything. Yeah, we're being scrutinized, and it's intense, but it's nothing we haven't handled before. It'll die down."

"Unless some nosy PI like me comes along and pokes the ant hill with a stick?"

"Unless that." She leaned forward and shifted a couple of files on her desk. "I wish I could help, Claire, but really, there's nothing there. We dragged—or rather, the Coast Guard dragged—the Bay. We searched the boat, the dock, the marina, the entire route of the race. Some of the Coasties even put in overtime, on their own dime, to look for a body. Nothing turned up."

"Interviews?"

"Half the participants in that race left town after the finish, before Allison's disappearance was even mentioned."

"No one missed her?"

"Not until the end of the race, when the race officials saw her bag was still at the pickup point. Then we got a call from race officials reporting her missing, and her boyfriend started yelling, and we stopped everyone we could and interviewed."

"You didn't follow up with the folks who left the race?"

Suzette sighed patiently. "Claire, I pushed the line as it was, since she hadn't even been missing twenty-four hours. You know when an adult goes missing, we can't assume the worst right away."

"You ran the boyfriend, right?" I tried not to tap my foot. I wished I could see her files.

"We ran them both."

Behind me, Wyatt snorted. "She don't miss a trick."

Suzette stared off at a corner of her cubicle, drawing on memory. "First was a guy named Marty Hancock, one of the contestants, called it in first when he waited for her at the finish line and she never showed up. Then a guy named Rafferty, Wayne Rafferty, one of the race sponsors, kicked up a fuss. He said Allison was his fiancée. We kept the two of them separated, and both men claimed her as a girlfriend."

"Busy lady," Wyatt chuckled.

"And you didn't think two-timing a guy is a motive? Come on, Suzette."

She raised both eyebrows. "Motive for what? Claire, we don't have a body. We don't have evidence of a crime. What we do have evidence of is a very unfortunate accident. If the woman was bouncing on two different beds, that's no business of ours."

"But if one of them found out about the other—" I knew Marty's reaction to Rafferty, or thought I did. But I had idea what Rafferty thought of his girlfriend's ex.

Suzette drummed fingers on the desktop. "I know. It bugs me, too. But again, I have no evidence, no probable cause, no reason to think either one of them is guilty of anything other than, at most, bad judgement."

"Do these two guys know one another?"

She shrugged.

I gave my voice the most formal Academy-style inflection I could muster. "So, Inspector, there's no reason, according to the San Francisco Police Department, that I can't look into this."

Suzette's cheek dimpled on one side as she suppressed a smile. "No reason at all. Now, Citizen, get out of my cubicle. And don't forget we're having lunch day after tomorrow."

"How could I forget?" I said as I rose. "It's your turn to buy."

Suzette's mention of food reminded me that it was past my lunch time. I headed down Bryant to Henry's, a cop bar and cafe. Heads turned when I went in, conversation muted, but no one actually ordered me out. Two of the three TVs on the wall were tuned to sports channels, the third ran a news show. I noted with dismay that Oakland was down two in the bottom of the eighth inning, with one out. I snagged a single table in a corner, and ordered a burger and fries. A guy in a leather jacket and a yellow Alcatraz Triathlon T-shirt came in and sat down at the next table.

"Hi," I said brightly.

He looked over at me with red-rimmed eyes under bushy gray eyebrows. "What?" he growled.

I pointed at his shirt. "Did you compete?"

He stared at me a minute and then looked away without answering. I guess maybe he was embarrassed, being as how he had a gut that looked like he was seven months pregnant.

Wyatt slid into a chair across from me. He made sure that our knees did not touch, so much so that half of the chair back protruded from his chest. It was a disconcerting look. The diners on the other side of me were engrossed in conversation or actively ignoring me, but just to make sure I pulled out my cell phone and pretended to make a call. No one pays attention to a woman talking to herself if she's holding a cell phone.

"You looking to share my fries, you're out of luck," I said. "Hey, is it me, or is every fourth person in San Francisco wearing an Alcatraz Triathlon T-shirt?"

"You're really going to take this case?" Wyatt said.

"Sure, why not?" I nodded my thanks as the waitress plopped down a plate in front of me with a hamburger slightly smaller than Milwaukee. "I could use the exercise."

"You don't need the money."

I squinted at him. "You think I do this for money?"

His shoulders rose and fell under the black jacket. "Reckon not. In any event, I don't think there's anything to find."

"You're such a pessimist," I said. He watched me as I polished off the hamburger. "First things first. We need to know if she came out of the water," I said. "Suzette won't let me access the file. I wonder if there's any way to get a list of witnesses, race contestants."

"I seen a newsreel about the race the day it happened," he said. "Likely there's more that didn't get shown on the teevee. How about you go ask if there's more?"

I blinked. "I can't believe it. You're getting to be downright media savvy." I punched a number I knew into my phone. "Next thing, you'll have a Facebook account."

A voice on my cell phone said, "Novak."

"Hey," I told it. "I'm looking for a liberal pinko media running dog. Know where I can find one?"

"They're all at a convention in Berkeley," the voice told me.

"Why aren't you there?"

"I'm only a moderate media running dog," he said. "Not pink enough yet."

"I need to see some footage of the Alcatraz triathlon," I said. "Stuff that didn't make the broadcast. You got any?"

"Miles of it," Art Novak told me. "Doesn't mean I can let you see it."

"Even if I show up with beer?"

"I'll leave the door unlocked." He hung up.

CHAPTER 3

Art Novak and I had met during one of my earlier cases, in the basement of the San Francisco Chronicle, which held the ancient, yellowing files of earlier San Francisco newspapers. At the time, he was a reporter for the paper looking for a break. My case gave him that break, and he'd parlayed it into a job as video reporter for the local TV news station, and still felt he owed me. I took a taxi to the address on South Van Ness, and found the four-story Sixties-era building that housed the station. I bypassed the showy front reception area, and instead walked around to the alley. Sure enough, the metal door was propped open with an old crate, and I stepped into a dimly lit hallway with a six-pack of local microbrew under one arm.

"Hey?" I called.

"Back here!"

I followed voices down an unlit corridor to a door and stopped in it, letting my eyes adjust. The edit suite was a large room with oak panel flooring, walls covered with posters, and big windows with vertical blinds. Several workstations stood against walls and crowded the floor, every one of them with a minimum of two video monitors; some had four. There were computer banks, video and DVR boxes, locked cabinets everywhere. Most of the stations were abandoned except for the litter of soft drink cans, candy wrappers and coffee cups. Somewhere in the pile to my left, a phone rang.

"Claire," a voice said. I turned and there was Art, as short, gorgeous and blue-eyed as ever. He kissed my cheek perfunctorily and led me over to a workstation in the corner, next to a radiator that probably hadn't worked since the Reagan administration. "I cued up the footage of the race," he said. "You want the whole thing?"

"Everything you have," I said. Wyatt stepped through the vertical blinds on the other side of the room and drifted over to stare into a monitor silently running a video of a car chase.

Art eased into a chair. He always looked better sitting down, where his body proportions didn't look so odd. His head was a little larger than it should have been for those shoulders, his arms were a little too long for his torso. I could never pin down what, exactly, made him look out of kilter, so I concentrated on his face. There was nothing wrong with those cheekbones or the laser blue eyes or the shock of black hair. "I shot some of this myself," he said. He tapped a couple of keys, and an image popped up on the screen. I caught a whiff of Art's aftershave. He wore jeans and a yellow T-shirt that said "Alcatraz Triathlon" in slanted letters across the front. It fit him very tightly. Very tightly.

"You're shooting your own stories? How egalitarian of you."

He shrugged. "I edit them, too, when I get a chance. Damn directors always want to mess with them."

"This is the start of the race?" I asked, leaning in to look. Across the room, Wyatt pulled himself away from the car chase and walked over. He stopped behind Art, leaning in for a look.

"There's the ferry taking the swimmers out." Onscreen, one of the Bay's commercial ferries, leased for the day, churned its way towards the Rock. Alcatraz Island squatted smack in the center of San Francisco Bay, looking forbidding and ugly and squat even in bright California sunshine. Wetsuited swimmers thronged the deck of the boat, elbowing each other, laughing, looking nervous. One couple was hugging one another. A redheaded guy was puking over the side.

"They all look alike in those wetsuits," I said. I pulled out my smart phone and dialed up the picture of Allison that Marty had sent to me.

"We can fast-forward through this if you want. Turn that wheel on the console next to you. Yeah, like that. It's sensitive, so be careful." He wasn't kidding; I barely touched the smooth knob and the image jumped forward. I dialed it back, and eventually found a speed that didn't give me motion sickness, while letting me see the footage.

"Okay, here they're arriving at the dock." Art pointed at the screen, leaning into me. "You know there's only one place to dock a boat that size on Alcatraz, right?"

"That's what I've heard," I said. "Oh, there they go."

Onscreen, the eager swimmers piled off the boat onto the National Park Service's big concrete dock. The piers supported a series of ramps that led up to a flat, paved area at the base of a steep bluff. A three-story former Army barracks towered over the paved area. The contestants trooped up the ramp; I slowed the playback to a funereal pace. I squinted at the screen, looking at every face. "There she is. Freeze this?"

"Okay," Art said. The scene went still, and I saw Allison Farley, half turned to speak to a woman behind her. She stood five foot nine, about one-forty, with a swimmer's slim build. Her brown hair was cut short, and she was tucking it into a light blue swim cap. I compared the image with the one on my cell phone.

"Looks like her," Wyatt said from behind Art.

"Well, now I can confirm she arrived at Alcatraz with the rest," I said. "Can we continue?"

"Sure," Art said, and tapped keys. "I recognize her. That's the woman who drowned." He looked at me curiously. "You're going to tell me what this is all about, right? Right?"

"Absolutely," I said. As the scene of barely organized chaos unfolded, I brought him up to speed. I carefully did not mention my client's name, or Art would be dogging his footsteps within the hour.

Art whistled. "If your client's right, and she's not dead, it's a helluva story," he said. He glanced at me out of those deep blue eyes. "If you find her, can I get an exclusive?"

"What's in it for me?"

"Dinner at Mekajiki, in Japantown. Asian fusion."

"Witch. You know I can't resist shrimp dumplings. Deal."

We watched more of the race footage: boring and disorganized, like most real-life events. On the turned-down soundtrack, I heard whistles and yelling as race organizers tried to line the contestants up in some kind of order.

"Ain't that your client?" Wyatt was leaning so far in his arm intersected with Art's shoulder. Neither of them seemed to notice.

I peered at the screen. "Can we freeze this? Right there, yeah. Can we zoom?"

"A little," Art said. He manipulated a few sliders, and the image enlarged and at the same time got fuzzier, more pixelated. "Who are you looking for?"

I poked a finger at the monitor. "That guy, right there. The wetsuit with the orange stripes."

Art tapped keys, and the image shrank, sharpened, then enlarged again. "This guy? Who's he?"

"Person of interest," I said shortly. I wasn't about to breach client privacy with a reporter.

"How come he ain't with that Farley gal?" Wyatt asked.

Marty Hancock stood impatiently in the second rank of swimmers lined up along the edge of the dock. I clicked through a couple of frames, and his number stood out clearly. It was good to have confirmation he was in the race, but otherwise didn't help me.

"Where is Allison Farley?" Wyatt muttered.

Onscreen, action picked up at the normal speed, and a race official standing on the edge of the dock raised a starting pistol. Just at that moment, one of the swimmers fell forward off the dock, arms windmilling, and hit the water with a mighty splash. Milling, yelling, confusion ensued. Two women wearing armbands and life vests jumped in after him, and a guy in a bright orange vest steered a Zodiac boat close in. The officials hauled the fallen man into the boat, which scooted away. The starter fired his pistol, and two thousand (less one) eager athletes leaped into the frigid waters of the bay, a mass of black neoprene and flailing limbs.

"And they're off," Art muttered. The vast majority of

swimmers wore identical black wetsuits, distinguished only by the occasional colored stripe down the side, difficult to make out once they were in the water. Onscreen, the images jiggled as the camera boat got under way. "This part makes me seasick," Art said. Indeed, the motion of the camera, the churning swimmers, all combined to render the scene turbulent and confusing. It was impossible to tell one swimmer from another. At least half of them wore blue swim caps like Allison's. "Where is she?" I groused.

A phone on the next console rang, and Art scooted his chair across the floor to answer it. I continued watching. The seething mass of swimmers looked like a random collection of arms, legs and heads. Officials in kayaks and inflatable boats kept pace with the crowd, and a Coast Guard rescue boat putt-putted along, keeping an eye out for swimmers in distress. Twice swimmers were pulled from the water, exhausted or hypothermic. I zoomed in, panned, enlarged— none of them were Allison. Several times I got lost and had to backtrack. Art kept up a low-voiced argument at the next desk, and Wyatt stood an arm's length from me, watching the swimmers and looking bored. It took over twenty minutes for the first swimmers to reach the shoreline at Crissy Field. The video feed switched to a land-based camera, to the relief of my queasy stomach.

"There's your client," Wyatt said.

On the monitor, Marty Hancock slogged out of the water and broke into a trot. He was already reaching back for the zipper pull on his suit as he jogged towards the assembly area. He passed the camera, and then another swimmer ran past. A few more, and then a mass of swimmers staggered or crawled out of the frigid water onto the grassy shore. A couple collapsed on their backs, breathing hard. "I don't see her," I whispered, glancing over at Art. He was still turned away, talking on the phone. "Do you?"

Wyatt shook his head, arms crossed, staring at the screen. "Not a sign of her."

The video went black, then another feed cut in. This showed

the assembly area, with swimmers stripping out of wetsuits. Underneath, most of them wore bike shorts and extremely tight shirts; as soon as someone shed a wetsuit, he or she would almost leap onto a bicycle and pedal away. My attention was drawn to a knot of spectators off to the side, dressed in street clothes.

"Who are those guys?" I mumbled.

Art was back. "Race sponsors," he said. "See? Deputy mayor there, representing Hizzoner. That's a Nike rep, and that woman with the red hoodie works for a bike manufacturer."

"That's Marty again," Wyatt said, bending closer. "He's not even looking for Allison."

I leaned away from Wyatt, which had me leaning into Art. Art didn't seem unhappy about that. "Can we freeze it again?" I said.

Sure enough, off to one side of the assembly area, Marty was faced off with a tall, rangy guy with brown hair. I hit PLAY and turned up the volume, but all I heard was a buzz of conversation, yelling, cheers, applause. "Who's he arguing with?" I said.

And it was clearly an argument: Marty was waving his arms, his body language showing threat and defensiveness. The tall man looked puzzled, then angry. He made a dismissive gesture and turned away, but Marty grabbed the man's arm and swung him back. Tall Guy shrugged him off, said something short, and stalked away. Marty stood glaring after him, then walked off camera towards the bicycle stands.

"Interesting," I said.

"That's Wayne Rafferty," Art said. "Owns a commercial real estate and contracting company. He's a major fundraiser for the Mayor, and bids on a lot of City contracts."

I made sure not to react to the name Rafferty. "Bad guy?"

Art shrugged. "Not that I've heard. At least, no worse than most guys who raise money for City politicians."

"How can a real estate developer afford to sponsor a race?" I asked. "I thought those guys were all jumping out of windows in this market."

"I did a profile on him three months back for the noon

Finance spot," Art said. "He's managed to keep his head above water with government work, refinancing, a bunch of tricks. His net worth is pretty high."

I cocked my head on one side. "So what's this guy's beef with Rafferty?" I asked, careful not to give my client's identity away.

"Beats me. Hey, that was my boss on the phone. I have a story down in Hunter's Point I need to cover. Can I drop you somewhere?"

I stood. "No, thanks." I put out my hand, and he took it and drew me close enough for a peck on the cheek. "Thanks again. For letting me look at the video," I said.

"You get what you needed?" Art opened a large cabinet and hauled out a camera case.

"Not sure what I needed," I said. "But I got something. I think. Listen, do you think you could ask around, see if any freelance photographers out there caught a shot of Allison?"

"The cops already asked."

"Yeah, but I'm offering money. Tell them there's a reward for any shot of Allison after the start of the race."

Art nodded. "Okay. I know a couple of guys. I gotta go." He hoisted the camera case. "See you, Claire. And don't forget about that exclusive, if this pans out."

"Sure," I said.

Art waved and left. Wyatt stood frowning down at a monitor, where an image of swimmers emerging from the water had frozen.

"What?" I asked.

He glanced up at me out of laser blue eyes. "Why didn't Marty stick around to see if Allison came out of the water? I know I would have, if my woman was in that race." He stroked one side of his mustache. "In fact, I didn't see those two together even one time."

"It was a busy race," I said. "And she had broken off with him."

He nodded, unconvinced. "You know the first suspect when a woman goes missing is the husband or boyfriend. Or former boyfriend."

"Does this mean you think she's just missing, not dead?"

"No, but I'll ride along and see how this plays out."

I collected my purse and started for the door. "I'm going to see this Rafferty character."

"Ten bucks says she's there, with her fiancé."

"I'm not betting against a professional gambler," I told him. He stepped through the wall and was gone.

I let myself out. As far as I knew, Art hadn't even touched the beer.

CHAPTER 4

I caught a crosstown bus; Wyatt didn't have to pay the fare, so he copped a seat next to the window. I sat across the aisle from him. It was the middle of the afternoon in the middle of a work week, so there were hardly any people on the bus, just a couple of tourists muttering to one another in German.

"Maybe we'll get lucky, and Allison Farley will be at home," Wyatt rumbled.

"You think she's shacked up with Rafferty?" I didn't bother with the cell phone ruse. The tourists stared at me, apparently talking to myself. Good; maybe they'd leave me alone. "We only know about the one night Marty followed her there."

Wyatt crossed his arms over his chest. "He said they weren't strangers. She spent the night."

"Sometimes you are so Victorian," I said, shaking my head. "Guess women didn't have one-nighters in your day, did they?"

He raised an eyebrow, and I suddenly remembered some of the rumors I'd read about Wyatt Earp. There was some evidence he and his brothers had run brothels, or at least acted as bouncers for them. But all he said was, "If she's home, you can send Marty Hancock a bill and be done with this."

"Be a nasty surprise for Suzette," I mused. "And for you, Mr. Pessimist."

"And the life insurance company," Wyatt said. At my look, one corner of the walrus mustache rose up in a half-smile. "Follow the money, Claire."

He had a point. It wouldn't hurt to look into any life insurance policies taken out on Allison Farley. In the meantime, I used my phone to discover that the address Marty had tracked

Allison to was owned by JackWay Holdings. I shrugged. That told me nothing, except that the house was probably a rental.

I walked down a quiet, tree-shaded street in one of the wealthiest neighborhoods in an already pricey City. I passed a short Hispanic woman walking three dogs at once, talking in rapid Spanish on her cell phone. I crossed Fillmore, a shopping street lined with jewelry stores, handbag boutiques, upscale salons and five banks. Across the street, I was once again in a quiet residential neighborhood.

The house Marty had tracked Allison to was a three story Victorian, light blue with white trim, set back from the street behind a miniature lawn and narrow iron fence. Classic bay windows on two floors sported butter-yellow shades, and pots of bright yellow flowers marched up the steps. A garage door at street level was closed. Nothing stirred but the leaves of the orange tree between the house and its neighbor ten feet away.

"Nice," Wyatt said. He stuck his hands in his pockets and rocked back on his polished boot heels, staring up at the house. "Cost a pretty penny, too."

I pushed the gate open and mounted the steps and rang the bell. Beside me, Wyatt passed directly through the wall and entered the living room. Through the glass inset in the door I could see him walking through the room—including walking through the sofa. I saw a narrow hallway that ran all the way to the back of the house; dark polished wood gleamed.

Wyatt wandered through the door at the end of it and disappeared. To the right of the entry, a carpeted stairway rose out of sight; to the left a buff-painted wall framed a large archway into a living room. Faintly I could hear rock music coming from somewhere. I rang the bell again, and heard a door slam upstairs. Feet trotted down the stairs, a shadow passed across the glass, and then a tall man wearing jeans and a flannel shirt with the sleeves rolled up to his elbows yanked open the door.

"Yes?"

"You're Wayne Rafferty," I said. "The developer?"

He looked impatient. "Yes? I'm extremely busy right now."

"My name is Claire Turnbull," I said. "I'm a private detective, and I'm looking into the disappearance of Allison Farley."

He scowled. "Have you been following me? Who the hell hired you?"

"Mr. Rafferty, I have—" I stopped because he turned and nearly leaped away. Only then did I hear that his phone was ringing.

Since he'd left the door standing open, I went inside and closed it. The hall smelled faintly of floor polish and oranges. I saw a modern kitchen through an open door further down the hallway, and heard a murmur of voices. I stepped into the living room on my left and looked around. It was immaculate, tidy, well cared for. Modern prints on the wall harmonized well with the clean, contemporary look of the furniture. I could practically smell money in the air.

Wyatt stepped through the wall next to one of the prints. One day he'll do that and run smack into me, and they'll be burying me the day after. Hopefully, not in the same cemetery as Wyatt. "Kitchen is neat as a pin," Wyatt said. "One automobile in the garage, a red one. I'll take a look upstairs now."

"Fine," I said. He circled around me and climbed the stairs. I had asked him once why he did things like that, climbing up a staircase as if he were real, rather than just levitating or something. He'd looked at me funny and said, "Habit." I'd left it at that. I stood examining a bookshelf which held a few volumes—mostly books on accounting and architecture—as well as framed photographs. I picked one up just as Rafferty came back.

"What are you doing in here?" he said loudly. His hand gripped a cell phone so tightly I could see white knuckles. "I didn't let you in. You're trespassing."

I turned to him with the framed photograph in my hand and held it up. "This is you, with Allison." In the photo, a grinning Wayne Rafferty embraced a smiling Allison Farley, his arms wrapped around her from behind. Her left hand lay over his, with a sparkly ring on it. "Is she here?"

"No. And I want you to leave. Right now." He strode over, snatched the photo from my hand, and set it on the shelf. He took my elbow to steer me towards the door.

I jerked my elbow out of his hand, stepping towards the open arch that led to the dining room. A glass topped table, surrounded by sleek black leatherette dining chairs, held a bowl of fruit. "Mr. Rafferty, it will only take a few minutes. Why won't you answer my questions?"

"I'm going to call the cops." He raised the phone.

"You can call the cops if you want, but then you might have to explain why you were arguing with Allison Farley's boyfriend at the race on Saturday, the day she disappeared."

He stopped, mouth open. "Boyfriend?" He glanced from me to the phone in his hand and then back. "Is he—do you know anything about this?"

His answer made no sense. "Has Allison called you?"

He stared, then shoved his free hand through his tousled hair. The belligerence was gone; I could see sweat on his forehead. "No. I don't know what you're doing or what you want," he said. "But I need you to leave." His voice was low, a little shaky. He avoided my eyes. "Please."

Something was wrong here. He wasn't acting like a grieving lover. "I want to know what you know about Allison's disappearance," I said. "Why don't we sit down and talk about it?"

He shook his head, his jaw clenching. "No. I want you to go."

I cocked my head. "Do you know where she is?"

"Get out."

"I will when you answer my question. Do you know where Allison is?"

He still wouldn't meet my eyes. "The cops said she drowned. She's dead." He said it loudly, as if trying to convince himself.

"Did you see her the day of the race? Did you see her get out of the water?"

He made an exasperated sound. "Dammit, will you go?"

I shrugged. "As soon as I get answers."

He stood like a clenched fist. "Very well. I did not see her the day she drow—disappeared. I don't know where she is. Where her body is. The cops told me she drowned. Her body hasn't been found. That's all I know." His eyes strayed to the photo on the shelf. "Except that I love her," he added very quietly.

"How long have you known one another?"

He didn't answer right away. Instead, he stepped past me to a cupboard, opened it and took out a bottle of Glenfiddich scotch. Putting down the cell phone, he snatched up a glass and poured a healthy slug and knocked it back. "About six months," he said. His voice was a little hoarse from the whiskey.

"Did you have a fight? Was there any reason she'd want to run away?"

He glared at me. "No. Hell, no. We were in love. We're planning to get married in eight weeks." He poured himself another dose. He didn't offer me anything.

"How long has she lived with you?"

"A little over five months."

"That's not a lot of time between meet and marry."

His mouth twisted up. "I didn't need a lot of time. The moment I met Allison, that was it."

"Where did you meet?"

He glanced down at the display on the cell phone. "Why do you need to know all this?"

"Maybe it will help me find her."

He looked at me out of red-rimmed blue eyes. "Find her? I told you, she's dead."

I crossed my arms. "You don't sound convinced of that."

He stared down at the empty glass in his hand. "The cops…"

"They've been known to be wrong."

He met my gaze again, and this time there was desperation in his face. "She's alive?"

I shrugged. "I don't know yet. I'm asking around. At any rate, don't you want to know for sure?"

His shoulders slumped, and he closed his eyes. He suddenly looked exhausted. "Yes." He swallowed. "To answer your question, we met when I was bidding on some commercial property she was selling. A building in the Tenderloin. I buy them, renovate, sell them."

"There a big market for those right now?"

He looked at me dully. "What? Oh, yeah, some. Even these days. Not much margin, but I get by, and in any case it's a long-term investment. Anyway, we met, then we had coffee, then we had dinner. Then I asked her to move in. A week later she did."

"Wow," I said. "Talk about your whirlwind romance."

A corner of his mouth curled up, fleetingly. "Whirlwind. Yeah, that's Allison."

"Did Allison have any enemies? Personal, professional? Sports rivals?"

"Not that I know of. She got along well with clients, everyone."

"Did you two argue?"

He stared at me over the rim of his glass. "That's ridiculous."

"She left one man for you," I said evenly. "Could she have left you for another?"

His fist tightened around the glass. "Go to hell."

"Did you know when you two met that she had a boyfriend?"

He shook his head. "You're off. Way off. There was nothing wrong between us. I want you to leave."

"I can't believe you had no arguments at all."

His lip curled, half smiling, half bitter. "She wanted to invite her bitch of a mother to the wedding. I said no. She didn't push it. That was the extent of our disagreements."

"Tell me about the day of the race."

He poured and drank, a little more slowly now. "What about it?"

"Just everything you remember."

He stared past me, thinking. "She left before me; she usually does on a race day. I found her breakfast dishes in the sink when I came downstairs."

"Did she pack her usual competition bag?"

He shrugged. "Sure."

"Why were you arguing with Marty Hancock?"

"Who?"

That was a mistake. He said it too quickly, and didn't meet my eye. "You know who he is," I said. "The ex."

"The little prick wanted her phone number. Wouldn't stop

bugging her, wanting to get back together." His gaze sharpened. "Do you think he did something to Allison?"

"When did you know she was missing?"

His hand on the glass tightened. "When she didn't cross the finish line. I was waiting for her, with champagne. But she never arrived, and then her bag was left unclaimed at the staging area."

Wyatt came down the stairs, then stopped and listened behind Rafferty.

"Were you the one who called the police?"

He shook his head. "The race director did, I think." He sighed, capped the whiskey and put it away. "Then all hell broke loose. Cops, Coast Guard, race officials."

"Mr. Rafferty, do you believe Allison is dead?" I looked at him keenly.

Wyatt walked around the table so he could see Rafferty's face.

Rafferty blew out his cheeks in a huff. "The cops haven't found a body," he said carefully.

"But do you believe it?" I pressed.

"I—"

His phone rang. He snatched it up, staring at the screen. "Hello?" His eyes went wide. "Oh. Yes. Yes, I will. Hold on." He looked at me and clutched the phone against his chest. "I … I have to take this. Can you go now? Please? This is a … really important business deal."

"Sure," I said. I wished I could see who was calling him. "See you at the memorial service?"

"What?"

"For Allison. You are holding one, right?"

He looked at me as if I were speaking Martian. "Sure. Whatever," he said.

I nodded, and walked out of the room. He followed me, still clutching the phone to his chest. He opened the door for me. "I'll be in touch," I said.

He closed the door in my face. As he turned away, he started up the stairs and out of sight.

I waited, but he didn't come back down.

Wyatt stepped through the closed door. "There was a

woman living here." He pushed his hat back on his head, letting his blond hair fall onto his forehead. "Women's stuff in the closets. Picture of her and him next to the bed. Suitcases are in the attic, so if she packed, she packed light."

"You think she took off?"

"I don't know." His gaze met mine. "Claire, there's something else. I saw signs of a fight in his home office."

"What kind of signs?"

"On the second floor, he's a got a bedroom made up with a desk, a computer, file cabinets. There's broken glass, a dent in the wall as if someone had thrown something. A coffee cup spilled on the floor, never cleaned up."

I met his gaze. "And in the rest of the house?"

He shrugged.

"What does that tell you?" I asked, already pretty sure what he would say.

"Guilty conscience," Wyatt rumbled. "I think maybe he had a fight with Allison and now he's sorry."

"So now you think he killed her?"

He shrugged again. "Either way, she's dead."

"Either way, there's no body," I said.

Wyatt nodded thoughtfully. "I'll stick around here," he said. "I want to hear who he's talking to."

"I think I need to talk to our client again."

Wyatt looked amused. "Our client? Does this mean I get part of the fee?"

"Don't get greedy. I'll see you later tonight, my place."

Wyatt turned away, turned back.

"What?" I said.

"Rafferty. On the phone. He didn't sound guilty. Or angry."

I nodded. "He sounded frightened."

Wyatt nodded once and then strode back up the sidewalk.

On the street, a man wearing earbuds jogged by, intent on his own inner world. Down the street a car honked. The sun shone hot and bright. I wondered where Allison Farley was, and if she could see the sun.

CHAPTER 5

I tracked my client down at his apartment, a shabby four-unit off of 28th Street, a couple of blocks from Dolores Street. It had once been tan, and someone had tried to paint it white and had quit halfway through the job. Marty lived on the second floor, the better to hear the Muni L line clank past day and night. His landlady lived on the first floor. When she answered the door, a cloud of tobacco smoke billowed out and I coughed.

"Yeah?" Fat and fiftyish, with a mustache. A cigarette bobbed between her lips. "We ain't got no vacancies."

I shoved my detective's license under her nose; she didn't even glance at it. "Can I ask about your tenants, Marty Hancock and Allison Farley?"

She drew in a lungful of smoke and let it out slow. "Who are you?"

I offered her a look at my license again and she ignored it, beady weasel eyes on mine. "I'm Claire Turnbull," I said. "I'm looking into Allison's disappearance."

"Yeah," the landlady said.

Patience, I told myself. "Can you tell me how long she's lived here?"

"Angie!" a man's voice called from the dark room behind her. "What the fuck is going on out there?"

Stolidly, Angie drew another drag. "She don't live here," she said, as if the man had not yelled.

"When was the last time you saw her?"

"Hey, close the goddamned door before the goddamned cat gets out!" The shout was followed by a bout of wet coughing.

35

"She don't live here," Angie said again. She closed the door in my face.

I went up the open stairs to 4-B. When I rang the door, Marty answered wearing bike shorts and a red T-shirt with a sports logo.

"Oh, hi!" He stepped back and waved me in. "Have you found her already? That was fast!"

The living room walls were plain white, relieved here and there by posters for races and triathlons. The bare wooden floor of the living room showed dust bunnies, and the furniture consisted of one large tan couch, a couple of crates that served as a coffee table supporting a collection of racing magazines, and a huge HD television mounted on the wall. The dingy curtains probably dated from the Korean War. The entire left wall was taken up by three racing bikes hanging from supports or propped against the wall; on the floor lay a couple of helmets, a spare set of racing pedals, and a bicycle tire repair kit. Off to one side sat a small rack with some weights and a barbell.

"You want a beer?" Marty didn't wait for my answer but headed for the narrow kitchen. I followed him. The kitchen was neater than the living room; in fact, it didn't look as if anyone cooked here at all. That suspicion was confirmed when Marty opened the white, beat-up refrigerator. Inside I saw lots of sports and protein drinks, a couple of beers. There were no dirty dishes on the counters, no toaster, no blender.

Marty handed me a beer and I leaned back against the kitchen counter. "You lied to me, Marty."

"No I didn't! I swear! Everything I told you was the truth."

"You didn't tell me you got into a fight with Wayne Rafferty the day of the race," I said. "What was it? You wanted her back? Did you tell him to dump her? Threaten him?" I thought of the fear in Rafferty's voice and face. "What did you do to Allison?"

His face drained of color. "You think I…you're crazy." He glugged beer. "You're out of your fucking mind. If I had done something to her, why would I hire you to find it out?"

"Maybe you think you're clever," I said. "I had a case not long ago, where a client tried to game me. Didn't work out too well for that client. I'm a little sensitive to that sort of thing."

"I didn't hold out on you." Carefully, he set the empty bottle on the counter top. "I just didn't think it was important. All I wanted was her phone number."

"Why? You already told me you followed her home. Did you want to call, leave messages? Talk dirty to her? Why do you want the number of a woman who's marrying another man?"

"He's all wrong for her!" Marty burst out. His face turned red, and a vein stood out in his forehead. "She's confused. Dazzled. He'll cheat on her, use her."

"That's her call, Marty."

His hand made a fist, then relaxed. "Just find her," he said. His voice was shaky. "I'm not a stalker. I won't hurt her. I…I won't even talk to her. I just want to know if she's all right. And I can't look for her myself. I don't know how, don't know where." He looked up at me, and there were tears in his eyes. "No one is looking for her. Nobody cares."

"I haven't found any evidence that she ever came out of the water," I said quietly.

He rubbed his eyes. "Look, maybe I can help. I can…I don't know. I can knock on doors or something."

I finished off the bottle and thought about Allison Farley. If it had just been a matter of finding her for Marty, I'd have quit the case right then. But there was the fact that Allison was missing and no one had seen her since the race. If she'd left Marty, that was one thing. If she'd left Rafferty, that was one more thing. But Allison Farley seemed to have left the world.

"I'll keep looking. But I'm telling you again: if I find her safe and sound, and she's gone because you were stalking her or harassing her or giving her any kind of hassle, you will have bought yourself a world of trouble."

"Just tell me she's okay," he said. His eyes looked haunted. "Tell me she's alive."

"If she is, I'll do my best to find her. But it will be up to her whether I tell you where she is."

"Great! Thanks! Oh, thanks so much!" He jumped to his feet, almost knocking over the beer bottle. A criminal waste. He smiled, and I discovered that my hunch had been right: his smile was off the scale of gorgeous. But I was beginning to think he was pretty dim behind that bright smile.

"As long as we understand one another." I stepped back to let him pass, and we went back into the living room. I took my phone out of my pocket, and when he turned to show me out, I snapped off a photo of him. He looked surprised. "What's that for?"

"Just being careful," I said.

He stuck his hand out eagerly. "We're okay now, right? You'll find her?"

"I'll try," I said.

"Great!" he said, and stood watching me as I went down the steps to the street.

CHAPTER 6

I live in North Beach, the old Italian quarter of San Francisco. Thronged with tourists year round, it has great restaurants and entertainment. But it also has some steep hills, and I live on one of them. I panted my way up from the bus stop on Columbus, almost wishing that the City had put stairs instead of sidewalks on the sides of the street. However, when I got to my three-story building in the middle of the block, I remembered why that would not be a good idea. The first floor is my favorite Italian restaurant in the world, Benetto's, and the smells coming out of it could put calories on a walking stick. I often eat there, so the more climbing I did, the better. As I arrived, Al the maitre d' was unlocking the front door for the evening.

"Claire." He nodded, his pale skin showing through the thinning black hair on his skull. He had a huge white apron tied around his expansive middle. He's one of the sons of the owner, Mamma Benetto.

"Al." I nodded back. I unlocked the gate to the building entrance, locked it behind me, and went up the narrow stairs. Coming from the bright daylight inside, my eyes had not quite adjusted, but I have climbed those stairs in the dark and trotted right on up. As I stepped onto the landing, the door to my right opened and a bicycle attacked me.

"Hey!" The wheel hit me on the shoulder and I dodged to my left.

"Oh!" Brown tousled hair, sparkling brown eyes, lean cheeks with a manly beard. Wide shoulders, muscled arms and a very, very tight bike shirt. He carried the bicycle on one shoulder as easily as if it were a towel. "I'm so sorry, I didn't see you." His voice was deep and warm.

Another tousled head, this time with black hair, peered around the edge of the door. "Claire! Darling, we didn't know you were home!" My neighbor, Justin, squeezed past the guy still standing in the doorway. His aftershave preceded him by seconds, and as he pressed a kiss to my cheek he appeared to be wearing nothing but an apron. A very small apron. "Here, let's just step by so Ronnie can get that thing through the door."

"Uh, thanks." The cyclist rotated the bike so it was vertical, and started down the stairs.

Justin grabbed his shoulder. "Wait! You haven't said if you'll be back for supper!"

The cyclist turned, and I saw that his helmet hung from one brawny forearm. "I dunno. Depends on how I do on California Street."

"You're riding up California Street?" I said, impressed. California Street climbs from the flat Embarcadero to the top of Nob Hill in a steep, uncompromising line.

"Up, and then down again," he said. He grinned, and his teeth were so white I needed shades. "Twice."

"Are you in training for something?" I dug in my trouser pocket for my apartment key.

He shifted the bike for a firmer grip. He looked capable of standing in that stairwell all day, hoisting a bicycle. "Just finished the Alcatraz, and I'm trying to stay in top condition for the Coast Classic next week."

"And he eats nothing but carbs," Justin said. "I swear I don't know where he puts them. Claire, this is Ronnie. Ronnie, Claire is my next door neighbor."

The cyclist freed one hand and extended it. "Ron Stedman," he said, glancing at Justin. "I'm staying with Justin 'til I leave for Monterey."

I shook a hand the size of a dinner plate. "Nice to meet you. Did you say you competed in the Alcatraz triathlon last Saturday?"

"Yes! And he finished in the top ten percent!" Justin crowed.

I'd found my key, but paused. "Would you mind answering a few questions about it?"

Ron smiled a little uncertainly. "Uh. Sure. Right now?"

Justin looked from one of us to the other, rather like a small owl. I was not exactly sure how to handle this. What is the protocol in asking your gay neighbor's new squeeze into your apartment? But I couldn't interview him standing in the hallway. The scent of basil wafting up the staircase decided me.

"How about both of you join me for dinner at Benetto's?"

Justin's eyebrows shot up. "But my truffle chicken—"

"Sounds great," Ron said. He looked at Justin. "I promise I'll have the chicken tomorrow."

Justin sighed. "Will there be tiramisu?"

"What's an Italian dinner without it?" I said. My gaze met Ron's and something heated the air between us. "Seven?"

"Seven thirty," he said, and his voice was a purr. "I'll need a shower." Nodding at me, he trotted down the stairs.

Justin fanned himself with one hand as I let myself in my apartment. He followed me, making panting noises. "Is he adorable, or what?"

I flung my purse onto the stand next to the door. It fell over, and Justin righted it. "I guess," I said. Justin always had the cutest boyfriends in San Francisco, a town full of beautiful men. "I'm sorry if I broke up your date."

Justin adjusted a framed photograph of Mount Shasta that Suzette had given me the year before. "Oh, it's not a date," he said absently. "And I had only just started the chicken. Maybe I'll marinate it overnight in pineapple and white wine. Or do you think lemon juice would work better?"

I yawned. "Not sure," I said. As Justin continued around my room, bending over, picking up things and tidying, I realized that I had been mistaken. He was wearing more than an apron. He was wearing a thong. I closed my eyes.

"Hmm. Three cushions on your couch, a throw, two books and an empty wine bottle. Also a new wine stain. Claire, you've been sleeping on the couch again," he said.

Eyes still closed, I shook my head. "Not sleeping, no."

A giggle. "Well, congratulations, then!"

"And not what you're thinking," I said. When I opened my eyes, he was folding the colorful quilted throw into neat thirds. "Justin, you're going to make some man a wonderful wife someday."

A big sigh. "Maybe, but where will I find him? The good ones are all taken." Considering the eye candy I had just met on the landing, I found this remark puzzling, but let it go. Traipsing past me to the recycling bin, Justin patted my shoulder. "But seriously, hon. Still not sleeping well?"

"Not sleeping at all," I said. "But I'm okay."

"I wish you'd see that neurologist I told you about," he said. "You know, the one who came to my Gay Pride party? He says they do things with brain chemistry today that can help."

My sleeping disorder is so far beyond conventional insomnia, it defies description. Since childhood, I have had trouble falling asleep or remaining asleep. It's not unusual for me to go up to three days without sleep. Oddly, my lack of sleep rarely impairs my day to day functioning.

"No time," I said. The truth was, I was tired of fighting it. Years of failed treatments, diagnoses that didn't pan out, and the well-meaning but useless advice of everyone in the world had made me weary of the subject. "I'm fine, Justin. Thanks."

He leaned back against my refrigerator, studying me. "You do look pretty normal," he said. "Is that a bruise?" He touched my jaw on one side.

"Got that at the dojo," I said. "My sensei was teaching me a new hold."

Justin smiled. Between the puppy-dog eyes and the chiseled cheekbones, he looked a little like Adrien Brody. "He needs to teach you better, then."

"She," I said. "My new sensei is a woman. And she kicks ass."

"Let me know if you need anything, then," Justin said.

As he passed me, bare butt and all, I shook my head. "You do remember that Benetto's has a dress code, right? I don't care if Mamma is our landlady, she's not going to let you in the door like that."

Justin stopped, posed, and cocked his head flirtatiously. "Really?"

"Seriously. Wear pants."

"Oh, all right. I'll be over at seven." He paused at the door, nodding at the window over the street. "And water that poor plant, will you?"

I called down to Al and made reservations at the restaurant, then went for a shower. I was towelling my hair dry when I heard someone whistling in my living room. I slipped into sweatpants and a tank top, and found Wyatt standing with his hands in his pockets, staring out of my front window and whistling to himself.

"Find anything useful, Marshal?" I asked. "A body in the basement?"

He turned, caught sight of my outfit, and frowned slightly. I get the impression Wyatt does not approve of modern casual female dress. But he only said, "No."

"Well, that's good news for the client, anyway," I said. I draped the towel around my neck and went to the refrigerator in my tiny kitchen for a bottle of water. "You calling it a night?"

"No, I was just coming to tell you I think I'll stay on there a while, see what he does."

I eyed him, cop to ex-lawman. "You're thinking the boyfriend is a good suspect."

Wyatt shrugged. "Still no evidence of a crime, but yes."

"This mean you no longer think she drowned?"

He sighed, and looked away. "Still the best answer. But I was thinking, while I'm following Rafferty, how about you follow our client? Or turn about."

I shook my head. "I have a date."

He froze in the act of putting his hat on. He looked at me quietly a moment, blue eyes intense. "A … date."

I squared my shoulders. "Problem?"

He shook his head, straightened, still holding his hat. "No, ma'am. Your business." His mouth made a tight, thin line under the mustache.

"I sense disapproval," I said.

He turned the hat in his hands, glancing away. "None of my business."

I sipped more water. I sensed a trust issue developing. "But I'm asking, so now it is."

He looked at me. "Who is this fellow? How well do you know him? What if he ... maybe I should come along. Keep an eye on him."

I smiled. "Thanks, Dad, but I don't think that's necessary."

He looked solemn. "Will you take your gun?"

I laughed. "Not on a first date." I turned over a hand. "Wyatt, we're eating at Mamma Benetto's. And I'll be with Justin, from across the hall." I explained about meeting Ronald.

Wyatt seemed to ease a bit. "So this is related to your, uh, investigation?"

"Absolutely," I said. "I want the lowdown on this race, from someone who was in it." Wyatt didn't need to know that Ron Stedman was also hotter than a hot thing.

"I'll be back after awhile, then." He put his hat on and turned to go (through my front window), but then turned. He looked past me, a little awkwardly. "Have a good time." He stepped through the glass before I could reply.

I stood for a moment, thinking about Victorian mindsets and modern social life. Then I went to dress for my date.

CHAPTER 7

I met Justin on the landing at seven. He wore a black T-shirt under a gray jacket, gray slacks and polished black shoes. His eyes widened when he saw me. "Oh, nice!" he chirped. "Purple suits you."

"Thanks," I said. I'd picked a short violet dress that gathered along one side, with long sleeves. I was wearing cork soled wedge sandals and carrying a tiny leather messenger-style purse. It did not contain a firearm. "And you're wearing actual pants."

Ron stepped out behind Justin and closed the door. He wore tight fitting jeans, a white T-shirt that looked as if it had been sprayed on, and a leather bomber jacket. I fought not to drool. "How was your ride?"

"I made pretty good time," he said. "Better than I thought I would. San Francisco suits me." We proceeded downstairs to Mamma Benetto's.

Al met us, smiling, and conducted us through the crowded restaurant with its traditional white tablecloths and flickering candles. He had saved us a booth near the kitchen, knowing Mamma would be out to say hello. There wasn't much room to maneuver in the little restaurant, and somehow I wound up next to Ron, across from Justin. I had thought Justin would want to sit next to his boyfriend, but it felt awkward to mention it so I said nothing. Al handed around menus and departed.

On my right, Ron fiddled with the table setting. "So. Justin tells me you're a detective."

"A private investigator," I said, reaching for my ice water.

I glared at Justin. "And he's not supposed to be talking about my cases."

"Oh, I didn't, Claire," Justin said serenely. "Not with real, actual names or anything. But Ron was asking about you and I—"

"What's good here?" Ron opened his menu in Justin's face. His thigh bumped mine; there was tension in him.

"Whatever Mamma has cooked up for the kitchen staff," Justin said before I could.

"She owns the building as well as the restaurant," I explained. "And takes it all very seriously. She cooks dinner for the employees every night, and it's always superb. Hey, Al," I said as he re-appeared, pad in hand. "What's Mamma working on tonight?"

He smiled smugly. "To start, a *zuppa Emilia*. Soup with millet, beans, chickpeas, and green peas, seasoned with pepper and garlic. Then a marinated calamari salad, *arista alla florentina*, four-cheese ravioli with the tomato-basil cream sauce, and *schiacciata* for dessert."

"What's this *arista* thing?" Ron asked.

"Roast pork with rosemary," I said. Everyone looked at me. "What? I don't actually have the menu memorized." Not quite, anyway.

Ron glanced at me, then at Justin. "If that's what you guys want, okay. But I don't usually eat pork."

"In that case, have the ravioli," I said.

"Ravioli's high in carbs. Gotta load up for the race. I'll have that," Ron said.

"Me, too," I said.

We gave salad and wine orders, and Al went away. The smells coming out of kitchen when he went through the door were magical.

"How long have you been a private eye?" Ron asked.

Private eye? Did people still say things like that? "Since I quit the cops," I said.

"You didn't like being a cop?"

"My husband was killed in the line of duty," I said. "And I kind of fell apart. I was putting lives in danger."

"I'm sorry to hear about that," Ron said. He put his arm next to mine on the table. "How long ago was that?"

"A while." This was a more intimate conversation than I was comfortable with, especially with Justin sitting right across from us. He was looking from me to Justin with bright, lively eyes. "How long have you been competing in triathlons?"

Ron leaned back into the corner of the booth so he could see both me and Justin. "In amateur events, about five years. Three years professionally, since then. This was my third Alcatraz event."

"Tell me about racing. Tell me what it takes to compete professionally."

He rubbed his chin, thinking. "It takes all your focus, all your concentration. It's a balancing act, trying to make sure you don't spend all your energy at once, but don't fall so far behind it takes a superhuman effort to catch up. You plan a race in micro-stages, you calculate every edge. Like the deadwater."

Justin looked at him. "Deadwater? Sounds ominous."

"That's a racer's turn. When you're swimming behind a boat, it leaves slack water in its wake. It's called deadwater, and it's easier to swim in because there's no turbulence or waves to fight."

"How much time can you gain doing that?" I speared a ravioli and it skipped across the plate.

"Maybe two seconds. That's what it comes down to, shaving a second here, a second there. Transitions, from one event to another, are where you can gain or lose time." He reached for a breadstick, broke it. "Like, when you're getting near the end of the swim, some athletes start taking off their wetsuits before they're even out of the water, trying to gain a half-second. You load your helmet, sunglasses and gloves on your bike before you go in the water, so you don't have to go through your equipment bag when you come out. This afternoon, I was going over a couple of shortcuts on the downhill part of my ride, like how fast I can get out of my bike shoes into my running shoes."

"What about the other people in the race? Are you paying attention to them?"

He shook his head, then straightened up as Al placed soups and salads on the table. "Not really. I mean, I'm aware of who's around me, who's ahead in the times, as much as I can be. But most of the time I'm concentrating on what I'm doing, what's coming up, where the exciters are—"

"Exciters?" Justin asked. "Sounds fun!"

"That's what they call the transponders used in race timing."

"Transponders?" I asked. I spooned soup; it was excellent, up to Mamma's usual standards.

"Race timers. You know, to keep track of times."

"You guys don't use stopwatches?"

Ron looked from Justin to me. "You know how many people run in some events? Thousands. There are more than a hundred and fifty thousand members of the various triathlete unions, and those are just the pros and semi-pros. The amateurs are easily three times that. This year's New York City Triathlon had to limit contestants to three thousand entrants. The London Triathlon had over ten thousand competitors one year. I can't even tell you how many thousands tried to get into the Iowa Athlete's Cup, which had a purse of $100,000. Now imagine trying to score a race that big with a stopwatch."

I dug into my salad. "So how do they score it?"

Ron ate some soup. "Every athlete wears an RFID chip. Some are ankle bracelets, some are tied to your shoes. When you pass a station, called an exciter, it sends out a signal that triggers your chip. The system then records your ID and time, so there's no mistake."

"And the people in charge can make sure you pass all the stations," Justin said, sipping his wine. "That would make it hard to take a shortcut."

Ron smiled. "Well, there are other ways to cheat."

"Like what?" I asked.

Ron shrugged. "One guy got caught entering a swim with fins. Then there's drafting. That's when one person swims directly behind or to the side of another. It's not technically illegal, but some of us think it's a gray area. And then, of course, there's doping."

"You mean drugs?"

"Steroids, hormones, you name it. Some athletes go so far as to have their blood hyperoxygenated, but not many. It's an expensive way to cheat."

The glimmer of an idea shone in my brain for a moment, but then Al was back with plates and more wine and it was five or ten minutes before we were all settled into our meals. Then I turned to Ron. "Is doping a big problem in triathlons?"

He shrugged. "Not as much as in, say, pro cycling. But I think that's because there just isn't as much testing. I think as time goes on there will be more and bigger scandals, cases." He forked up ravioli. "Man, this is fantastic."

"Don't you get tested before and after a race?"

He shrugged. "Not routinely. And in any case, there are ways around it." He caught my expression and shook his head. "No, I don't use drugs. And I don't cheat. But I know how it's done. Any competitor would. Diuretics, sample swapping, there's lots of ways. Is this what you wanted to know about? Cheating? You think someone cheated in the Alcatraz race?"

I ate some ravioli. "No, sorry. Got off on a tangent. I'm looking into the disappearance of Allison Farley."

"I thought that was settled. Didn't she drown?"

"Well, they never found the body. So her boyfriend says she may still be alive."

"Did she run away?" Justin asked, sawing at his roast pork.

I shrugged. "Right now, I'm just trying to find out where we lost her." I explained about the footage of Allison on Alcatraz. "So we know she was at the start of the race. You were in it," I said to Ron. "Can you kind of take me through it?"

"Sure." He reached for some of Mamma Benetto's homemade sourdough bread. "You jump into the water at the starting gun, of course. Damn, but that water was cold!"

"I don't know how you stand it," Justin said. "I tried swimming at the Marina Green once. I thought my balls would never come back down again."

"I made good time," Ron said, ignoring him. "Twenty-seven minutes, thirteen seconds. I came out of the water near the Penguin Club." The Penguin Club was the oldest swim club in San Francisco, with facilities near Fisherman's Wharf. "I climbed out of my wetsuit. I had my bike shorts and tank on underneath, but I lost some time getting into my footgear. It's hard to put socks onto wet feet."

"Why don't you skip the socks?" I asked.

"If I developed blisters I couldn't run the race. So I got into the socks, then the shoes, jumped on my bike. You know the bicycle course?"

I shook my head.

Justin cut in. "It went down Bay Street, hooked up with Marina Boulevard, went by Crissy Field, then got onto Lincoln. Then it wound through the Presidio, through Lincoln Park to Ocean Beach, and then headed back through Golden Gate Park. Then they reverse the course on the way back." He sipped wine. "I ran that same course last year in the Zippy 5K." The Zippy 5K race was a San Francisco tradition, a race based on a popular comic book character.

"I thought you finished that one in the top ten," Ron said.

Justin shrugged modestly. "Just saying, I know the route."

I cut in. "What's to prevent you from taking a shortcut along, say, Highway One? It would take you right across to Doyle, back at the Marina."

"Or Arguello would take you to the golf course at the Presidio," Justin said. "You could cut right through to Doyle again."

Ron shrugged. "Sure. But of course that would mean my chip wouldn't register at any of the stations."

I chased an errant ravioli across my plate. "Why not get someone to take your chip past those stations, while you cut across?"

Ron looked at me with some amusement. "Are you accusing me of cheating in the Alcatraz race?"

I felt my face go hot. "Sorry. No. Just thinking out loud." I focused on my rapidly disappearing ravioli. "What would happen if someone got caught doping?"

He shrugged. "He'd get fined, probably. He'd forfeit any prize money. And of course, his sponsors would drop him."

"How much would that cost him?"

"Everything." He reached across the table for the salt shaker. "A lot of pros, even the ones who aren't in the very top rank, depend entirely on endorsement money."

"You don't," Justin said, pouring wine.

"True," Ron said. He smiled at my raised eyebrow. "I'm a history teacher. American history, Sacramento City College. Great gig for a racer; I get most summers off."

"Alas, he's just passing through," Justin said, sighing. "Are you sure I can't persuade you to stay longer?"

Ron shook his head. "Just this week, I'm afraid. But have I answered all your questions?"

"Pretty much," I said. I reached into my purse for my cell phone. "Can you tell me if you saw any of these people?"

He looked doubtful as he glanced at the screen display. "I was pretty much concentrating on the race. Is that the dead woman?"

"Allison Farley."

"No, sorry, I can't say I saw her at all, or if I did I didn't recognize her."

I swiped the screen and held it out. "This guy?"

Ron did a double take, his eyes flicking up to mine. "I don't know his name, but yeah, I've seen him at other races." He looked warily at me. "Is this guy the reason you're asking all these doping questions?"

I looked at the screen, at the picture of Marty I'd snapped off that morning. "He's my client."

"He's your client?" Ron's hand made a fist on the tablecloth. He looked from me to Justin, and now his expression was neutral at best. "I thought this was a friendly dinner. Now, I'm thinking maybe not."

Justin frowned. "Claire, what is this?"

"What's up?" I asked Ron. "You know him?"

"I don't know him personally, not his name or anything, but like I said, I've seen him at races."

"And?"

"And he's rumored to be a drug dealer, selling enhancement drugs to athletes."

I closed my eyes. "Well, hell."

Justin said sharply, "Claire? Did you know about this?"

"No," I said. "But at this point, I'm not surprised."

Ron had imperceptibly moved away, and now was sitting about as far from me as it was possible to get in the cramped booth. "I think I'm done here," he said, and his tone was neither neutral nor friendly.

Sighing again, I signaled to Al for the check.

CHAPTER 8

After a strained and awkward dinner, Justin and Ron walked me up to my landing and went into Justin's apartment. I opened the door and found Wyatt waiting for me in the living room. He stood with his hands in the pockets of his black pants, but he had left off his coat and hat. His gold-on-black brocaded vest looked good against the white shirt.

"How was your dinner?" he asked.

"Strained and awkward," I said. "Our client may be dealing drugs."

"That's bad," he said.

I told him about my conversation with Ron.

"If he was selling illegal drugs, and she found out about it…" Wyatt mused, stroking his mustache. "Did you search his apartment?"

"Didn't know about the drug thing," I said.

"I can do it," Wyatt said. "'Cept for closed drawers and such. But I can take a look around." Wyatt could not affect the physical world (apart from me, personally), so I knew he could not open doors or drawers or anything else. But he was invisible and inaudible, the perfect spy. When people don't know a spy is around, they sometimes leave stuff in the open where he can see it.

"Thanks." I was quiet a minute, studying him. "You think Marty killed her?"

He looked back at me, his blue eyes hooded, sober. "Maybe that's the real reason she left, because she found out about the drugs. And maybe he didn't want her talking about it to her new fellow."

"If she found him dealing, turned him over to the police, he'd lose everything," I agreed. "But remember, she was alive at the start of the race."

"And he was swimming in that same race." Wyatt pushed off from the wall, his hands in his pockets. His watch chain arced across his waistcoat in a ripple of gold. "He could have dragged her under."

I knew he was right: it was possible. But was it likely? "But then why hire me?"

"On the other hand, her fiancé doesn't seem to be mourning her," Wyatt said. "I spent all evening with him."

"Tell me about it," I said.

"He did a lot of drinking and a lot of pacing. He's as nervous as a cat on a hot sidewalk. Every time the telephone rang he jumped a foot. I looked in all the rooms. The bedroom still has dresses in the closet. Women's gear in the bathroom. Shoes on the floor, scattered around."

"So he hasn't packed away her belongings," I said. "Maybe he thinks she's coming back."

Wyatt looked away, a shadow in his eyes. "Some people mourn that way."

I paced a bit. "Does Rafferty act like she's dead? Like he's mourning?"

"Folks mourn in different ways." He looked at me. "How did you?"

I thought about the weeks following my husband's death, years ago. Jack had been a detective on the SFPD, like me. He'd been on a case in Hunter's Point and caught a bullet; he died on the operating table. It had been a very dark time in my life after that. "I stared at walls a lot," I said tightly.

"Angry or sad?"

"Angry."

Wyatt nodded. "I can see that. And sad, I can see that. But Rafferty's not angry, and he's not sad. He's scared."

I looked at him speculatively. "Is he? That sounds more like a man afraid of being found out. Like a man with a guilty conscience."

Wyatt gave me a long look. "Maybe that argument at the race wasn't about Allison at all. Maybe it was about something else. A deal gone wrong."

"You think Rafferty was buying? Selling?" I frowned, trying to fit the puzzle pieces together. "Did he have any visitors while you were there? Send or receive any packages?"

"Nope. And the only things he said on the phone were yes and no."

"Could you see the caller ID?"

Wyatt nodded. "Once. It said 'Harrington'."

I got up and went over and sat down at my desk and turned on my computer. A few minutes' search in the financial databases, and I had him. "Jackson Harrington," I said, leaning back in my chair. "Lives in Pacific Heights. Partner in JackWay Holdings."

"JackWay. Jackson plus Wayne," Wyatt mused.

"Yeah, I guess. Looks like he's a contractor. Rafferty's house is owned by JackWay."

"Makes sense," Wyatt said. "Rafferty buys property, Harrington builds on it. They sell it and both clean up. Nothing wrong with any of that."

"Not a thing," I said, closing the laptop. "And none of these things, in themselves, mean squat. But while Rafferty may be in real estate, his partner is a contractor. Which means he buys and sells imported products, finishes, and so forth. Hires day laborers off the books. Might have an import license. I need to check him out."

"Makes sense." Wyatt put his head to one side, squinting those blue eyes at me. "Not such a clean case as you thought, huh?"

"Marty may or may not be dealing drugs. Rafferty may or may not have a guilty conscience. No one can find Allison's body. The more I investigate, the less I know."

"You want to quit?" Wyatt's voice was neutral. "Nobody'd blame you if you did."

I got up and went to the refrigerator in the kitchen and drank some cold water. I went and stood and looked out of my front window at the dark street beyond. Below, I heard noises and saw people coming out of Benetto's, the warm yellow light spilling out into the street and then disappearing as the door opened and closed. Finally, I said, "No. I don't want to quit."

"You got some reason to keep on?" There was no challenge, no judgement in his voice.

"Nothing but my gut," I said.

"Good enough for me," Wyatt said. I turned, and he was beside the door. "I reckon I'll go on back and keep an eye on Rafferty. You?"

I nodded at the laptop. "Research Rafferty. Look up Marty's financials, see if there's any interesting large transactions. And I'll talk to Suzette, see what she knows about doping."

"I'll say good night then, Claire." He nodded and stepped through the door.

I changed into jeans and T-shirt and called Suzette. "Hey."

"Hey," she answered. I heard the TV on in the background.

"You watching the game?"

"Yeah," she answered. "Giants are up by two in the fourth inning. You want to come over and watch?"

"Which one are we ogling?"

"The new shortstop."

"The tall guy with the curly hair?"

"And an arm made of solid gold—that was way outside! No way that was a strike!"

"I'll be right over."

Suzette lived in a neat little condominium in a tall building six blocks from me. I stopped in a corner grocery on the way over and bought microwave popcorn and soda, then rang her doorbell about a half hour after I'd called. Suzette answered wearing pajama bottoms and a T-shirt. She should have looked like hell but she looked like a model wearing designer pajama bottoms and a hundred-dollar T-shirt.

"How are they doing?" I asked as I walked into the kitchenette.

"I should arrest them for loitering," she said. "They got Buster Posey on but can't hit him home. Dammit, why were you swinging at that pitch? Oh, hell, that's the inning. Need some help?"

I punched buttons on the microwave. "Yeah, but not with popcorn. It's this Farley case."

Suzette yawned. She was sprawled across her silver-grey sectional sofa, her feet up on the quilted-leather hassock in front of her. Her tan walls were decorated with framed photographs she had taken. The HD television on the opposite wall shone big and bright, with the players splashed against the deep green of the ball field. Being summer in San Francisco, naturally everyone in the stands was wearing long sleeves, hats, hooded sweatshirts and warm-up jackets. I'd heard rumors that in other cities, baseball was played in the heat. I didn't believe it.

I sat down on the sofa with the bowl of popcorn between us. Suzette stared at the screen, where the Colorado Rockies were flailing at unhittable pitches thrown by Tim Lincecum. "Beautiful slider. Did you see that?" She dipped her hand into the bowl of popcorn without looking. "So what do you need in the Farley non-case?"

"I'm hearing rumors that the ex may be dealing."

She turned her head and looked at me with no expression. "Do tell."

I did. I told her about Ron, the race and Ron's suspicions. Onscreen, Lincecum humiliated the Rockies and strode off the field with a cocky look on his face. Pablo Sandoval waddled to first base, went through his usual kicking and spitting warm-up, settled the bat on his shoulder and prepared to further embarrass the Colorado bullpen.

When I finished, Suzette ate more popcorn and stared at the screen. "So really all you have is a rumor. Guy didn't even identify Marty by name."

"That's right."

"And your only other evidence is that Marty lied about Allison."

"Yup."

"Well, hell, Claire, he's practically convicted already." She

57

scowled as Pablo swung at a pitch two feet over his head. "The Panda just can't lay off the high ones, can he? Claire, do you seriously want me to run drug records on a guy who's not even a person of interest, in a case that's closed?"

"Seriously, frivolously, trivially, however you need to do it," I said. "Preferably quietly, but it's up to you."

She snorted as Pablo hit a ground ball to third which hit the base, took an odd hop over third baseman Chris Nelson's head and headed for deep left. "And how am I supposed to convince the Captain to let me do this?"

I shook salt onto my popcorn. "With your winsome charm…He missed the cutoff man."

"Doesn't matter. No way Pablo can turn that into a double. He'll stay at first. Everything you've told me still doesn't add up to Allison Farley being alive."

"Are you going to run Marty through the DEA?"

Suzette sighed. "Sure. Now can we watch the friggin' game?"

We ran out of popcorn by the seventh inning, but by then the Giants had the game locked up anyway.

I didn't really sleep after dragging myself home from Suzette's, but I did lie down a while. In the morning, Wyatt greeted me as I padded into my kitchenette, wearing a sweatshirt over pajama bottoms. My hair was a mess. I didn't care.

"Good morning." There was a certain tension in his voice.

"Good morning," I said, yawning. He wore a green brocade vest under the usual black suit. Very spiffy. "What's the occasion?"

He straightened. His expression at all times was perfect for a poker game, but now I detected a hint of a flush along his cheekbones. "Nothing special," he said, his voice rumbling. "Something wrong with the way I look?"

"Not at all," I said. I set up the coffee maker. "Something on your mind?"

"I came back last night after Rafferty went to bed," he said. "You weren't here."

I peered at him. His posture was stiff, tense. He turned his hat around and around in his hands. "So?"

He cleared his throat. "What you do on a … a date … is your business," he said. "But it would be nice if you left me a note."

I smiled. "Worried about me, Marshal?"

"There's a lot of strange men out there," he said. "A lot of dangerous men. I've seen them."

You've been one, I thought but did not say. I poured coffee into a cup. "I was with Suzette." I told him about my evening, and watched the tension leak out of his shoulders. Sipping my coffee, I said, "So what was your evening like?"

Wyatt shrugged. "Boring. Rafferty paced, drank, and spent a long time with his head in his hands. He received some telephone calls. Couldn't tell who he was talking to, couldn't get a look at that tiny screen. Mostly he said yes, no, and 'have you got it all'? Mentioned a meeting with some bankers to sign some papers. Sounded like a business deal."

I raised an eyebrow. "So why isn't he at his office? Why is he at home?"

"Don't know yet. Reckon if I keep an eye on him, we'll find out. 'Less you want me to tag along with you today."

I squinted at him. "I hear some disapproval."

He met my gaze squarely. "If I'd lost my Sadie like that, well, I wouldn't be much interested in business a while."

"Some people find solace in work," I said.

"Yeah," Wyatt said. "But why isn't he at his office? I ain't no builder, but I know it can't be done from home. He should be out on the job."

I was quiet a moment. "Guilty people don't always act like it. I need more coffee."

An expression flitted across his face, something between amusement and wistfulness. I felt sorry for him, a man—a ghost—who had loved coffee and could no longer enjoy it. Wyatt shifted his feet. "What are you doing today?"

I finished my coffee. "I thought I'd stop by and talk to the race director today. Then see about Rafferty's partner. He was on the other end of at least one of those business calls you say Rafferty's taking."

"That would make sense. In which case, we're wasting our time on him," Wyatt said gloomily. "You should be looking for Allison, since you're the one who thinks she may still be alive."

"Then you'll be glad to hear my next stop after the race director will be Allison's mother." I put my coffee cup in the sink. "When girls run away, sometimes they run home to mom."

"I'll be back later tonight, when I get a chance." Wyatt stared out the window, at the sky. He looked restless.

"I'll leave you a note if I have to go out," I said. "I wouldn't want to worry you."

"Appreciate it," Wyatt said. He put on his hat, turned, and stepped through the wall. Some day I'll get used to that.

Chapter 9

Fifty-Two Fremont Street was a ten-story beige building with frameless windows near the Embarcadero, on the flat infill that used to be Yerba Buena Cove. The lobby was large, composed of various shades of marble, and had all the personality of a refrigerator. I checked the big wall directory and rode the elevator up to the sixth floor. Cornerstone Home Imports had half the floor, starting with a reception area tiled in its own products. My flat-soled shoes echoed on the polished floor as I approached the receptionist. She was a young black woman with very short hair and a wide, friendly smile.

"May I help you?"

I handed her my card. "I would like to speak to Kenneth Mannheim, please."

She frowned, looking at my card that had my name and "Private Investigations" on it. "Do you have an appointment?"

"No. But tell him it's about Allison Farley."

Her eyes flicked from me to the card and back. "Please have a seat. I'll be right back."

Actually, it was fifteen minutes before she returned, in which time the phone rang seven different times. I stayed on my feet, looking at samples of tile made from porcelain and clay and natural stone and bamboo and vinyl and, for all I knew, moon rock. They were framed and mounted on the wall like artwork.

The receptionist came back. Her smile was only half the wattage it had been, but it was there. I admired her professionalism. "Mr. Mannheim can see you now."

She led me through the door and down a short corridor

to a room I really couldn't call an office. It was about forty feet square, with rows of tables holding crates of tiles, most of them even more exotic than the samples on the reception area walls. There were glass tiles, river rocks, granite counter tops, and mosaics. One table held nothing but various cans of grout and setting compounds. Men in jeans and T-shirts that said "Cornerstone Home Imports" on the back were moving and shifting and carrying crates. One of them, a medium sized guy with gray hair and thick shoulders, came over to me.

"Ken Mannheim," he said, holding out his hand. "What's this about Ms. Farley?"

"You were the director of the Alcatraz Triathlon," I told him. "Can I speak to you about it?"

"I don't know what I can tell you I haven't told the cops," he said. His blue-gray eyes held steady on mine. He had rough, reddened skin, a man who spent a lot of time outdoors. It was an incongruous look for a manager with an office on the sixth floor of a sleek office building.

"Anything you can help me with would be good," I said. "Maybe you could start by telling me about the race, how it's set up, how you run it."

He nodded, ran a hand through his close-cropped gray hair. I could just see him in a windbreaker on the sidelines, with a whistle around his neck on a lanyard and a clipboard in his hand. "Okay. Let's go to my office. Bob, make sure these samples get shipped out on the two o'clock truck."

He led me back to the short corridor, all the way to the end, and ushered me into a cramped office consisting mainly of a desk, two chairs, one window and about fifty boxes stacked on top of one another. He sat down behind the desk, shoved a stack of call slips out of the way, and sat with my business card in both big hands. "This is some insurance thing, isn't it? You working for Allison Farley's insurance company? Well, I can tell you right now there was no scam. The poor girl drowned, and I'm sorry as hell, but it happens. So you should tell your client to shut up and pay up and let the rest of us get on with our lives."

"You're certain she drowned?"

"Absolutely. No question. We looked for her for days. There was no sign of her body, but she never came out of the water. If you're thinking she faked this whole thing, maybe to collect on insurance, all I can say is that she fooled me, the Coast Guard, the San Francisco PD, the National Park Service, Search and Rescue, and about two hundred volunteers anxious to find her."

"How sure are you that she never came out of the water?"

"You ever run in a race? Even a local 3K charity run?"

I shook my head.

"The chip timers—you know about the chips every contestant carries? Okay, we had ankle chips on every runner, and mats reading them as they came up the dock. Those are flat mats with embedded antennas that read the RFID chips when people walk over them. That's why we insisted on the ramps, even though the Park Service wanted to just let everyone jump onto the dock. Since all the contestants had to walk over the same mat, we read chips on every one of them. Everyone was accounted for."

"And in the water? Do you have mats or readers or antennas in the water as well?"

He shook his head. "No, but why would we? It's not like a foot race, where someone can take a shortcut. Of course, we've got race volunteers in kayaks to make sure no one wanders off course."

"Who sets all this up? Who keeps track of it?"

"I do." He squinted at me. "I shoulda quit my job when I took this race on. The meetings, the red tape, the scheduling, the hassles. I had to learn, in two weeks, the most complicated race management software you can imagine. And then there's the insurance people, the cops, the National Park Service guys. It took me two months to get permission to have the swim start at Alcatraz. The damn Rangers didn't want to close the Rock for the race, or have our people set foot on it."

"So this is the first time swimmers have actually begun the race at Alcatraz itself?"

"Yeah. That was one of the big draws. People wanted to say they did the big swim, the one those prisoners who escaped did."

Clearly, Mannheim didn't believe the FBI claim that no prisoner had ever escaped the Rock by swimming. "What would have happened if the Park Service had said no to starting from the island?" I asked.

"We'd have done what we did last year. The swimmers would have dived off the ferry parked right next to the Alcatraz dock."

"I saw footage of the swim. One guy jumped in early."

Mannheim made a disgusted sound. "He said he was pushed. I don't believe it. Guy disqualified himself and was bitching about it. But the Rangers weren't amused. Herding those swimmers up and down those ramps was no picnic."

"I'd like to talk to the Park Service folks who helped you set all this up," I said. "They might have some insight into how Allison could go missing."

"I doubt it," Mannheim said. "But here…" He rummaged in his desk and came up with a dog-eared business card. It belonged to someone named Chrystal Richards and had the Park Service logo in one corner.

"Thanks." I thought of Allison Farley, last seen ascending the ramp to the dock on Alcatraz Island, under the looming barracks of the crumbling prison. "How hard would it be to lose someone in that crowd?"

He looked at me strangely. "Everyone went into the water who was supposed to, I'll guarantee that."

"How can you be sure?"

"There was an antenna on the edge of the dock. It triggered Allison's chip. We've got the readout; I handed it over to the cops. She went into the water, all right."

This was news. "You're sure? Could she have climbed out again? How do you keep count of the swimmers who reach shore?"

"They have to cross a mat coming out of the water. Allison's chip didn't trigger the waypoint. And the dock antenna didn't register a second time."

"Nobody sounded an alarm?"

"No." He sounded defensive. I could understand why.

"No one thought it was odd she didn't come out of the water?"

"The volunteers thought she was one of the ones pulled from the water by the safety officers. In that case, no one would have expected her chip to register. Or maybe they thought it malfunctioned, or fell off during the swim."

"And her chip never registered anywhere along the rest of the course?"

He shook his head. "None of the waypoints logged her. And before you ask, yes, they've been checked and they were working fine. I've been all over this with the cops. If you're looking for insurance fraud, you're going to have to look somewhere else." He clenched his jaw, unclenched it. "I've had all the insurance investigators I want to see, ever, for the rest of my life."

"How so?"

"The athletes' organization, the City, the Park Service, they all sent investigators. The race was insured, and those guys have been all over my ass. Now you come along. If I never hear about this damned race again as long as I live, it'll be too soon."

Something he'd said nagged at me. "How often does a chip fall off during a swim?"

"Oh, for God's sake."

"What's the range on one of those things? Ten feet? Fifteen?"

He glared at me. "We went all out on this one. Top of the line, fifteen thousand dollar system. Those chips will read within fifty feet of an RFID reader. The Coast Guard towed three of them readers back and forth over the swim area, and never got a ping. The Bay is only twenty feet deep at that point, so the chip would have been triggered even if it was lying on the bottom, under a foot of sand. It wasn't there."

"So her chip didn't fall off."

"No," he said grimly. "I think it got swept out to sea with the rest of her."

That seemed to be the popular opinion. I nodded at him. "Can I get a list of the volunteers for the race?"

"Why?"

"I would like to talk to them."

"Again, why?"

"Maybe they saw or heard something. Maybe they don't even know it. I'll talk to them, ask questions, find out."

"They've already been hassled enough by the cops," he said. "I don't want to bother them any more than they have been. They're just ordinary people who were generous enough to donate their time to this race. They didn't sign on for a police investigation. Or to get hounded by you."

I kept my expression and my tone as mild and non-threatening as possible. "I won't hound them. I'll be polite. But I can probably get a list from the website, or from one of the sponsors, like Wayne Rafferty."

He frowned. "You've talked to Rafferty?"

"Yes." I didn't need to tell him Rafferty had practically thrown me out.

He stared down at his hands, now clenched on his desktop. Finally he shook his head in resignation. "You got an email address?"

I handed him my card.

"Okay. I'll send it to you. You swear you won't harass any of these good people?"

"I promise I'll be gentle," I said.

CHAPTER 10

O ut on the sidewalk again, I took a minute to call Chrystal Richards. No one answered, so I left a message asking for an appointment.

Next stop was Rafferty's place of business. While I didn't expect to find Allison there, I thought a list of Rafferty's job sites might prove useful. Especially if I decided I was looking for a body. I wasn't at that point yet, but it was sure looking as if Allison was dead.

Wayne Rafferty may have lived in Pacific Heights, but he made his living in Dogpatch. This was originally a working-class neighborhood near Potrero Hill, so named for the packs of dogs that used to scavenge the butcher shops in nearby Butchertown. Both those old sections of San Francisco now had tonier names, but the blue-collar industrial tone of this eastern area near the Bay didn't lend itself to upscale nick-names. The construction offices of JackWay Holdings were on Minnesota Street, not far from the abandoned PG&E power plant. I took the light rail down Third Street, got off at 23rd Street, and walked four blocks.

This part of San Francisco was positively tropical, with more sunlight per year than the rest of the City combined. Right now it was a little confused, as the aging industrial district underwent "an ongoing transition to renovated hipster lofts", according to my cell phone's browser. New condominia stood next to crumbling brick warehouses, and the flat terrain made it easy to walk along, looking at gas stations and self-storage facilities and RV parking lots. I passed a diner that had clean windows and a boxing gym that had plywood over the windows. The neighborhood was an interesting mix of vacant lots, run-down auto stores, upscale boutiques and small businesses. JackWay Holdings turned out to be a large portable building behind chain link fences and a parking lot half-filled with trucks of every shape and description.

As I walked into the open parking lot, I passed a sign that said, "Hard Hats Required". However, the three guys I saw loading lumber onto a flatbed at the far end of the lot were wearing San Francisco Giants baseball caps. I didn't think those would protect their heads from rain, let alone falling objects. The front door of the building listed JackWay Holdings, Rafferty International, Harrington Construction and WayJack Designs. I guessed the partners had stopped creating companies because they ran out of ways to combine their names. I pushed the door open and went inside into a narrow, vinyl-floored office. A metal desk blocked entrance to the hallway beyond, with no one sitting at it. Signs saying "NOTICE: HARD HATS REQUIRED" and "AUTHORIZED ENTRY ONLY" lay in a pile along one wall. A bookshelf held three-ring binders, and a large wall calendar hung against another wall. The air smelled of sawdust and burnt coffee.

"Hey?" I called out.

"Who is it?" someone called from the rear.

"Jackson Harrington?" I called back. "I need to speak to you."

A man with black hair and blue eyes and a day's growth of beard stuck his head out of a door farther down the corridor. "If this is about that invoice, I—oh. Hi." He emerged more fully, and I saw that he was tall, well-built, tanned and handsome. I couldn't complain about the scenery in this case, that was for sure.

"Jackson Harrington? I'm Claire Turnbull."

He walked up the hall towards me, carrying a rolled up blueprint in one hand. He wore a flannel shirt over a white T-shirt, jeans and work boots. "I gotta say, you're the best lookin' bill collector they've sent yet. I might even have to pay you." He scooted around the desk to my side and then half-sat on it.

His visage was frank and open and genial, but his eyes looked wary.

"I'm not here to collect a debt, Mr. Harrington—"

"Call me Jack."

"Jack. I'm a private investigator, and I'm looking into the death of Allison Farley."

He looked blank. "Allison is dead. What's there to look into?"

"You know her body was never found. My client is seeking … closure."

He folded his arms over his chest. "Did Wayne hire you? Look, I know he's going through hell. God knows I wouldn't wish this kind of pain on anyone. But what does he think you can do? I mean, to be blunt, the girl is dead and gone. This kind of thing won't help Wayne get past it."

"Did you know Allison?"

He shifted his weight, uncrossing his arms across his chest, then sticking his hands in his pockets. "Yeah, I knew her. We met at Wayne's a couple of times, she went along on a couple of business dinners we had with clients."

"Did she and Wayne get along well? Any arguments or disagreements?"

He was silent a long moment, looking away. "I don't know if I should be talking about this. This is Wayne's private business."

"And Allison's," I said. "I don't think she'd mind me asking questions about her business, if it clears things up."

He swung a leg casually against the desk. "I…" He let out a big sigh and pushed his hands through his hair. It was thick hair, wavy, and when his hands left it, it lay across his head in a tousled wave that would have cost him a hundred bucks at a salon. Men get all the breaks. "Look, there might have been some … friction there."

"Like what? Fights? Screaming matches? Cold silences?"

His mouth quirked up a bit at the corner. "Nothing that obvious. Just a feeling now and then. Especially when we were all out together, having dinner or something. Allison would start to say something and Wayne would cut her off. Real casual, nothing obvious, but there were some things he didn't want her to talk about."

"Like what?"

"Money," he said bluntly. "I'm pretty sure they were having trouble over money. Allison spent money like it was going out of style. Wayne's no tightwad, but it bothered him."

"Was it her money? Or was she spending Wayne's?"

He shrugged.

The door behind me opened and a big Hispanic guy wearing a hard hat, jeans, boots and a denim shirt walked in and shut the door behind him. Ignoring me, he said to Harrington, "We got a mess out on the Turk Street rehab. Jorge ain't showed up and we got no backhoe. I called his number and his old lady said you let him go. What's the deal? You didn't tell me?"

Harrington stood and folded his arms. "Not in front of strangers, Enrique." He gestured to me with his head.

Enrique sent me an uninterested look and charged on. "Yeah, but we need that backhoe to finish the trench work. We been waiting all day. You need somebody to drive it, I can maybe pull Guillermo off the waterfront job—"

Harrington held up a hand. "Not now!" He looked at me. "We're done here. I have work to do. You got any more questions, ask Wayne."

The two men stood looking at me expectantly. I smiled back in a friendly manner. Enrique looked from me to Jack Harrington and back. I continued to smile.

Finally Harrington said, "I think you should go now."

"I don't mind staying," I said brightly. "I can wait until you've finished."

Harrington strode over to the front door and yanked it open. "Goodbye. Please don't come here again."

Enrique stared at Harrington, then at me.

I stepped out into the bright, hot day, with the sun beating back from the blacktop of the parking lot in front of me. The door shut behind me and I leaned against the wall next to it.

From inside, I heard raised voices.

"How am I supposed to finish the trench job you keep firing guys without telling me?" Enrique said. He sounded puzzled as much as angry. "This is what, the fourth time this month you done something like this? Man, we can't get no work done at all. And what happened to the cement mixer? I needed it for the foundation work, but I went into the yard today and it's gone. You fire it, too?"

"Look, you know how it's been, with the bills and the shitty economy. We all gotta do the best we can with what we've got."

"Yeah, but what have we got?" Enrique said. "We got no cement mixer, nobody knows where the backhoe is, and I'm short four guys."

"I'm on top of it." Harrington's voice sounded hard, defensive. "Didn't you pull Tom and Jorge off the Park Service job? They're skilled labor, and you have them digging trenches."

"Hey, that ain't on me," Enrique said defensively. "If you was on site more often, you'd set things up like you want to. If I gotta handle these guys, I do the best I can. We need you on the work site, not here in the office."

Harrington's voice had some snap to it. "Look, I had to rent some equipment out a couple days. It's just a short-term thing, but it brings in enough money to pay your wages. But I can't cut deals like that if I'm out in a hard hat supervising ditch diggers; I have to be 'here in the office'. So don't bring this beef to me."

"Maybe I should take it to Mr. Wayne."

"You go right ahead." Harrington' voice now sounded as hard as granite. "You go right on ahead and bust in on him while he's going crazy over Allison. Don't even think about how he's got more on his mind these days, like mourning for her, arranging a funeral, getting rid of her things and dealing with her mom. Yeah, you don't think about any of that. You go right on over there and knock on his door and insist on bothering him with work shit at a time like this."

I had to hand it to Harrington, it was as masterful a guilt-trip as I'd ever heard put down. There was a long silence, and then Enrique said, "I'll get on back to the trench job. We got shovels, we still know how to dig. But the site boss is gonna scream at us."

"Tell him to call me." Boots moved towards the door and I sidled around the corner. Enrique slammed out and down the steps and stalked away across the blacktop. The door had barely swung to behind him when Harrington stomped out. He, too, strode away and was quickly out of sight among the parked trucks. In a moment one of the trucks roared to life and pulled out of the parking lot.

I waited, listening to the wind whispering among tall weeds at the edge of the lot, bringing the smell of the Bay. The brackish water lay about five hundred yards west of me, close enough that gulls wheeled in the air over my head in their ceaseless search for discarded French fries. The only sound I could hear was a distant radio station playing Tejano musica, all the way across the parking lot.

I slid around the corner, eased up to the front door, looking around. I didn't see anyone. I tested the door; sure enough, in his haste, Jack Harrington had not pulled the door all the way to. It opened quietly when I pushed on it. I stepped inside and closed it behind me; the lock clicked shut.

I wasn't sure what I was looking for, but something in Harrington' whole manner had me hearing alarm bells. I glanced over the surface of the reception desk. Circulars, car wash flyers, and local discount coupon books mixed in with invoices, bills of lading, and a surprising number of unopened envelopes stamped PAST DUE in angry red ink. I opened one, from a supplier of insulation, and found a collection notice for three thousand dollars. Another one showed a bill that was six months overdue for five thousand dollars worth of window frames. At the very bottom was a notice from a bank threatening repossession of a truck.

I stepped around the desk and made my way down the narrow central hall. On the left was a tiny modular bathroom with a shower. On the right was a storage room holding boxes of plumbing supplies, tubs of roofing compound, cans of paint, and a small desktop-sized copy machine. I lifted the top and found that whoever had made the last copy had left the original on the glass. I took a look; it was a signed bill of sale, conveying ownership of one used backhoe to Allied Machinery Resellers in Burlingame for forty three thousand dollars. I didn't think Enrique was going to be getting his backhoe back.

At the end of the hallway was a larger office, with locked file cabinets, a battered computer, and another metal desk. The computer was on, but the screen saver demanded a password to unlock the screen. I tried a few obvious ones, to no avail.

I searched the drawers but did not find a sticky note with the password written down on it; apparently Wayne and Jack were too savvy to give a thief that much help. The drawers held mostly boilerplate contracts, standard invoices to be filled in by hand, and a half-empty bottle of whiskey.

The top of the desk held several construction drawings; from what I could make out, JackWay Holdings was building an addition to a private school on Turk Street, as well as a small apartment complex in the Western Addition and a shopping mall in San Mateo. An ashtray held a motley assembly of keys. More paperwork showed them doing some renovation work on Alcatraz for the National Park Service and subcontracting for some major re-landscaping of a couple of San Francisco city parks. The ugly thought crossed my mind that a guy who owned (or used to own) a backhoe and a landscaping contract would be in an ideal position to bury a body.

On the floor next to the desk sat a small shredder, the kind that sits on top of a trash can. On the desk above it was a cardboard tray marked SHRED. There were papers lying in it; the laziness of the human animal never ceases to amaze me. I went through the papers; most of them were things like receipts for nails. I figured Jack Harrington didn't want his company's credit card numbers to fall into the wrong hands, and routinely shredded them.

Two items caught my eye: deposit slips. They were to the Peninsula Bank of Daly City and showed deposits of forty three thousand dollars and twenty three thousand dollars. Was the first one for the backhoe? If so, what was the second one for? I searched but did not find a check book or bank book of any kind. They were probably in the locked files. But if those deposit slips were genuine, then Jack Harrington had enough money to pay his bills; why was he ducking them? Was he just a cheapskate? Or was there something really wrong with JackWay Holdings?

This portable building had thin walls. I heard voices; at least two men walked by outside the building, speaking rapidly in Spanish. I decided I had learned something, though not what I had come for. I left everything as I had found it and gingerly let myself out the front. Two men were talking nearby, but there were two parked trucks between them and me. I walked nonchalantly out the front gate, holding my breath. No one yelled or followed me. The distant music of Tejano carried on. The gulls continued their quest for fried potato products. I walked on in the quiet noon and headed for the light rail station.

CHAPTER 11

I took the light rail back downtown and got on BART. The Bay Area Rapid Transit system was not always rapid, but it was pretty comprehensive. I was too early for the afternoon commute crowd, so I almost had the car to myself. A pair of brown-skinned teenage girls shared a seat between them, frowning furiously at their smartphones as their fingers danced rapidly over the miniscule screens. I could only assume they were texting one another, being as how they were separated by a yawning gulf of four inches. A guy with a face like tanned leather and a tangle of brown-gray hair slept in the back, wearing a spanking new yellow Alcatraz Triathlon T-shirt. His head had fallen back on the head rest and his mouth was open, making it plain to everyone that he had no teeth. I doubted he had acquired the T-shirt by crossing a finish line.

I settled back and watched the Peninsula spin by and thought. I still had no concrete evidence that Allison Farley was alive. I still had every possible reason to believe she'd been shark bait for the better part of a week.

But one of the things I had learned in this business was to pay attention to my gut; it was one reason I would never make a detective on the PD, as Suzette had. She had to stick to the rules, to hard evidence that would stand up in court. All I had to do was satisfy my conscience and my clients, and I had fewer rules to break to do it. And, never to be discounted, I had an invisible partner who could follow anyone, see or hear anything. So far all that had gotten me was the uneasy feeling that something was very, very wrong with this case.

Marty Hancock could be dealing. Wayne Rafferty was so

broken up over his girlfriend's death he spent all his time talking business on the phone. His partner seemed to be running the business in his absence, but was juggling a lot of debt. Allison Farley had spent a lot of Wayne's money. And she and Wayne may have fought. I did not like the outlines of the picture this was drawing for me

I rode the BART all the way to the end of the line, in Millbrae. Here, the San Francisco Peninsula divided the Pacific Ocean from San Francisco Bay, along the spine of the northern Santa Cruz Mountains. There were spots along this commuter corridor where one could stand with one foot on the North American tectonic plate, and one foot on the Pacific plate, straddling the infamous San Andreas fault. Right now, I just needed to cross three miles of suburbia. It took a forty-five minute wait, and then a leisurely trip in an empty bus threading through shopping malls, parks, schools and residential neighborhoods.

I had begun to wonder if my car wouldn't have been a better choice, despite the long commute and the parking dilemma, when the bus finally pulled up at my stop. I got off and was hit by a blast of dry heat—unlike San Francisco, Burlingame enjoyed warm, hot summers. Sweat popped on the back of my neck. It was like being on another planet. By the time I'd followed my cell phone's map (two blocks west, one south), I was wishing I'd worn fewer clothes.

The apartment building was old, worn, and probably no longer met seismic codes. Long, jagged cracks radiating from the corner of each window testified to the fact that it had weathered at least one earthquake. I did not find this comforting, however. Either a building is tested and made stronger by a shock, or it is weakened by one. Unless you're an engineer, you won't know until the next temblor. I climbed the steps and found myself facing one door and six mailboxes. I saw that K. Hille lived in 2B and entered the tiny lobby.

After the outdoor glare, I took a minute to adjust my eyes. I wished I could adjust my sense of smell. I smelled grease that had been re-used too often, trash bins that had been emptied too seldom. Somewhere a dog barked; from the sound of it, it was a very small dog with a very large ego. I found myself facing stairs and took them, reluctant to put my hand on the greasy-looking bannister. Apartment 2B was past the turn of the landing. I knocked on the door loudly.

"Who is it?" The voice on the other side of the door could have belonged to a frog, if it smoked a lot of cigarettes and drank a lot of whiskey. "I'm paid up this month." A long, hacking cough followed this statement.

"My name is Claire Turnbull," I said. "I'm an investigator. I need to talk to you about your daughter, Allison."

There was a long silence, and the sound of someone moving around. Then various and assorted locks and chains were unlocked and unchained, and the door creaked open. A wide, jowly face peered through the slit. "What about her?"

"May I come in? I don't really want to talk in the hallway."

"I don't know you." More coughing. I hoped it wasn't contagious.

I pulled a business card out of my inside jacket pocket and poked it through the crack. "I won't take much of your time," I said.

The face studied it for a while, then the door opened just enough to let me in. "Come on, then," the voice said.

I stepped inside, and my eyes instantly watered. It could have been the smell or it could have been the blue-gray fog that passed for an atmosphere in the crowded living room. I heard locks locking behind me, and then Kandace Hille waddled past me.

She was in her late fifties or early sixties, about five-three, one-ninety. Her hair was mostly gray with streaks of brown, worn shoulder length. It had not had contact with a comb—or with shampoo and water, for that matter—in a long time. Her face was round, almost sexless, with bags and wrinkles and jowls tugging it out of shape. The rest of her had also apparently lost the war with gravity, but it was hard to tell under the layers of sweaters, vests and shawls. As she passed me, I got a whiff that told me she didn't bother with showers or baths.

God knows what color the walls of the room had originally been; right now they were a uniform tobacco brown. A single greasy window let in whatever light made it through the dingy white curtains. A television, a couch, two wooden chairs and a side table holding a lamp, a TV remote control and cigarettes completed the decor. The carpet showed beige under stains, ashes, gouges and assorted ground-in food. A few framed photographs on the walls hung crookedly; from what I could see, they showed a barely-clad blonde and a stripper pole in various poses I didn't care to examine; apparently Kandace had been quite a dish twenty years and seventy pounds ago.

Through a half-open door I saw a short hallway and another open door, probably to a bathroom. I figured there was a kitchenette and a bedroom somewhere in between, and the thought of what those rooms would look like depressed me.

I coughed as the woman plumped herself down on a sagging couch, reaching for the cigarettes. I doubted the landlord would approve of her smoking, but then I doubted that Kandace cared. She lit up, drew in a long breath, and blew out a cloud of smoke to join the haze in the rest of the room.

"Whatcha want?" she said.

I hadn't been invited to sit, and didn't really want to. I was afraid I might stick to something. I remained standing. "Ms. Hille—"

"Call me Kandace," she said, and coughed. "I don't do that 'ms' shit."

"Kandace," I said. "I've been hired to look into your daughter's disappearance."

Her eyes narrowed. "Who hired you?"

"I'm afraid that's confidential."

"Shit." She leaned forward, stubbed out her half-consumed cigarette in an overflowing ashtray. She reached for her pack and lighter again. "You're workin' for the goddam insurance company." She lit, drew, coughed, expelled smoke. "Goddamit, why can't they just pay up like they're supposed to."

"You're expecting an insurance payout?" I sidled slightly to my right to avoid the stream of smoke. I wondered if there was any actual oxygen left in the air of the apartment.

"Of course." Cough, hack. "Put in the claim the day after she drowned. What the hell is taking so long?" She looked at me out of small, stupid eyes. "Some kinda paperwork or shit I gotta fill out?"

"I was actually hired to find out what happened to her."

A slow blink greeted this, and a blank stare. "She drowned. Somebody paying you to find that out? You got a nice scam going, then." What might have been a smile, in some version of hell, curved her mouth for a moment.

"My client is not sure that happened." Despite the condition of the furniture, I decided it would be better if my eyes were on the same level as Kandace's. I slid onto the very edge of a wooden chair facing the couch. "I'm so sorry for your loss, and any distress this may cause you. But as you know, Allison's body was—"

"Charla."

"Beg pardon?"

"That's what I named her. Charla. I thought it sounded nice."

"She changed her name?"

Kandace shrugged, the mounds of fabric going up and down. "When she left. Guess the name I give her weren't good enough for her." She coughed again. "Probably wanted to start clean."

"Why would she need to start clean?"

Kandace eyed me suspiciously. "You sure you ain't working for the insurance bastards?"

"Positive," I said. "Why did your daughter change her name?"

"Her business," Kandace said shortly. "Ain't got nothing to do with the insurance, anyway. When do I get the check?"

"Ms. Hille—Kandace, when was the last time you heard from your daughter?"

She shifted her body, getting comfortable. I got a whiff of body odor and resolved to breathe through my mouth. "Not since she took off. First I heard of her in three years or more is when the cops come to tell me she's dead." More coughing. Kandace's rheumy eyes went soft, looking not at me but back into a dark past. "Worked my ass off keeping that girl fed. Worked nights, days, whatever. Every bar, every strip joint from San Francisco to Morgan Hill. Ruined my health. And what does she do? Soon as she can, she takes off on her own, leaves me to rot. Ungrateful." A coughing fit mercifully cut this rant short.

"Did she ever send you any letters, any—"

I wasn't sure at first what sounds Kandace Hille was making. I finally figured out she was chuckling and coughing at the same time. "Letters? That's a good one. Never even sent me a goddam birthday card. No, no letters. I spent every dollar I made on her, put fancy clothes on her back, but she don't give me a dime."

"That's a shame," I said, putting as much sympathy as I could into my voice. "She seemed to be doing so well for herself. It's a shame when a girl is ashamed of her roots."

This hit a nerve. Kandace's face flushed. "Ashamed," she spat. "Thought she was better than her own mother, didn't she? Changed her name. Didn't introduce me to her friends. Never came around, even when I—" More coughing. Kandace reached over and pulled out a drawer in the side table. She hauled out a half-empty bottle of liquor and unscrewed the top. Between racking coughs, she swigged down a generous portion of it. She set it, still opened, on the table beside her. "Cough medicine," she said abruptly. Her filmed-over eyes blinked, stared into the corner of the room as if seeing something in her past. "Bailed her ass out more than once. Worked an extra shift to pay for that fancy rehab. And what does she do? Takes off before she's half done, sticking me with bills to pay even though she ain't there no more." Her gaze fastened on me. "So I got something coming. I got something coming from the goddam insurance. She owes me. They better pay up. You make them pay up."

Her grief underwhelmed me. I had to struggle to keep an

expression of sympathy and understanding on my face. "Must be hard for you," I said. "Rehab can be expensive."

"Damn right it is," Kandace said. She drank from the bottle again. "Judge sent her twice, once when she was thirteen, and then when she was seventeen. Little bitch never learned nothing. Got out, came home, and right away got doped up again."

I glanced around the grim apartment. If I was a young girl and lived here, with this toad, I might reach for the nearest opiate, too. Kandace sucked down more amnesia juice from the bottle, and I decided I'd heard everything she had to tell me. "Thank you for your time," I said, getting up.

Her eyes watered as she looked up at me. "Don't forget," she said, and a whining note came into her voice. "I got something coming to me. You tell that insurance company to pay up."

At the door, I turned. "Was there a memorial service for Allison?"

Kandace stared at me. "Memorial service?"

"I thought so." I opened the door and trotted down the stairs as fast as I could. Outside, I took in several deep breaths, thanking God for the oxygen factory that is the Pacific Ocean.

CHAPTER 12

I was so glad to breathe actual air again I didn't even care that it was hotter than hell. But I was not going to go through that public transit mess again if I could help it, so I grabbed a cab in downtown Burlingame and told the driver my address. I was relaxing in the air conditioning when my cell phone dinged to announce an incoming message. It was from Mannheim, and it was the list of volunteers who had taken part in the race. I scrolled idly through the list, noting who lived out of town and therefore would be difficult to track down, when one name jumped out at me.

"Son of a bitch!" I said, sitting up straight.

"Say what?" the cabbie said, frowning into his rear view mirror.

"Not you," I said hastily. "I've changed my mind. Drop me at Civic Center."

"You got it," he said, and switched lanes. In a few minutes, we were pulling up in front of City Hall. I paid him, exited into the cool gray of San Francisco, and trotted up the steps.

Inside, the fifth largest dome in the world soared more than 300 feet overhead, higher than the U. S. Capitol Building. Polished marble floors echoed to the clatter of many feet.

As always, I paused a moment in the huge Rotunda. President Warren G. Harding's body had lain in state here after his death in San Francisco; Joe DiMaggio and Marilyn Monroe had been married here. George Moscone and Harvey Milk had died at the hands of an assassin only a few yards from this spot, and right here at the bottom of the sweeping Grand Staircase the mayor of San Francisco had personally performed some of the first gay weddings in California. For my money, the City Hall of San Francisco is one of the most beautiful buildings in the world. I will admit that I have not seen them all.

I climbed the smooth granite steps, found myself confronting the enormous double oak doors of the Board of Supervisor's meeting room, and turned left. A marble-floored gallery ran around the second-floor level of the vast open space, and I strode down it quickly, dodging messengers, secretaries, lawyers, the odd security guard, and tourists.

At the far end, directly opposite the top of the Grand Staircase, the huge doors of the Mayor's office matched those of the Board of Supervisors. I pushed through the doors and confronted a beehive of activity. Thanking God this was not an election year (or I wouldn't even have gotten in the door), I stopped in front of a desk where a girl with a pink streak dyed in her hair spoke earnestly into headphones.

"He absolutely, positively cannot make it tonight," she said forcefully, her eyes on a flat computer monitor. "We have to reschedule for Tuesday at four. No. Yes. Yes. No. I'm afraid not. Okay, thanks." She hung up, glanced up at me, and pointed to a row of chairs where people sat waiting. "If you'll take a seat, I'll—"

"I'm not here for the Mayor," I said. I laid my business card in front of her. "Is Roland in?"

She squinted up at me, picked up a phone, and murmured into it. She hung up, shrugged, and said, "He said to come on in. You know the way?"

"Unless he's moved since last week, yes."

I threaded my way past desks, workstations, monitors, and haphazardly placed chairs. Phones rang, faxes hummed, people talked or whispered or even shouted across rooms. How anyone got any work done in that environment baffled me.

Roland Ewing and I had met a few months ago on a case, and had dated a few times since. We hadn't progressed much beyond movies, restaurants, and a goodnight kiss. It wasn't so much lack of interest as lack of time: every night I was free, he was hung up at work, and vice versa. We liked each other, and there was a buzz under all our conversations, but so far everything was on a back burner.

Roland had a title I could never remember, which roughly translated as Mayor's Right Hand. His office was small, neat, and tucked away around a corner; the Mayor had to make do with a Medici palace. I pushed open Roland's door, nodded to his aide Peter, and got waved in.

"Claire! What a nice surprise!" Roland rose to his full six feet two inches, a bright smile on his handsome face. Today he wore a navy suit, blue shirt and blue paisley silk tie, slightly unknotted. Like every other male in San Francisco, he sported a manly one-day growth of beard. He came around the desk, caught my hands in his and gave me a peck on the lips. I caught a close-up shot of blue-green eyes with a twinkle in them. "Can I get you something? Coffee? Tea?"

"No, thanks." I let go of his hands, a little reluctantly. "I'm actually here on business."

His eyebrow, the same dark brown as his curly hair, flicked upward. "You want something from the Mayor?" He gestured to a chair.

I sat and pulled out my cell phone. "No, from you. I found your name popping up in connection with a case."

He grinned as he sat back down behind his desk. "Should I be flattered? Or should I call my lawyer?"

Since Roland is, in fact, a lawyer, I smiled back at him. "I just need some information."

He spread his hands wide. "Who doesn't? It's the currency of politics."

"You volunteered at the Alcatraz Triathlon last week."

He blinked. The grin faded into puzzlement. "Uh. Yeah. Since the Mayor is a supporter, of course I had to be there too."

"Can His Honor take a step in any direction without you?"

"Of course not," he said. "I am his eyes, his ears, and his feet." His gaze narrowed. "This have anything to do with that woman who drowned?"

No one ever called Roland slow. "I'm not sure she drowned."

Roland sat forward and put his hands flat on the desk. "Explain?" he said quietly.

I held back my client's name, but gave him the rest. Roland listened, fully focused, his eyes never leaving my face. "So I'm talking to anyone who had anything to do with that race," I finished. "What do you remember about it?"

Roland got up, stepped over to a case of vitamin-spiked water sitting on top of a file cabinet. He opened one and took a long pull. "Mostly I was there to meet and greet, shake hands. A lot of the Mayor's donors were there, and a few we wanted to hit up for campaign donations. I remember when the commotion started, with cops coming up and asking questions. They questioned me and the Mayor, but we didn't know anything. I don't even know what she looked like."

"I bet you knew her boyfriend, though." I swiped my finger over the phone display, calling up some pictures. "Here." I held out an image of Wayne Rafferty I'd pulled off a local gossip website.

Roland peered at it, nodded. "Yeah. Rafferty's been a contributor." He sat back down, assessing me. His eyes were cool now, the political animal looking out at me. "You're linking this woman's disappearance to the Mayor's office? Because of her boyfriend?"

I shook my head. "Take off the politician's hat for a minute," I said, irritated. "This has nothing to do with the Mayor's office." I caught a flicker of emotion across his face, and felt a chill. "Or does it? What do you know about this?"

He sipped water, still watching me. "About the drowning? Not a thing." He glanced past me, checking to make sure the door was closed. He leaned forward, arms on his desk. "But Claire, since we're friends, I'll tell you. Rafferty may be tied to the Cogent Fund mess."

"Ah, hell." I slumped in my chair. The Cogent Fund had been a venture capital organization that blended private and state investment money to bankroll construction projects in the Bay Area. The idea had been to jump-start some economic recovery for the City, creating jobs and bolstering local businesses. But after sixteen months and no action, the state had called for an audit, only to discover that the money had vanished and no one quite knew where it had gone. Two construction companies had already shut down, four insurance companies were on the rocks, and suspicion had fallen on a half dozen state agencies and private builders. There were reports of kickbacks, bribes, embezzlement, corruption.

"The District Attorney is talking about taking the case to the Grand Jury next week," he said. "I haven't seen the files, but rumor has it that Rafferty's name is on the list."

"Damn all politics! This is just going to screw everything up." I jumped to my feet and started pacing.

"It's only a rumor," Roland said. His green gaze followed my pacing. "I have no confirmation. All I know is that the DA is looking at him, along with others. They say he may have taken contracts and then not done the work, cut corners, substituted substandard materials. The DA is looking at fraud, embezzlement, maybe even money laundering charges. There's talk the Feds are getting involved." He lounged back in his padded leather seat. "Where does that put your drowning victim?"

"Allison was in commercial real estate. There are a couple of real estate agencies involved in Cogent, aren't there? A savvy commercial real estate agent might make a tidy fortune off that, if she didn't mind the risk. And if she wasn't involved, if she figured out a scam Rafferty was running, he might have had her disappeared. Was Allison tied to Cogent?"

Roland shrugged elaborately. "Her name hasn't come up, that I know of. Have you talked to the police?"

I stepped past him to stare out of his window. Below, people on the sidewalk walked and talked and bought and fidgeted. "I talked to Inspector Melton," I told Roland. "But I don't know if she knows about this connection. Don't worry, I'll keep your name out of it. But I think she needs to know."

I heard him behind me; he put his hands on my shoulders, turned me. "Claire, I think you're chasing smoke and shadows. This Allison woman is dead. She's been dead nearly a week now."

I turned, leaned my head on his chest. It felt good. He smelled good. I sighed, and wished I had more time to spend like this. I wasn't sure what we were at this point—friends? Allies? Potential lovers? "Things keep getting in our way," I murmured.

He rested his chin on the top of my head. "Yeah," he rumbled. "But we'll work it all out. Give me a call when you're free. Maybe we can get out of town for a weekend or something."

I kissed his cheek, refusing to let myself linger on it, and said goodbye.

Out on the sidewalk, I pulled my cell phone out and called Suzette.

"Hey, Claire," she said. "I'm walking to the morgue, got a hit and run vic."

"Can I have five minutes?"

"You got three."

Rapidly, I filled her in. In the background, I could hear people talking, the echo of noise off white tiles, a PA announcement. Suzette said nothing until I'd finished. Then she said, "Well, hell."

"I know. It's a mess. Harrington said she was becoming too expensive for Rafferty. My source in the Mayor's office possibly links Rafferty to Cogent; my own paranoia puts her in it, too. Her mom says Allison was busted in juvie, had drug troubles. She changed her name, her address, everything."

"No law against making a new start," Suzette said. "But dammit, none of this means anything if we can't show that a crime was committed. The coroner has already ruled accidental death."

"Maybe we can come at this from another angle. Did you run my client yet for drugs?"

"Working on it," she said tersely. "Keep me in the loop. What's your next move?"

I glanced at my cell phone list. "Got some more volunteers to interview."

"About the race?"

"Yeah," I said. "But now I'm going to be asking about doping, too."

"And since I'm on the way to the morgue, I'm gonna see if the ME is in. I want her to re-examine that ruling of accidental death."

"Give her my love," I said, and hung up.

The phone immediately rang, but the display showed nothing but a phone number. I answered it. "Claire Turnbull."

"Is this Claire Turnbull?"

Some people don't listen to anything you say. "Speaking."

"You called and asked for an appointment," a breathless female voice said. "Would, um, tomorrow at two be all right?"

"Sure," I said. "But first I have to know who I'm seeing."

"What?"

"Who is my appointment with?" I tried not to grit my teeth; that makes it harder to hear people.

"With me, of course." She, whoever she was, actually giggled.

I decided subtlety was wasted. "Who are you?" I asked.

"Oh. Didn't I tell you? This is Chrystal!" She announced it as if I had won a prize.

"Ms. Richards? Of the Park Service?" I frankly didn't believe it. Every government official I had ever met was a grown-up. When had the Park Service started hiring teenyboppers?

"So can you? Be here at two? 'Cause if that's no good, we can meet later. Or anytime at all, really. I just have to know so I can tell my supervisor."

"Let me just check and make sure I've got the right Chrystal Richards," I said. "Were you the Park Service liaison for the Alcatraz triathlon?"

"Oh, yes! I work with the race directors every year!" There was some background noise—a ringing phone, a distant announcement over a PA system. "So is two o'clock okay?"

She hadn't even asked what I wanted to talk to her about. "Sure," I said. "I'm not sure how to get there, though. It will depend on whether I can get a ticket in time." The only public access to Alcatraz Island is to buy a ticket on a tour. And since Alcatraz tours are the most popular tourist attraction in the city, tickets tend to sell out days in advance.

But Chrystal giggled again. "Oh, that's no problem! I'll give your name to the ferry guys and they'll let you on board for free, since you have Official Business." I swear I could hear the capital letters when she spoke.

"Then I'll be there at two," I told her.

"Great! I'll be in the administration building, Room 30."

CHAPTER 13

It was early evening and the fog was rolling in, grey and cold. I like grey and cold, it suits the City's flare for drama, but now I was tired and hungry. It was too far to walk home, so I caught a cab, deciding Marty could afford the expense. By the time it dropped me in front of Benetto's, the day had grown dark and dreary. This was the San Francisco of Sam Spade, of the ominously quiet alleyways and the noisy beggars.

As I paid off the cabbie, I was thinking of Alcatraz, sitting cold and aloof in the middle of the Bay, of the anger housed in its walls for so long, and the desperation that had driven so many into the chilling waters of San Francisco Bay. The government claimed that no escapee had made it off the Rock alive, because of the currents and the sharks. One would think that the two thousand swimmers a year of the Alcatraz Triathlon would have proved the government wrong; had Allison Farley proved it right?

I climbed the stairs to my apartment and noticed that Justin's door was closed. He was out with his buddy Ron, apparently. I opened my door and was completely not surprised to find Wyatt Earp standing in my living room again.

"Howdy," he said, and took off his hat. It was such an old-fashioned moment, I almost laughed, but thought that might hurt his feelings.

"Hey," I said. "Any news?"

"No."

"Things got more complicated this afternoon," I said. I told him about my trip to see Allison's mother, and then my visit with Roland. Five sentences into that last, Wyatt started scowling. He was still scowling when I finished. I walked to my fridge, got a beer, opened it, and leaned back against my counter. "What's eating you, Wyatt? You don't trust Roland?"

"I don't trust a politician," Wyatt rumbled.

"Well, who does?"

"Never yet met one didn't have more slick moves than a greased-up rattler. Might be you should look for more connections between the Mayor's office and this Rafferty fellow. Might be more there than campaign contributions."

"Well, keep an eye on Rafferty, see if he's making any slick moves," I said. "I'm going to dig into Allison Farley a little more, too. Strikes me that a commercial real estate agent with a history of drug abuse, a contractor with an import license, and a land speculator with money troubles might have a few slick moves of their own."

"I think we ought to look at the island."

I sipped beer. "Alcatraz? The cops and Feds have been over it with a fine-toothed comb."

He set his jaw stubbornly. "Don't hurt to look a second time."

"I won't argue with you," I said. "I'm never satisfied 'til I've gone over the ground myself. I've got a two o'clock meet set up with a Park Ranger." Actually, I suspected Wyatt was getting bored with his baby-sitting job. I didn't blame him.

"I want to be there," he said.

I kept a straight face as I said, "And if Rafferty suddenly makes a break for Mexico, or goes to dig up Allison in his rose garden? Don't you want to be in on that?"

Wyatt snorted derisively, set his hat on his head, and pulled the brim low. "Good night, then," he said formally. He was polite enough to exit through my door, though he didn't bother to open it.

I settled in for a rousing evening of microwaved Swedish meatballs, beer, and lots of digging. I subscribe to a lot of investigative services, like credit bureaus, driving records, and insurance databases. For a small fee, you can find out a hell of a lot about people online, even those who don't think they're giving out information. Even if you don't post information yourself, it can be posted or leaked by your bank, credit bureau, school, or even an eighth cousin posting a genealogy. Death records, vehicle registrations, website archives, parole offices, even the Postal Service's tracking databases can give an experienced investigator a clue. My personal prediction for the future is that people will be scrambling not for fame, but for fifteen minutes of anonymity.

Of course, the downside to this flood of information is that you have to sift through the trivial to find the significant. I discovered that Allison and/or Charla Farley had been an average student in middle school, skipped her measles vaccination in fifth grade, and had garnered two parking tickets last month. Her real estate license was up to date. More to the point, her credit cards were maxed out and three had been suspended for lack of payment. The San Francisco County website listed dozens of deeds, conveyances and trusts with her name on it, something I expected from a real estate agent. I decided that as a last, desperate resort to force myself to fall asleep, I might read through some of them.

My conversation with Harrington had made it sound as if Allison was planning a fairly large wedding, and she liked to spend money. Women who like to spend money like to spend it on weddings, and that usually includes things like engagement announcements and registries at bridal outlets.

I went through every bridal registry in the Bay Area, along with the society section of every blog, website and paper in five counties. I couldn't find any evidence that Allison Farley had been planning a wedding. Of course, not everyone wants to post their whole life on the Internet, or advertise to potential burglars what silver pattern to look for after the honeymoon. Still, I thought it was odd that there was nothing about her upcoming wedding.

I was deep into a search of national bridal registries when my phone rang. Without taking my eyes from the screen, I answered it. "Yo."

"Chigger's in town, but we need a minyan," said a raspy female voice.

"Nice to hear from you, too, Dani," I said.

"We're on at three. You in?"

"Yeah."

Dani hung up without saying goodbye. I hate it when she gets chatty like that.

I logged off and went to change. A night at Nicky's meant black jeans, black T-shirt, and a leather jacket. Alas, mine was brown, but I hoped in the dark no one would care. I was half-way out the door when I stopped myself. I scribbled a note for Wyatt and left it stuck on my computer monitor, then headed downstairs.

The night was cool and hazy with fog as I walked down my street to Columbus Avenue. Columbus runs diagonally across North Beach, cutting brashly across the staid grid between Washington and Montgomery streets. Behind me, Fisherman's Wharf was still brightly lit even though the tourists were long since tucked into bed; ahead lay the Transamerica Pyramid and the financial district. A few lonely cabs and single cars drifted by, and the sounds of rock music pounded out of a few pubs still open.

When I reached the corner I turned, and nearly tripped over a Harley Davidson motorcycle illegally parked on the sidewalk. I stepped around it, around the one next to it, and detoured around the other four also illegally parked. I passed four guys furiously smoking outside the entrance to Nicky's and then swung on in.

The joint had opened on Montgomery Street in 1860 as a saloon called the Monte Carlo; at various times its upstairs has been a brothel, its downstairs a speakeasy. During World War I, many departing sailors downed their last shot-and-a-beer at the polished oak bar. When the owner died after the Great War, Nick Tatum bought it. He named it, modestly enough, Nicky's Jazz to cash in on the new music craze. The doors have never been shut since then, even during Prohibition. Nicky's was the first club to hire black musicians on the West Coast, and as far as I know, the tiny stage has been continuously occupied since December of 1929. There are no locks on the doors or hours posted, because Nicky's just simply never closes.

I've often wondered how the present owner, Edie Wong, manages to maintain the smoke-filled atmosphere of a classic blues club in a city where indoor smoking has been banned for decades. Maybe she has fog-catchers on the roof funneling San Francisco's major atmospheric phenomenon down into the first floor of the building. The bar, hundred-and-fifty year old polished oak, was on my right as I walked in; two-top and four-top tables ranged three deep against the wall to my left. Dead ahead was the stage. There were about a dozen people in the place, including the gray haired man asleep in the corner, snoring. At this time of the night, or rather morning, the only patrons left were either musicians waiting their turn on stage, or die-hard fans of jazz and blues. And Harley riders; two of the tables had been shoved together to accommodate six or seven motorcyclists. I turned my attention to the stage.

Nicky's has a unique policy: anyone can step up on stage and play, it doesn't matter what music it is. Jazz, blues, folk, rock and roll are all welcome. There have been country singers and opera divas on that stage. The one inviolable house rule is that you never leave the stage empty; there must always be someone on stage playing, singing, or tuning up. Right now it was Mike Shipperton, blond with blue eyes and a perpetual squint, perched on stage on a high stool with his guitar under a baby spotlight. Smooth chords purred out of the beat-up speakers flanking the stage. Shadowy figures behind and around him were setting up instruments. I stood at the bar and waited.

The bartender slid a short whiskey across to me. "Hey, Claire."

"Frank." I sipped. Frank Wharton has been tending bar at Nicky's since before God was old enough to buy a beer.

"How's your mom?" He took my money and brought me change.

"Okay. She and Angus are in Hawaii at a charity surf meet." My mother and a few hippie friends, including Angus the Bear, had founded a commune in Marin County in the Seventies. Now it was a world-class retreat, spa and herb farm, but Mom was still a hippie. She just had more money to give away these days.

His eyebrows went up. "Didn't know Amethyst surfed."

"She doesn't. Angus is teaching her."

He nodded again. "Say hi for me."

"Will do." I waved my glass at the bikers in leather and chains gathered around the tables. "Who are the riders?"

"Washouts," he said.

Plenty of riders want to be Hell's Angels; relatively few actually make it into the club. The ones who don't make the cut join the Washouts, and proudly wear their failure as a badge. They were knocking back boilermakers around empty baskets of fries, caught up in an argument conducted mostly in snarls.

"Jazz fans?" I asked skeptically.

Frank shrugged. "Probably got run out of every other biker bar in town."

"Need some help keeping them in line?"

"Nah. Trong's keeping an eye on 'em."

I took my whiskey with me to the stage.

"Claire." Daniella "Dani" Soto is short, fiery, Hispanic, with a voice that can make angels weep. She's the front for Ad Hoc Committee, the cover band I've been playing in for ten years. As I climbed up the steps to the stage, she adjusted a microphone on a stand. "Glad you could make it. How's business?"

"Pretty good. Thanks for steering that fraud case my way." Dani is a claims adjuster with one of the largest insurance firms in the US; we met when I was starting out as a private investigator. We'd hit it off, and the jobs she'd thrown my way had kept me eating for the shaky first couple of years. It had been several more months before I'd learned that she played in a band. I'd been humming Ray Charles one day, she'd joined in and I'd learned what an incredible voice she had. At her invitation, I'd dusted off my long-ago piano lessons and discovered a way to kill time at night while the rest of the world was asleep and I wasn't.

On the stool, Mike grinned at me and kept on with his meandering solo. A baby grand piano slid out of the darkness at the back of the stage, barrelling towards me. I dodged out of the way. "Hey!"

"Sorry, Claire," a deep bass voice rumbled. The piano rolled to a stop in midstage. A burly black man with a shaved head emerged and stuck out a hand. "Didn't see you standing there. Edie says she got it tuned last week."

"Thanks, Carl." I pulled over a stool and positioned it, opened the keyboard, and touched a few notes. Smooth, clear. Good. I hated playing a badly tuned instrument, and mine was the only one on stage that depended on an outside professional to stay playable.

Carl Stone propped open the lid for me, then stepped over to open his own instrument case. Hauling out his big bass, he set it up and glanced at me. I gave him an A note, and he started tuning up. I heard Mike right behind him, and then a soft clatter from the darkness behind Doug; Chigger was setting up his drum kit.

A tall, lanky black guy in a black suit and black fedora stepped up on stage carrying a horn case. "Children," Doug Sheckley said. "Let the service begin." He flipped latches, opened the case, and drew out a gleaming saxophone.

A few soft brushing sounds from Chigger, then Carl swung in with the deep, walking bass notes of Mancini's classic "Peter Gunn", moving up and down the E string. Two bars later I came in with the same beat, and then Doug soared in over the top with alto sax, weaving in and out of the dark, rolling beat.

We've been starting every set with this song ever since I got my PI license; the rest of the band thinks it's a hoot, especially Carl, who's a cop. I personally considered it sheer hubris to introduce a band that included a cop, a PI and an insurance investigator with the most famous gumshoe theme in history; even worse, the original pianist on the song had been none other than John Williams and I am not in that league. But Dani had once said if we could get to the end without being

lynched by the audience, we would be fine. She was right, and
by the time Doug's sax slammed us home in the last breathless
bars, the applause was actually audible. Before it died away,
Dani stepped up to the mike, took a breath, and launched into
Lenny Cohen's "Blue Alert".

I have to half-fake the piano part on that one—the original used a Hammond organ, not a baby grand—so I was concentrating so hard on the keys I didn't even notice when Wyatt showed up. I only knew that when we got to the end, there
he was, leaning against the back wall of the stage, arms crossed
in front of his chest, eyes half-closed. Did he like jazz? Blues?
It had never occurred to me to ask.

He stayed where he was through Susan Tedeschi, John
Coltrane, Miles Davis, Oscar Peterson, and my own version of
Sonny Clark's "Deep in a Dream". He opened his eyes when
Doug came in with the sax about midway through, nodded
once at me. Was that a smile? It was too dim to tell, but it was
nice to see him there.

Dani signalled for a break, and Doug started a slow, meandering variation on a Stan Getz number. I sat back from the
piano, flexing my fingers to relax them. Wyatt opened his eyes.

"Interesting," he said. "Didn't know you played."

I turned to face the wall, under the pretense of flexing and
examining my hand. "We get together once a month or so," I
murmured. "When everyone's in town. What's up?"

"Not a thing," he said. "Rafferty's drunk hisself to sleep. I got
nowhere special to be." He glanced around the room. "Always
liked this place. Ain't hardly changed a bit since 1945 or so."

Now and then I forget that Wyatt's been hanging around
San Francisco since the nineteenth century. I glanced around
to make sure no one was paying attention. "What do you like?
I'm taking requests."

A corner of his mouth turned up. "Anything by Stephen
Foster or Gilbert and Sullivan."

"I'll see what I can do." I got up and went to the bar to find
Dina, passing Doug who was still tootling away.

Dina was talking to a couple of bikers. Dina will talk to

anybody, anytime, anywhere—I've always thought she should have been a politician or an ambassador or something. She glanced at me when I came up. "Hey, Claire, this guy was asking if you know anything by Brad Mehldau."

"Sure," I said. The man turned around and I found myself facing a huge guy wearing a bright yellow Alcatraz Triathlon T-shirt under his leathers. It seemed that every third person I saw in San Francisco this week was wearing one.

"You competed?" I asked. I may have sounded a tad skeptical, since the man in front of me easily topped six five and weighed over 240 pounds. If he jumped in the Bay he'd sink like a stone.

He rumbled, "Security." Looking at me out of small eyes lost in a thicket of beard, he swigged beer. "Got the T-shirt for free."

"Security?" I signaled to Frank for another whiskey. "Didn't know you guys were into triathlons."

Big Guy shrugged and drank more beer. "Just a gig. You gonna play any Mehldau or not?"

"Sure." I took the whiskey from Frank and knocked back half of it. "If you tell me who hired you to work security for two thousand runners."

Wyatt Earp suddenly stepped through the bar. I mean he stepped into it, and wound up emerging from the middle of it like a bust of himself. "Claire, who is this?" he asked sharply. "He looks dangerous."

Big Guy snorted at me. "Hog was on that. Red bandana, over at the table."

Wyatt followed me silently across the room to the group of bikers. He took up a stance across the table from me, arms crossed, scowling from one to another. "Hog" turned out to be a mid-sized guy with a deep tan, graying hair and very used leathers. He eyed me suspiciously when I approached and straddled a chair. "I'm swapping beer for information," I told him. "You the one they call 'Hog'?"

"Who's asking?" His breath told me he was well into a six-pack already.

"I'm trying to find out what happened to Allison Farley," I said. I nodded at Frank, who started drawing a pitcher of draft beer. "Cops think she drowned. You guys were there. What do you think?"

"I think you better get out of Low-Rider's chair," he said. Snickers greeted this around the table.

"Claire, don't mix in with these people," Wyatt warned. I ignored him.

"Just keeping it warm," I said easily. But out of the corner of my eye, I kept an eye on the bearded biker. "He said you were running security for the Alcatraz race." I punched up Allison's photo on my smart phone. "Did you see her anywhere, before or after the swim?"

"No. Get lost."

"Aw, come on. You'll hurt my feelings. Can you at least take a look at her?" I turned the screen so the others could see the picture.

"Ain't nobody saw her," Hog snapped. "Mind your own business."

"This is my business," I said, and put some iron in my voice. "Her boyfriend wants to know what happened to her. We're paying for information."

That definitely got their attention. Four pairs of eyes were riveted on me.

"How much?" the woman across from me said. She had braided her hair into cornrows, and wore five or six silver rings in her left ear. "Whaddya wanna know?"

"I said shut up," Hog snarled.

"Fuck off, Hog," she said placidly. "I don't answer to you." She looked back at me. "What do you wanna know?"

"You saw her?" I showed the photo again. The woman peered more closely.

"She was in the paper the day after. Drowned or something. How much money you paying?"

"If you can prove you saw her after the swim part of the race, there's five hundred in it." Five was a little high, but I thought it was worth it.

Wyatt sighed. "Throwing money away again."

"Nobody saw her," Hog cut in loudly. "She drowned. Don't you read the papers? Now get out of here."

The woman looked disappointed. "I seen her before the swim, not after. She was gettin' on the ferry."

No one else would admit to having seen her. Damn. I had hoped this was a new set of witnesses who would help out. I was putting the phone back in my pocket when a question occurred to me. "Do you guys do this a lot? Ride security for races?"

"First time," the woman said proudly. "The Boltheads got hired every year before this. This is our first year."

"Really?" I said. Frank arrived at the table with a pitcher and several mugs. I took the pitcher from him and held it hostage. "So why this year? You guys win a lottery or something?"

The woman's eyes were on the pitcher. "Ask Hog. He's the one with the connections."

I looked around at Hog, whose red-rimmed eyes looked a little bleary. "Must have been your lucky day," I said evenly. "Beating out the Boltheads for a plum gig like that."

"Nothing to it," the woman said. "I told you. Hog's connected. Used to work for one of the sponsors."

The connection in my head was almost an audible click. "JackWay?"

"I told you to shut the fuck up," Hog snarled. He rounded on me with an angry glare. "You, too. We got nothing to say."

The woman glared at Hog but said nothing more.

"I think you've got all you can get out of them," Wyatt said.

I shrugged and set the pitcher down on the table but held onto it. I let my eyes meet those of everyone sitting around the table. "Five hundred," I said. "My name's Claire Turnbull, and I'm in the book."

"Paying too much," Wyatt muttered again. "But I'll stick around here, listen to what they saw when you leave."

Dani fell in beside me on the way back to the stage. "I think the guy in the red bandana is in love with you," she said.

"He's staring a hole in your back."

"Yeah," I said, climbing the low steps. "I think he wants to eat my liver."

"I think I know him," she said speculatively. "If I'm right, he's Dan Shaeffer. Ran into him on a case about a year ago, involving stolen merchandise. Not a nice guy."

"You think? He doesn't bother me. Listen, I have a request from someone." I told her my idea. She laughed, and went over to murmur in the ears of the other band members.

Mike grinned at me. "The Brubeck version?"

"Sure, why not?" I said. I sat down at the piano, waited for Carl to start the one-two on his bass, and then started the intro on the second bar. I leaned over to Mike's microphone. "This one's for Wyatt," I told the audience.

I met Wyatt's startled gaze across the room. He stood next to Low-Rider, arms folded. And throughout our entire rendition of Stephen Foster's "Camptown Races", as re-interpreted by the Dave Brubeck Quartet and now the Ad Hoc Committee, Wyatt Earp grinned from ear to ear.

CHAPTER 14

I actually dozed off on my couch after coming home from Nicky's at dawn, so the phone waking me up at nine in the morning was an unpleasant surprise. I yawned and answered. "Mrfgrhp."

"Good morning, Sunshine," Suzette said, a note of amusement in her voice.

"What?" I'm not at my best in the morning, sleep or no.

"I've got a meeting with a detective from Narcotics today. Thought you might like to sit in."

"Why?" I rubbed my eyes. What was that smell? Oh. Me. I needed a shower.

"I asked around about Marty Hancock, like you asked. A friend of mine in DEA tagged me back, and I figured you'd want to be there when she briefs me."

"Your lieutenant won't mind?"

"What she doesn't know won't hurt her."

"Please tell me Vic is not in any way associated with this meeting."

"Vic is not in any way associated with this meeting," she said. "In fact, he's on another case today."

"Then I'll be there. Your office?"

"No way," she laughed. "Henry's, noon. And you're buying."

"Damn," I said, but she'd hung up.

I showered, ate, and spent an hour at the computer tracking down the rather colorful record of one Dan "Hog" Schaeffer, biker president. Frank the bartender had told me his real name after the bikers had left. I found court cases covering theft, assault, battery, and plenty of traffic citations. Three convictions for dealing, reduced to time served—apparently he'd made a deal with the DA. He'd done a couple of months for stealing bike parts from a junkyard, which told me he was a cheapskate as well as a thief. I mean, if you're going to steal bike parts, why not steal new ones? Most of all, I wondered why a guy with a record of drug dealing, assault and battery would be considered a good security guard. I ran a search of employment records, and sure enough, JackWay Holdings popped.

"Interesting," I murmured to myself.

"What's interesting?" a deep voice said behind me.

I yelped and spun, jumping out of the chair. Wyatt Earp stood on the other side of the room, hands in his pockets. Today he wore a white shirt, brown pants, and a black vest with his watch chain looping across it. But he was without a coat, and his sleeves were rolled up to his elbows. He looked more casual than I could remember having seen him. Still, I snarled at him. "Don't do that!"

"Sorry," he said, with no trace of sorry in his voice. "Didn't mean to startle you."

"Bullshit," I said. "You love watching me jump."

Was that a twinkle in his eye? Did tough lawmen in the Old West actually twinkle? "You did look funny," he admitted.

Scowling, I stomped off into my bedroom. We have an agreement: Wyatt is only permitted to visit my living room. He has given me his word not to enter any other room in my apartment. Otherwise, the lack of privacy might drive me mad. Knowing I had more than one stop to make today, I pulled on gray pants, a gray knit turtleneck, and a black jacket to cover my gun, which I wore in the middle of my back. This meant I didn't have to carry a purse, which I prefer not to do anyway. I have walking boots in every color available, so I was ready to go in a matter of minutes.

I walked into my kitchen, which is divided from the living room by a pass-through and bar. I grabbed a yogurt out of the fridge and leaned back against the door to eat it. "Is there a reason you are disturbing my chi this morning, Marshal?"

He raised one eyebrow at my use of Chinese but otherwise remained dead-pan. "I went through Marty's apartment. He's out."

"Canada," I said. I dug for a strawberry buried in the yogurt. "Race."

He nodded. "If he has drugs, he didn't leave any out where I could see them. But he's behind on the rent. One of the opened bills on his desk showed he's behind on a credit card by three months."

I frowned. "Great. Will he be able to pay my bill?"

Wyatt shrugged. "I hope you got a big retainer."

I sighed. "Even if he turns out to be a deadbeat, I can't drop the case now." I filled Wyatt in on my research on Dan Schaeffer and his connection to JackWay. Scraping the last of the yogurt out of the carton, I said, "And on top of everything else, Suzette has set me up with a meeting with a narcotics cop. I think there's something on Marty."

"If he's selling illegal drugs, will that implicate you?" Wyatt's eyes went dark, as I'd noticed they did when his temper was up.

"Doubtful. And since I'm the one bringing this to Suzette, that would work in my favor," I said. I glanced at the clock on the microwave. I told him the address for Henry's and then said, "Afterwards, I want to talk to the Park Rangers on Alcatraz about the race."

Wyatt nodded in agreement. "I'll meet you there." He glanced away, then back to me. "Thanks for letting me know where you're going to be."

"Be nice if you could do the same," I said.

He nodded.

"Too bad they didn't have phones in your day," I said. I nodded at his watch chain, stretched across his flat stomach.

"Who says we didn't?" He said, a note of irritation in his voice. "The day of the street fight in Tombstone, someone telephoned to the mine owners. Dick Gird arrived with a vigilance committee while the bodies were still warm."

I blinked. Wyatt almost never spoke of the gunfight near

the OK Corral in Tombstone, the street fight that had made his name a household word. "So they had 9-1-1 back then?"

He glared at me, then relaxed. "You're funnin' me."

"I've always wanted to ask." I nodded at his watch chain. "Why do you have a watch in the afterlife? And a gun?" Most days, he wore his Colt .44 Peacemaker in a shoulder rig. "And a hat and boots and all the rest. Were you buried with them or something?" And how weird were these questions?

He got a distant, frosty look. "I don't know. I only know that I can only go where I went in life, or possess things I had in life. I had a telephone, of course. My phone number in Los Angeles was—"

"Stop!" I said, holding up a hand. "You're hurting my head. Wyatt Earp, with a telephone?"

"And a car and a radio," he said testily. "I used to listen to baseball and boxing."

I rubbed my eyes. It was hard sometimes for me to remember that Wyatt's life had covered such a long span of American history, from the Gold Rush to the Great Depression. "Well, maybe we can work on getting you a cell phone, though God knows what the roaming charges would be, on your side of the Great Divide," I said. I tossed the carton in the recycle bin. "Meanwhile, I need to get moving."

"Likewise," he said. He seemed to be in a thoughtful mood. He straightened, stuck his hands in his pockets and sauntered through a wall.

I'm old fashioned; I used the door.

Henry's was usually packed at lunch, so my strategy was to get there early. As it was, I got the last four-top in the place, bullying a couple of rookie cops out of the spot. I had barely sat down when Suzette walked in with another woman. Conversation dimmed, eyes focused on the two women. They made quite a pair: Suzette tall and elegant, the other woman shorter but just as striking, with red hair, brown eyes in a delicate face, and a classy medium blue suit. The patrons of the bar made them as cops, and conversations resumed.

"Hey, Claire," Suzette said as she pulled out a chair. "This is Special Agent Leesa Kern, from DEA. Leesa, Claire Turnbull."

Agent Kern eyed me with some misgiving. "Civilian?"

"Used to be on the job," I said. "Six years."

"Suzette briefed me on the case." Kern said. "You're working for Marty Hancock?"

I signaled for the waitress, in the forlorn hope we might be able to order within an hour. She stalked by, ignoring us. "He hired me to find his missing girlfriend."

Kern exchanged a glance with Suzette. "You really think she's alive?"

I shrugged. "Probably not. But he's paying me to find out what happened, and I am."

Kern's expression was a shade short of an outright sneer. "So you're investigating until he runs out of money, or what?"

I looked at Suzette. "She here for a reason, or just to bust my chops?"

"Let's get something to eat," Suzette said reasonably. She lifted a hand, and the waitress was instantly at her side. How does she do that? We ordered—burgers and fries all around—and settled in with our sodas.

"It's not as simple as Suzette thinks," I said. "Which is why I need info from the DEA."

As I filled them in, Kern listened with that intense cop focus that misses nothing, and gives nothing away. By the time I'd finished, the burgers had arrived, hot and juicy. Kern leaned back, sipping on her soda.

"You realize that possession, sale and use of performance enhancing drugs is not my concern," she said.

"Yeah," I said. "So why is a second-tier triathlete even on the radar?"

Kern leaned forward. "It's not the PEDs we're interested in. It's the meth."

I inhaled slowly. "Yikes. You think Marty's dealing speed?"

Kern shrugged. "We've got informants who link him to a couple of dealers. A DEA bust last year turned his name up in a couple of address books. And there's a pattern we're piecing together: every time Marty is in a town for a race, meth sales go up."

"Maybe it wasn't Marty doing the dealing," I said. "Allison had a history of drug abuse." I told them about my visit to Allison's mother, and her account of Allison's juvie record. "So you've got a woman who may have been using or dealing drugs from her teens upward, who travels from town to town for race meets, and is now living with a guy with ties to the Washouts."

Both women stared at me. "The Washouts?"

I explained the connection between the bikers and Rafferty's company. "And I'm not completely oblivious," I said, speaking to Suzette. "I know bikers are a prime force in the movement and distribution of drugs."

Kern stared at the table, thinking. Her fingers drummed on her thigh. "Rafferty. Hm."

"And JackWay deals with importers," I added. "The director of the race is also a subcontractor for JackWay, and he brings in building supplies from all over the Pacific Rim. Lots of money changing hands over international boundaries."

Kern looked at me, her eyes narrowed. "Not just drugs, then—"

"But money laundering," I finished for her. "I can keep up that far." I looked over at Suzette. "Still think Allison Farley drowned by accident?"

Suzette looked thoughtful. "I think I need to talk to the LT," she said.

I glanced at my watch and rose. "Let me know what she says," I said.

Agent Kern frowned at me. "What's your hurry? Where are you going?"

"To prison," I said, and walked out.

Chapter 15

Getting to Alcatraz was a lot easier in Al Capone's day; all you needed was a federal conviction and a reputation. Nowadays, tickets sell out days or even weeks in advance in tourist season; October might not be the height of tourist season but it's still no picnic getting onto the island. So I was glad that Chrystal Richards had arranged for me to ride the ferry out to Alcatraz for free. It was a crowded ride in the big double-decker, one where I had to decide whether to risk windburn on the exposed upper deck or toxic poisoning from the diesel fumes below. I opted for fresh air and stood at the rail, watching Alcatraz approach.

The island holds a lot of buildings for only twenty-two acres. Sitting smack in the middle of San Francisco Bay, the Army took one look at it in the 1840s and commandeered it for defense. For a hundred and fifty years it bristled with cannons and redoubts, with a dilapidated lighthouse beaming through the fog, the Army's reluctant concession to the needs of sailors. Then the Feds moved the Army out and turned it into the most notorious prison in America, housing celebrity felons like Big Al, 'Doc' Barker, Mickey Cohen and Machine Gun Kelly.

When the operating costs topped three million dollars a year, the Feds abandoned it. Indians took it over for two years, and then it was deserted again. San Francisco debated with the federal government over what to do next, until someone got the bright idea of turning it into a tourist attraction.

Now, after losing money for a century and a half, the crumbling concrete pile had suddenly become the number one tourist attraction in the Bay Area, and the government was making a profit off of it at last.

The island itself is not very impressive, rising less than a hundred feet above the waterline. The five story main building lay on the long axis of the island, a no-nonsense block of cells and windows, like a five hundred foot long Parthenon.

Other buildings crowded the top of the island, and sheer cliffs fell to the sea for more than half of its shoreline. A tall lighthouse blinked regularly, guiding shipping around its base, and one squat water tower on spindly legs rose on its eastern shore. As I leaned on the rail, tourists of every kind crowded up and down the ladders from below, eager to document this moment for future generations.

"Regardes-moi, Alain! Michelle! Ne retourner pas! Regardes le camera!"

I got nudged by a skinny woman with a camera and a sun hat, who was positioning her mate and offspring for a photograph with the island in the background. They snapped picture after picture while I studied the shoreline, gauging the distance, the current, the swimming conditions.

The shore we were coming up on showed a steep, flat face descending almost to sea level, then terminating in a narrow paved path no more than a foot above the water. It was ringed with fences, walls, and other impedimenta to escape. The floating dock was on the island's leeward side, facing towards Berkeley and Oakland across the water. The big double launch chugged in, backed slowly, and finally sighed languidly into its berth.

A crewman opened the door, extended a short ramp, and tourists began filing out. The ramps leading up from the boat zigzagged back and forth, with several hairpin turns. I hung back until the last of the tourists had puffed their way up to the plaza level, and then followed.

This was the same ramp Allison Farley had walked up a little more than a week ago. As far as anyone knew, it was the last time anyone had laid eyes on her. It was ridiculous to believe I might find some sign of her passing or her fate, but I scrutinized the ramp anyway. It was nothing special: wooden slats covered with a tar paper walkway, worn through in spots from millions of feet.

We emerged onto a concrete open area, dotted with benches and kiosks. Overhead, a looming three story building dominated the scene, and a broad, sloping ramp led off to the left. A Ranger in a Smoky the Bear hat and a bullhorn was gathering people for a tour. I wandered off to the right, and stood looking over a railing onto a roped off area. Wyatt Earp stepped out of some shadows and came to stand beside me.

"Mighty pretty view of the city from here," he said.

We stood looking at San Francisco across a mile and a quarter of open water for awhile. It sat gleaming and white on its hills, with spires and buildings and the Ferry Building and ships nosed in here and there at the piers. "Must have driven the prisoners crazy to be so close to that, and so far," I said.

"Not just the prisoners," he said. "Although they used to say the worst part was being able to see and hear the New Year's Day parties from San Francisco."

"Frustrating," I said.

"The soldiers weren't crazy about it, either. They didn't get shore leave much more frequently than the prisoners did later."

I stuck my hands in my pockets. "You knew them?"

He shrugged. The wind whipped my jacket, but didn't touch him at all. He stood looking out across the water, maybe into the past. "Used to come over to watch the fights. Back in the 1920s, before the Bureau of Prisons took it over, they'd stage prize fights in the laundry or the mess hall. They set up a ring, put gloves on the boys. I refereed one or two myself."

I remembered that, in his day, Wyatt Earp had refereed more than eighty fights on the West Coast, including one very notorious bout for the heavyweight title. "You ever get in the ring?"

He snorted. "I was a mite old for it by then. And my eyes weren't so good any more. 'Sides, the warden woulda had a fit if a civilian got in the ring." He looked down at his hands, and made two slow fists. "But in my day, I would have won a couple of bouts, myself."

I looked up and past him, up at the steep hillside above us. "You know this Rock pretty well, then."

Wyatt shook his head. "Nobody knows it well. Men have been tunnelling and hacking and building and tearing down and covering over for a hunnerd fifty years. God knows what's buried under some of these buildings."

I cocked my head. "Tunnels?" I looked around the assembly area behind me. "Could Allison have wandered off and gotten lost in some underground tunnel? Or fallen in some pit?"

"More likely fell off over a railing and broke her neck," Wyatt said. "If you wanna search Alcatraz, we're gonna need more time or more men."

My cell phone dinged in my pocket, reminding me of my appointment. "Let's go talk to a Ranger," I said.

Wyatt followed me up the single rickety stair that climbed from the assembly area to the looming bulk of Building 64, which beetled over the plaza like a three-story cliff. Wyatt peered at the wooden stairs and handrail. "Hmm," he said.

"What?"

"Just remembering that this was built with convict labor," he mused. "More'n a century ago."

"Oh, thanks," I said. If it collapsed under us, Wyatt wouldn't be hurt, but I might be joining him on the other side.

Room 30 was one of several whose doors were on one of the long verandas; as I walked I could look down on the tourists milling about beneath me. I knocked, and was told to come in. Wyatt, of course, simply stepped through the wall.

We entered a large room that smelled of old wood. Dust motes danced in sunbeams streaming through uncurtained windows, and the walls were covered with Park Service posters encouraging people to visit other places than this one. Four desks pretty much filled the room; behind them, uniformed women typed on computer keyboards or spoke into telephones. The nearest woman rose as I came in. "Ms. Turnbull? I'm Chrystal Richards."

The voice on the phone had conjured a mental image that

did not match what stood before me. She should have been young, short, plump and giggly. Chrystal Richards was in her late fifties, had the tall, rangy figure of a women's basketball coach and dark brown hair cut short. She wore the standard dark green uniform of the Service, but not the hat. I shook her hand and thanked her for seeing me.

She did not offer me a chair, but remained standing. "How may I help you?" Watching her talk was like watching Katherine Hepburn talk with Marilyn Monroe's voice.

"I have some questions about the triathlon last week. You were the Park Service liaison?"

"Yes," she said. She leaned against the desk. I remained standing. "I worked with the race director and several sponsors, planning the event."

"I'm looking into the disappearance of Allison Farley," I said. I filled her in quickly on my investigation, including my conversation with the race director. "So I know she made it as far as the dock out there," I said, tilting my head. "But I'm wondering if she could have wandered away or been taken away, maybe somewhere on this island."

Chrystal crossed her arms, showing thin shoulders. "We searched the whole island," she said defensively.

"I am sure you did," I said. "My client only wants me to go over it, give him the picture. He's really cut up about her accident."

Sympathy flitted across Chrystal's sunburned features. "I'm not sure what I can do to help you."

"Ask her about the shoreline," Wyatt said. "Used to be some tidal caves along it."

I glanced at a map on the wall. "I understand the shoreline of Alcatraz Island is pretty rough," I said.

"It is," Chrystal said shortly.

"But there have been reports now and then of caves at the tideline. I'm thinking perhaps her body could have washed up in one."

"Like I said," Chrystal said, shifting her stance. "We searched the island very carefully."

"Right. But that was a week ago. Bodies of drowning victims can float to the surface days later. Has anyone checked lately to see if she's washed up here?" I said.

Chrystal got a thoughtful look on her face. "Not that I know of. But we don't really have the manpower to launch a full search right now."

"How about if I take a look around?"

Wyatt wandered over to study the map.

Chrystal frowned. "Oh, you can't do that! You'd need special permission!"

"So who do I talk to about that?" I tried not to sound impatient. I was growing weary of bureaucratic obstacles.

"Oh, that would be Senior Ranger Thompson. But he's in Sacramento right now. He'll be back Monday, though." She perked up. "Would you like to make an appointment?"

By Monday what little evidence remained after a week would be gone. I smiled and said, "No, thanks. I guess I'll go on back and call him from my office."

"It's no trouble!" Chrystal sounded as if she lived for nothing but making appointments for her boss.

"No, thanks." I eased towards the door. "I'll call him myself. You have a good day."

"You, too!" she said brightly.

Wyatt followed me out onto the veranda. We were well past noon and into the early afternoon, and while the weather remained calm and sunny, that could change as soon as the fog drifted in past the Golden Gate. I glanced right and left; the veranda was deserted, and the Rangers below were busy shepherding tourists and giving lectures.

"You want to search the shoreline?" Wyatt said. "I think I remember a way down to it from the Parade Grounds, if you don't mind a scramble."

"I would like to actually do something today," I said crossly.

Reaching the dock and assembly area, I fell in behind a group of tourists puffing their way up the steep eastern ramp that ran through the Sally Port, with its big cannon mounts. Wyatt kept pace with me all the way up, except when I had to stop and doing a little puffing myself at the switchbacks. The main road at Alcatraz zigzags from the waterline to the crest of the island, a climb of some thirteen stories. Wyatt strode on and then turned to wait, visibly impatient, as I caught my breath.

Fuchsias and climbing roses spilled over the concrete barrier walls, and ivy cascaded down the reinforced brick walls rising over the walkway. I thought of murderers and thieves tending these plants with loving care, so carefully that half a century after the prisoners left, their flowers remained behind. It kind of put Big Al and Machine Gun Kelly in perspective.

"Come on," Wyatt said impatiently.

I panted and blew my way to the top, resolving to get in more road work in the weeks to come. Finally I arrived at the windswept Eagle Plaza in front of the main door to the massive main cellhouse. The 84-foot-tall lighthouse, which overlooked the dropoff to the Parade Grounds below, dominated the site. It was a lonely, windswept place, full of sunshine but not hope.

It was far from empty, however. The western side of the Plaza, including the lighthouse, was surrounded by a chain link construction fence with HARD HAT AREA signs all over them. A neatly lettered sign informed visitors that something called slope stabilization was being performed on the ruins of the Warden's house.

Behind the fence, men were hammering and sawing, and yelling over the racket of a portable generator. Another generator purred away on the opposite side of the plaza, in support of some reconstruction on the burned-out warden's house.

"Used to come and watch Indian dances here," Wyatt said, pitching his voice over the noise.

"Indian dances?" I turned to him. "You mean from the Occupation?"

"Yup," Wyatt said. "Back in 1969, the Indians took over the island after the Federals shut down the prison. They'd hold dances and sing. Sure were different from Apaches in my day." He turned slowly. "We need to go past the lighthouse and then down that walk."

"Right." I started off, searching for a way past the construction fencing. A Hispanic man with a white hard hat and a bright orange safety vest watched me, frowning, but said nothing. I edged around a corner where two sections met, stepped over a bed of begonias, and only then realized I was alone. I stopped and glanced over my shoulder. Wyatt stood a little forward of where I'd left him, but even at this distance he looked different. Odd as it sounds, he looked almost pale. And his right arm seemed to be missing.

"Wyatt?"

I retraced my steps, aware of the Hispanic workman still watching me. I took my cell phone from my pocket and pretended to make a call, staring at Wyatt.

His right arm and part of his hat faded into nothing, like a weathered photograph. He stood stock still, blinking, swaying a bit.

"Wyatt? What the hell?" I felt my heart thump heavily. Was he finally, after so many years, fading away as most ghosts do? Had his end come at last? I felt a spike of anxiety. "Are you all right?"

He turned his head slowly towards me, as if moving against his will. "Generators…" he whispered.

I glanced behind me. Of course. The only force that could really affect Wyatt was a strong electrical field, and in following me he had walked right between two powerful generators. There was so much static electricity I could even feel the hairs on my own arms rising.

"Okay, slow and easy," I said. "Can you take a step back?"

He looked at me with a grim expression. After a long moment, he stepped slowly backwards on his left leg, dragging his right side. He took a deep breath (leading me to wonder how a ghost could breathe, and whether he could suffocate) and did it again. His arm faded in like a movie special effect, and his whole body straightened. This time he took a step back with his right leg and then he was whole again, if looking pale in the strong sunlight.

"Better?" I said.

His mouth made a dour line. "Some," he said. "Reckon I'm not much use around them machines."

"Do you need to sit down or something?"

He shook his head, not meeting my gaze. It occurred to me that he was embarrassed. He probably thought his one vulnerability made him look weak, and if I knew anything about Wyatt Earp, I knew he was a proud man. So I made my expression as neutral and casual as I could, and stood looking about the plaza like any other tourist.

Off to my left, fences with scaffolding and other construction structures, surrounded a crumbling two-story house. The fences held signs listing the construction firms hired by the Park Service. A rock escarpment covered with low-growing bushes was roped off and some men with shovels were digging compost into the soil.

"Looks like we can't go that way," I said. "Any suggestions?"

"Look at this, Claire." Wyatt pointed at an array of signs naming the contractors. "See anyone you recognize?"

I scanned the list, and stopped. "Cornerstone Home Imports. JackWay Holdings. Wainwright Contractors." My gaze met his. "Interesting coincidence. These are all sponsors of the race."

"Reckon that's how they got the contracts," Wyatt said. At my look, he smiled. "This don't even qualify as proper graft."

"I'm wondering how many of those sponsors are part of the Cogent Fund mess," I said, thinking of my conversation with Roland.

Wyatt shrugged. "Wouldn't be the first time public money got piped away. I remember after the '06 quake, when City Hall collapsed. Newspaper reports said you could have crumbled the 'bricks' with your bare hand; the builders had skimped on the materials and billed the city for prime supplies. Might be these folks are doing the same." He was looking better now, his posture straight and all his limbs visible. He squared his shoulders and adjusted his hat. "You go round the fence. I'll cut around these machines and meet you beyond it."

I skirted the construction fencing. Wyatt walked through a pile of building materials between the main cell block and a broken staircase. He also walked through a stack of cement bags, a pile of lumber, and a stone wall. I climbed, scrambled and inched my way over various similar obstacles, and found myself in Off Limits territory. I looked around; there were no Rangers in sight, nor any construction workers, but one could appear at any moment. I strode quickly down the gravel path until bushes hid me from above. Wyatt met me at the bottom of some disintegrating concrete steps, looking none the worse for his brief fade-out. "Where to now?"

Wyatt pointed to a low walkway skirting the island, several dozen feet above the waterline. Below, where land met sea, all was shattered black rock and dashing waves. "The way down is pretty steep," he said. "There are spots where you can stand up straight and bite the dirt."

"You've been down there before?"

"Prohibition," he answered tersely.

"They were running hooch to a prison?" I asked, startled. "And weren't you, uh, dead?"

"It was still an Army base back then," he said. "I'd come and watch. I hated Prohibition. Made us a nation of hypocrites." His jaw worked. "They didn't repeal it until after I died. Last alcohol I ever drank in my life was in a speakeasy."

He sounded as angry as I'd ever heard him.

I buttoned my jacket against the cold, and started climbing down the Rock.

CHAPTER 16

I scrambled down the hillside, half-sliding, half-falling, until I reached a narrow strip of sand no wider than I was. Water splashed and gurgled at my feet. Under the water, not more than four feet from shore, I saw the deep blue-green of deep water. No gentle underwater gradient here; Alcatraz was the top of a mountain with an abrupt drop-off.

In front of me, the narrow strip of seaweed-encrusted rock and sand curved out of sight; behind me, it petered out along a rocky strand. "Guess I'd better go this way," I said. "You go that direction. Don't get your boots wet."

Wyatt harrumphed and turned north. I inched my way along the shelf of sand, knowing that if I fell in, the combination of shockingly cold water and fast currents would take me half a mile from shore in minutes, helpless in the pull of the tide. Rocks slid underfoot as I crept around a bend. And there I saw a dark opening in the rock, right before me. "Wyatt!" I yelled.

He was instantly beside me. I pointed, he looked, and under the mustache a white grin flashed. "Good work, Claire." He strode off, more or less walking on the waves, while I crept slowly around the curve to the opening of the tidal cave. The entrance was about as tall as Wyatt, the walls dripping. "Tide comes up to the roof in here," Wyatt said, scanning the roof. "This must be Hamilton's cave."

"Who?"

"Floyd Hamilton," Wyatt said. "He rode with the Clyde Barrow gang."

"Bonnie and Clyde?" I stared at the waves washing in and

out, trying to determine whether the tide was rising or falling. "Aren't they a little after your day?"

"I kept up with the news," Wyatt said. "'Specially Texas outlaws. Got a partic'lar interest in them. Anyway, Floyd got sent to Alcatraz, but busted out in 1943 with a couple other fellows. They climbed down from the laundry, then tried to swim, but couldn't manage it. His partner was captured, but Hamilton hid out in the cave until he couldn't take the cold and the wet any more. He clumb back up and snuck back into the prison. Them hot showers and dry blankets probably looked a lot better after two nights in a tidal cave," he said.

"He broke into Alcatraz?" I eyed the sand in front of me; it was littered with junk left behind by the tides.

"Yup. Funny thing was, he hid out behind some boxes in a storage room. Wouldn't never have been found, except a guard went looking for some tools and stumbled across him."

I stopped. "So you're saying that a massive manhunt, including the Coast Guard and every guard on Alcatraz, somehow missed a guy hiding right here on the island?"

Wyatt met my eyes. "Don't go thinkin' that, Claire," he said. "Hamilton was in the cave less'n two days; she's been gone a week. Don't go thinkin' we're going to find her in this cave. Unless her body's washed up here. Watch your footing, it looks slippery."

He was right; seaweed and algae coated the sharp rocks jutting out of sand and water. I glanced around at the bleak and empty beach, the gray water, the distant shoreline. I imagined huddling here in water cold enough to numb your limbs, with the wind making it even colder, hungry and maybe wounded. And then the tide coming in, rising higher and higher in the cave...I picked my way carefully along the strand.

Wyatt strolled onward, head bent. He stopped and pointed. "Something here, Claire."

A bit of blue rubber lay half-buried in the sand. I tugged it free; it was a torn balloon. "Not a swim cap," I said.

We approached the tidal cave, which was a yawning mouth in the rock, here on the northwest tip of the island. I glanced up at the rock beetling out overhead; I knew no one could see us from above. I hoped the tide was going out. I hoped I would be able to retrace my steps to the top, or else I'd have to call for help to get home. And that would be embarrassing. Inside, it smelled like low tide—dead fish, seaweed, salt. Strands of seaweed were caught in a few boulders. The ground was soft sand, now absolutely blank of any imprints after a week of washing. The walls looked wet.

"Nothing here but trash and seashells," Wyatt said. He crouched down and walked into the cave.

I knelt and swept my hand back and forth lightly over the wet sand, looking for anything buried in the layers built up by the tides. I turned up some broken seashells, several bits of plastic cups, a fistful of anonymous pieces of paper that had once been cups or boxes or other trash.

Wyatt came back. "Goes back about forty feet," he announced. "Ground is clear except for some old tires. I walked right through several cobwebs stretched from wall to wall, so no one's been back there in a while."

Disappointed, I duck-walked back out of the sandy cave. Sunlight slanted through the fog and bouncing off the water. I squinted in the glare, and suddenly something winked at me out of the corner of my eye.

I knelt, and felt around and in between a couple of rocks. Something was wedged there; I fished it out and held it up.

"What's that?" Wyatt bent close. "Poker chip?"

It looked a little like one: silver, metallic, round. But on the face of it I read ALCATRAZ and the number 1131. That was Allison's number in the race. "It's her RFID timing chip," I said.

Wyatt met my eyes. "Washed in with the tide," he said.

"Or left here when someone held her hostage?" In my mind's eye, I saw a bound and helpless woman. "Could be she left this here deliberately, like a bread crumb trail. You sure there's no sign back there?"

"Look for yourself," he said, a little testily. "Ain't been a living soul in here in months, maybe years. Could be she lost that during the swim. Or her body got washed in here temporarily, that got caught on the rock and torn off."

"You sound like Suzette Melton," I said.

"Good," Wyatt snapped. "She's a woman with some sense."

I thought about ignoring Wyatt, exploring the cave myself. But the wind was cold, and I was afraid the tide was turning, and besides, did I trust his abilities or not? If the famous old lawman said there was no sign, then there was no sign. "I'll turn this over to her," I said.

"And close this case," Wyatt said. "You ain't never gonna find her body. You've found this chip, so you can bill your client and let this go."

I was tempted. But I'm also stubborn, and I couldn't forget the look in Marty's eyes, in Wayne Rafferty's. These men would be haunted until I knew the full truth. "Maybe she is dead," I said. "But that doesn't mean we know what happened."

Wyatt snorted and turned away.

I put the chip in my pocket and turned to retrace my steps. Wyatt guided me back up, directing and encouraging me as I scrambled and climbed back up to the walkway. I made it without incident, and finally stood again on the windswept plaza in front of the main cellhouse. A woman fussed with a baby in a stroller, while her husband took pictures of the San Francisco skyline. Some teenagers larked about at the base of the ruins of the warden's house, which was now a burnt-out shell. I sat down on a bench.

I stared out over the slopes covered with shrubs, green and alive under the sun, reclaiming rocky slopes and tumbled concrete ruins. Life, as always, reclaiming death.

"I'll catch the ferry back," I told Wyatt. "I'll need to get this chip to Suzette right away."

The mother with the stroller was whispering urgently to her husband, glancing over at me. I smiled. She blanched and tugged at her husband's arm.

"If you're going back to the mainland, then I'll go back and watch Rafferty," Wyatt said. "Ain't no more I can do here." Before I could respond, he tipped his hat and strode forward.

Before his foot hit the ground, he had vanished; that was a new trick.

I sat in the sunshine, staring up at the lighthouse towering over me. Even in the daylight, I could see the rhythmic flash of the light, warning away the huge tankers and cargo ships chugging through the Bay. Of all the many industries that had once made this island busy—the laundry, workshops, and the tailor shops—only the lighthouse still performed its original function, still had a job. My eye took in the scaffolding surrounding it, the generators that had afflicted Wyatt. I saw only one workman, pushing a wheelbarrow full of broken bricks towards the cliff edge. I wondered how many tons of discarded building materials had gone over that edge during the island's long occupation.

It took me less than two hours to get home; nobody checked tickets on the return trip. Unlike every other administration that had run Alcatraz, they weren't worried about people leaving it.

No one lingers on the Rock who doesn't have to.

CHAPTER 17

The afternoon was slanting towards evening by the time I got back to my street, and my aches had aches. I had scraped myself raw here and there, and there was something wrong with my ankle. All I wanted was food, spirituous liquors, and a soaking bath. Not necessarily in that order. I pulled myself up the stairs to my place one step at a time, holding onto the railing.

I thought about the tag in my pocket. Had it fallen off of Allison? Why hadn't it responded to the Coast Guard's exciters? I could answer that one myself: it was bent. But was that an accident or had someone deliberately disabled it?

I was pondering this when I reached the landing and Justin's door opened almost in my face. I braced for impact, but this time it was only Ron Stedman, without his bicycle.

I stopped. "Hi."

He stopped. "Hi."

"Um." I was tired, I wasn't ready for this conversation, but I didn't know when I would see him again. "Look, about the other night. I wasn't trying to accuse you of anything."

His expression stayed neutral. "Apology accepted." He shifted from foot to foot, and now I saw the duffle hanging off his shoulder.

"You going to work out?"

His mouth tightened. "Leaving, actually. I wanted to get to Monterey today, maybe get in a few miles on the course."

"Oh." Damn. "Look, I didn't want to leave things the way they were," I said. "Can I buy you some carbs downstairs before you go?"

I could see the "no" in his eyes. He looked away, then he looked back. Something relaxed in him, and he shifted minutely. "Okay," he said. "But I've got to be on the road in an hour."

I turned and made my slow way downstairs. I heard him behind me, his tread sure and strong. I caught a toe and tripped. His hand seized my elbow, steadying me. "You okay?" His voice in my ear sounded intimate and close.

"Yeah. Did a little rock climbing today. Might have pulled a muscle." Several, in fact, but I wasn't going to let him hear me whine.

He stepped down beside me, looking me over. "Your jacket is torn. You weren't using climbing gear? Where were you?"

"Alcatraz."

He blinked. "I think I need to hear this."

"I climbed into a tidal cave."

A hint of a smile. "Okay, I definitely need to hear this."

I glanced over my shoulder up at the landing. "Is Justin in?"

"At work. Watch the bottom step."

Ron helped me down and through the gates. My calf muscles were screaming in protest, and I thought about the hot bath that, in a perfect world, was already waiting for me upstairs. But a chance to sit across from a handsome man and eat tiramisu was not to be missed.

Al met us at the door, where he had been wrapping napkins around place settings. "Claire! Come in!"

He led us inside. It was the middle of the afternoon, and the restaurant was nearly deserted. He put us in the front, at a window overlooking the sidewalk, so it would look as if there were more customers than there were. Ron waited until I was seated before he sat down opposite from me. He put the duffle on the floor and clasped his hands before him on the white tablecloth. "So, have you found that missing girl yet?"

Before I could reply, I saw a large form rushing towards me from the kitchen and braced myself. Two huge arms crushed me to a bosom redolent of garlic. "Claire! *Cara mio!*" Mamma Benetto embraced me with all the fervor of an Italian summer.

"Where have you been?"

"I was in here last night," I said. "Al will tell y—"

Mamma dismissed this with a wave of her hand, turning her brilliant dark eyes on my companion. "*Si*, he tell me. And with this handsome young man, yes?"

I cleared my throat. "Mamma Benetto, this is Ron Stedman."

Ron, looking slightly amused, held out his hand. Mamma seized it in hers. "Ah. Strong. Calluses. You work outdoors, yes?"

"They're from riding my bicycle," he said.

Mamma raised an eyebrow. "A bicycle?" She shrugged elaborately. I could see her already writing him off as a dilettante tourist. For some reason I cared about what she thought of this guy. Maybe because I cared about what he thought of me.

"Mamma, we don't need anything special," I said, trying to forestall the kind of interrogation I knew her capable of. "What do you recommend today?"

Ron's instincts were as good as mine. He caught Mamma's sleeve. "No tourist food," he said with a brilliant smile. I could see her melting under its warmth. "What have you made for your own lunch today?"

Mamma beamed. There is nothing she loves more than a good eater with a hearty appetite. "*Tortellini al Brodo. Prosciutto crudo, mortadella*, sausages I made myself last fall. A simple broth sauce to cover, yes?"

"Oh, yes," Ron breathed, mesmerized.

"And for me," I said. But I wasn't sure she heard me. Mamma and Ron's gazes had locked, each apparently finding a kindred spirit in the other. "And maybe a salad?"

Mamma nodded slowly, still looking at Ron. "I make double for you, I think." She winked and walked away.

Ron watched her while I pondered the accuracy of old bromides about the way to a man's heart. I cleared my throat twice, but it wasn't until Al came over with water and place settings that Ron came back to earth.

"I believe you have made a friend for life," I said.

"Homemade sausage," he said, his attention still on Mamma. "She really makes it herself?"

I smiled. "She does, with herbs my mother gives her. My mom won't even tell me what herbs they are."

He fiddled with his place setting, unwrapping the napkin and toying with the fork and knife. "So. How did you come to be climbing Alcatraz without proper gear?"

I sobered a little, wondering how much to tell him. "I'm still looking for Allison Farley," I said. "I was looking for her body, actually." I told him about searching for the tidal cave, but not what I found in it. He watched me without saying anything, until I finished up by saying, "At any rate, I didn't find her body."

"So you think she might have washed up on the island," he said thoughtfully. Al brought salads, and we pushed at lettuce and arugula for a minute. "But that doesn't have to mean she was dead."

"Well, well," I said lightly. "Finally someone besides my client who doesn't assume this is a lost cause."

"I've been thinking about what you said the other night." He shook grated parmesan on his salad. "I was in a race two years ago, this guy jumped in at the start and didn't come up. I heard about it later. A lifeguard missed him, went back looking, and brought him up. He'd been under about twenty minutes."

"He survived?"

Ron nodded, reached for bread. "The water was fifty-five degrees Fahrenheit. Maximum survival time, unprotected, in water that cold is about fifteen minutes. But the mammalian diving reflex kicked in and saved him."

"The what?"

Ron smiled gently. "I researched it, having a personal interest in it, so to speak. I hope I never experience it personally, but you never know."

"How does this reflex work?"

Al brought two plates of aromatic pasta and all conversation ceased as we reverently regarded our food. Ron looked up at me, and his eyes were smiling as warmly as his mouth, and I felt a nice little tingle go all the way down to my toes.

Ron stuck a fork in his tortellini, tasted it. His eyes closed.

"I know what you're thinking," I said. "But forget it. A dozen men a week, and some women, propose to Mamma Benetto. She is faithful to her late husband's memory."

Ron swallowed, ate more tortellini. "He must have died a happy man."

After our first hunger had been slaked, I brought us back to point. "So how does this reflex work?"

He kept his eyes on his food as he answered. "There's a nerve in the face, the trigeminal. When very cold water hits it, it can trigger a cold shock response. The doc I talked to said that it can cause bradycardia, which is a fancy term for your heart slowing down. That can cause dizziness or faintness, and you'll slip under without a struggle."

"Allison would have been wearing a wetsuit, right?"

"Sure. But it's the shock of cold water against her unprotected face that may have triggered the response. That can cause dizziness. She could have slipped under without a struggle."

I thought about this while Ron worked systematically through a huge helping of tortellini, three helpings of bread, and his salad. I let myself appreciate his lean and muscular form, and decided that road work was a first class means of burning off Mamma Benetto's cooking. I picked up my water glass, sipped it, thought about ice cold water.

"So these people who go into this shock response, do they ever wake up spontaneously?"

He looked up at me. "You think this Allison passed out when she hit the water, then woke up on her own, maybe in that tidal cave?"

Ron shrugged. "I'm just mentioning the possibility. I'm not a doctor." He glanced surreptitiously at his watch. "Just thought you would want to know about it."

I nodded thoughtfully. "I'll check it out. Thanks."

Mamma bustled over. "I got a *torta della nonna* in the oven, if you can wait a little." At Ron's look, she explained. "Custard pie, with almonds and pine nuts."

I stifled a moan. "Yes, please," I said quickly.

Ron smiled again, and my heart did that little skip thing. "Sorry, Mrs. Benetto—"

"Mamma," she said immediately. "Everybody calls me Mamma, especially those who like my cooking." She cast a glance at the clean plate Al was taking away.

Now Ron treated both of us to a full-bore grin, and I do believe it cast shadows across the tablecloth. "I will call you nothing else," he said. "But I'm afraid I really have to go if I'm going to get to Monterey in time." He reached for his wallet, but Mamma waved her hands.

"No, no," she said firmly. "Is my treat. I get you a cannoli to go, yes?"

"I won't say no," Ron said.

"Wise answer," I said as Mamma strode off with her usual energy. "I could not live with the shame if my dinner guest turned down homemade cannoli." I was fighting a vaguely disappointed feeling. I stood up and tossed my napkin on the table. "Thanks for the tip about the diving response."

"Sure," he said. Al brought over a small white sack. Ron gestured for me to precede him out of the restaurant.

On the sidewalk, we paused. It was awkward, and it wasn't. There had been a spark, then a shimmer, then anger and mistrust. We were now back to the shimmer. I wasn't sure what to make of it.

Ron stuck his hand out. "I'm glad to have met you, Claire. Do me a favor and say goodbye to Justin. I thought he'd be home when I left but it didn't work out that way."

"I'll do that," I said. His hand in mine was hot and strong. I could feel the calluses Mamma had mentioned. "Will you be back any time soon?"

Ron shrugged the duffle back up onto his shoulder. "Maybe. We usually get back together for Grandma's birthday."

I blinked. "Grandma?"

The breeze flipped his hair into his eyes and he shook it back. "Yeah. We usually drive up to Vallejo for Grandma's birthday; it's right before Thanksgiving."

"So…you're cousins?"

He looked at me oddly. "Yeah."

"Oh. I thought you were…um." I felt like an idiot, but wisely decided to shut up while I could. I thought about Justin, wandering around my apartment, straightening cushions and talking about his guest. *Oh, it's not a date…*

Ron looked puzzled, then laughed. "Oh. Oh, that's funny." He chuckled. "No, I'm not gay. Justin and I have always been buddies, but not that kind. He didn't tell you? His mother is my mom's sister." His smile faded, and a different look came into his face. Maybe he was realizing what that misunderstanding might have cost him. Or us. He glanced away, and now the smile was gone.

"Well, I…" he said. He cleared his throat. "I have to get going, or I'll be hitting rush hour traffic."

I took a deep breath. *Another one that got away*, I thought. "Yeah. Have a safe trip."

He stood a moment, then nodded. "See you around, Claire."

I wasn't the only one on the street enjoying the view as he swung easily down the hill, with the sun gilding his hair and his shoulders wide under the leather jacket.

I went back into the restaurant for some cannoli.

CHAPTER 18

I was tired, my muscles ached, and I was full of carbs. And I had just missed a chance to get to know a really good looking guy. The situation obviously called for chocolates or wine or a bubble bath or all three at once. Instead, when I entered my apartment I went straight to the computer and logged on. My subconscious had probably kicked into self-preservation mode, but in any case I was curious about this mammalian diving reflex.

I had eaten all the cannoli and was deep into the National Institutes of Health website when I heard a cough behind me. I jumped, but had already recognized his voice when I turned around. "Wyatt?"

"Yup."

The room had grown dark while I was busy, and now was illuminated only by the glow of the computer screen and the light filtering up from the street below in my front windows. I heard a horn blare on the street, heard laughter as someone walked by outside. But in here it was dark and quiet and a little cold. "So how is Wayne Rafferty?" I asked him.

I could barely make out his white shirt peeking through the lapels of his jacket. "Asleep. Or passed out again. Hard to tell."

"And you're bored." It was not a question.

He stepped forward and I saw him shrug. "What are you working on?"

I told him about the mammalian diving reflex. Halfway through, he squinted at me. "Where did you find out about this?"

"From Ron Stedman, the guy across the hall. We had a late

lunch at Benetto's." As I spoke, I felt his gaze sharpen and focus on me.

"Another 'date'?"

"No," I said. I felt a little defensive, and that made me irritated. "He was leaving for Monterey, and we had lunch. We talked about the case, and he said he'd encountered the mammalian diving reflex in a race. I was looking it up."

"You trust him?"

"I don't have to trust him." I waved a hand at my computer. "I trust the NIH, though."

He rubbed his mustache and shifted from foot to foot. He looked uncomfortable. "Wish you'd have let me know about this date," he grumbled.

"What the hell? Are you my chaperone now, Marshal?"

His glance turned to a glare. "Young women can't be too careful."

"And you would know this from personal experience?" I blew out my breath in exasperation. "Wyatt, I can take care of myself. I was a police officer for several years, I am trained in the martial arts, and a lot of times I am armed with a deadly weapon. So can you please back off on the fatherly concern? You're starting to overstep."

He looked startled, then angry. "I'm only looking out for you," he said.

I swung around on my chair, rubbing my eyes. "Oh, knock it off," I said. "That's what every overbearing male in the world has used as an excuse—"

"I seen rape," he said abruptly. His voice had turned hard and cold. "I seen rape. Murder. Women beat bloody. I seen what men can do to women who they get backed into a corner. And I couldn't do a God damned thing about it." He looked down at his hands. "Couldn't touch them, couldn't stop anything. Useless. It…it tore me up inside, being so helpless." He met my look again, eyes bright and hard. "If it happened to you, I … I don't know if I could stand it. Being so *useless*…"

He turned away, strode to the window and stood looking out over the street. "You know what it's like," he said quietly.

"You know what it's like to watch someone suffer and die, and not be able to do anything."

I remembered the waiting room at the hospital, the pacing, the other cops coming in silently to offer a word, a shoulder, then leaving again. Endless hours of waiting and hoping and praying to every god with ears. I remembered the terrible, sinking feeling when the doors opened and the surgeon came through with that sad look in his eyes, the solemn and neutral expression on his face. I closed my eyes. "Yes," I said. "And that's why I'm looking for anything, anything that might help me find Allison Farley. For Marty Hancock's sake."

He waved a hand at the computer. "This is just raising false hope, he'll—"

"False hope is better than no hope!" I let my anger show. "Why should I cut it short? What's the advantage? So Marty can suffer that much sooner? Is that better for him? Or does it just satisfy you? Are you so bitter and twisted you think everyone should suffer as well?"

Wyatt stared at me. "Bitter? Twisted? Is that what you think I am?"

I stood up, pacing. "No. Not really. But you have to admit, from the very beginning of this case you've been nay-saying me, telling me I was wasting my time." I stopped, closing my eyes. "I know what it's like to hope." I opened them again. "Right now, my client has hope. Maybe he's got no good reason for it, but he's got it. Why should I take that away from him?"

"Claire." Wyatt's tone was subdued. "Sometimes it's good to be mule-headed about something. I admire anyone who don't quit at the first sign of trouble. But you got to realize, you're lookin' for the impossible."

"I want to find her," I said. "Or at least to find out what happened."

Wyatt stood in front of me, hands in pockets. "This is personal," he said. "Why?"

I ran a hand through my hair. "Jack. I remember what it was like when he died. I know what it's like to need to know, to be unable to rest until you do."

"You think you're the only one?" Wyatt's tone was harsh; he was almost shouting. "You think you're the only one to hope and pray and be helpless while he dies? You think you're the only one who's had to watch someone you love die almost in your arms?"

I stopped pacing. "You're talking about your brother, Morgan." I knew that his younger brother Morgan Earp, who had stood at his side during the famous gunfight near the OK Corral, had been backshot and murdered a few months later. "I'm sorry."

Wyatt looked away; even in the dim light of the window I could see the flush along his cheekbones, the big hands curling into fists. "Yeah," he said. He looked back at me. "Don't mix 'em up."

"What?"

"Don't mix 'em up, your husband, my brother. They're not like this case. Marty Hancock ain't you and he ain't me, and what happened to him losing his gal ain't what happened to us."

"How so? She disappeared, everyone says she's dead. He needs to know if she's alive or dead. I would want the same, wouldn't you?" It took me a minute to continue because my throat was too tight to speak.

"They never found out who shot Jack," I said. "They had the bullets from the gun that shot him. They had testimony from his partner. But they didn't have a suspect, a witness, nothing. The police department put it down to 'gang warfare' and held his funeral."

"You think they were wrong?"

I shook my head. "No. Suzette headed the investigation; she wouldn't have skimped or covered up. But there was nothing to find. And in the end, all they could do was recommend counseling so I could find 'closure'." I said the word angrily. I looked Wyatt in the eye. "So I know what Marty feels. And Wayne. They need to know. They don't need 'closure', they need facts. Whatever I can get for them, I will."

Wyatt nodded. "Of course you will."

We were silent a moment. We had gone from Wyatt fussing over me like a Victorian uncle, to bonding over shared grief. Life with Wyatt Earp was never dull. At least he wasn't talking about Ron Stedman any more.

I rubbed my eyes. "I'm tired. There's a forty percent possibility I could actually get some sleep tonight."

He raised an eyebrow. "Forty percent?"

"I made the number up." I stepped over, shut down the computer. "And it looks like this theory won't work anyway. Even if Allison passed out in the water and survived, there was no one to haul her out, revive her. I can't even find out if you can revive on your own."

"So this is a dead end?"

"Guess so." I yawned, which was a good sign. "Feel free to sack out on the couch if you like; I'm off to bed."

The corner of his mouth twitched up. "Good night, Claire." Of course we both knew he didn't need a couch, and I suspected he never slept anyway.

"Good night, Wyatt," I said.

He stepped towards the door, then turned back. "You tell Inspector Melton about that tag yet?"

I yawned again. "In the morning."

He nodded, stepped through the wall and vanished.

I made it all the way to the bedroom, fell face down on the quilt without taking off my clothes, and slept. Finally.

Chapter 19

Still sore from all my rock-climbing the day before, I got a late start in the morning. I left several voicemail messages with Suzette, to no avail. I decided to go to my office and lock Allison's tag in my office drawer, the safest place I knew. Besides, I needed to check my mail and pay some bills. I stopped at the coffee bar on the ground floor and treated myself to a vanilla latte, then grabbed the mail from my lobby mailbox. I decided to work off the calories by climbing the stairs. By the time I got to my floor, my quads were petitioning for reassignment.

I pushed open the stairwell door, and the smell hit like a brick, a ripe, stomach-turning stench. The stairwell door was in a little angle from the main corridor. I set my coffee cup on the floor and pulled my Colt out of the holster in the middle of my back. I held it next to my ear, with the barrel pointing up, and sneaked a peek around the corner.

The floor of my corridor has a worn gray carpet running down the center and an elevator in the center. Doors line the hall on either side, with alabaster sconces lighting the length all the way to the end, where a window lets in the cool gray light of San Francisco. That's where my office door is, at the far end of the hallway. The light fell on a dark lump on the carpet outside my door.

Seeing no one in the hallway, I eased around the corner and walked carefully down the way. As I approached the elevator, it dinged. I hesitated, and it opened. A short, fat black haired lady in a business suit one size too small stepped out. She glanced at me, then brought her hand up to her nose.

"Oh, my God, what's that smell?" She stared at my gun. "Claire? What's with the piece?"

"Hi, Shirley," I said. "I'm just checking it out. Why don't you go in your office and close the door?"

She blinked watery eyes. "What's going on?" She looked up and down the corridor, then saw the lump in front of my door. "What's that?"

"Go in the office, Shirley," I said. I kept my voice down, but something in it made her step back, and then sidle past me to the door of the CPA's office where she worked.

"I'm calling the building manager," she said. "Should I call the police?"

"If we need cops, I'll make the call," I said. I wondered if the lump was a stink bomb. Or any kind of bomb.

The door slammed behind me and I stepped closer. The smell was enough to gag a maggot; I tried breathing through my mouth but didn't like thinking about whatever molecules from it were entering. It wasn't big enough to be a human, and it didn't move. I stuck my gun back into my holster and bent over it.

Someone had dumped a pile of rotten fish guts on my doorstep. Liquids I didn't want to identify had soaked into the carpet; something, maybe blood, had splashed onto the wooden jamb. I was searching my pockets for a handkerchief or a tissue, when I heard the elevator behind me and turned. A lean older man in khaki work clothes emerged. He instantly recoiled as Shirley had, clutching his nose. "What the hell?"

"Hi, Mr. Rhodes," I said.

"Christ, what is that?" The building supervisor looked at me suspiciously.

"Fish innards," I said. I was trying to breathe through my mouth but it was hard to do that and talk, too. "I'd say they were a day or two past their sell date."

"God Almighty, what a stink." Rhodes' Southwestern twang flavored his speech. "You musta really pissed somebody off."

"Yeah," I said. I felt anger rising in me; whoever had done

this probably wanted to scare me, but had succeeded only in pissing me off.

Rhodes squinted at me. "You're gonna pay for the cleanup."

I raised an eyebrow. "Not to get technical, but this stuff is in the hallway. That's your territory, not mine."

"Hey, this is one of your clients," he said. "Your fault. You pay."

I shook my head. "I'm sorry this happened, but you can't prove I had anything to do with it. It might be a random act of vandalism. Maybe they were aiming at the lawyer next door, and missed." I nodded towards the offices of Schuster & Fitch, between me and the elevator.

The door of the CPA's office opened and Shirley stuck her head out. "You gonna do something about that smell, Mr. Rhodes? We've got all the windows open and we can still smell it way over here!"

"As soon as Ms. Turnbull here agrees to pay for—"

"How about you clean it up, and then we argue over the bill?" I snapped. "And maybe we'll discuss how a vandal got into this building, carrying a bucket of fish guts, and nobody noticed. Maybe we'll discuss better security in this building."

Shirley paled. "Oh. Oh, my goodness! Mr. Rhodes, she's right! Why, that person could have brought a bomb or something! Oh!" She disappeared back into the office and closed the door.

"Dammit," Rhodes said, glaring at me. "Now you got that woman all riled up. She'll nag me night and day to hire a security guard downstairs, and how much will that cost?"

"I'm sure you'll find a way to pass on any new costs to us tenants," I said coldly. I dug into my pocket for my key. "I have to check out my office. Can you get this cleaned up?"

He glared at me. "I'm not forgetting this," he said. "You bring any trouble on this building, I'll be talking to management about cancelling your lease."

With the number of vacancies currently plaguing downtown San Francisco offices, I doubted this. I unlocked my door, stepped over the mess on the threshold, and entered.

Inside, the smell was even worse, being close and warm in the room. I quickly raised all the windows, glad my building was old enough to have openable windows. I sniffed deep, inhaling the clean smell of San Francisco. One of the great advantages of a waterfront town was that the breeze constantly moved any stink from the City out over the Bay, leaving us with the fresh, salty tang of ocean air. Even so, I caught a nasty whiff of the present on my doorstep. I checked my boots to make doubly sure I hadn't stepped in any of it.

I pulled my chair over to the window to check out my mail. Third down in the stack was a plain white envelope with no return address or stamp, just my name printed in block letters. Someone had shoved it through the slot, someone who had been in the lobby. I had an idea I knew who. Sure enough, when I slit the end (carefully) and gently pried the envelope open, I found a single sheet of paper, torn from a memo book. I handled it only by the corners. In the same block letters, in the middle of the page, I read the note:

SHES DEAD. LET IT ALONE.

"Seriously?" I asked aloud. "Dead fish on the doorstep, and a hand-printed note? What is this, the Forties? And you didn't put the apostrophe in front of the S."

I put the paper on my desk and rummaged in my drawer for an evidence bag. I use them occasionally, and by a miracle actually found one large enough for the paper. I eased it in, sealed it, and wrote my name and date on the tag. If nothing else, Suzette might get a laugh out of it. I would have joined her if I wasn't convinced the stink of that little offering on my doorstep was in my clothes, my hair, my soul. So not funny.

I picked up the phone and called Suzette. This time, I got her.

"Someone's been watching too many Godfather movies," she said after I filled her in. "You're assuming this is not a practical joke? Someone ticked off at you over a prior case?"

I shrugged. "Could be. The perp didn't even get specific as to who the 'she' was who is dead."

"But you're assuming it's Allison Farley."

"Only 'she' I'm looking for right now," I said. "Does this bother you at all? That I start looking into a case, and get this amateur stunt on my doorstep?"

There was silence, and I imagined Suzette staring at the far wall. "Well, it's annoying. We can stretch a point and call it an implied threat. But as you say, there's no direct tie to the Farley case. Which is, I remind you, officially closed."

I let my temper show a little. "Maybe you'll take this more seriously. I found Allison Farley's timing chip."

"Where?" she demanded. "When?"

I told her about my trip to the prison island, skimming over the part where I trespassed to find evidence. "I've got the chip here, in an evidence bag," I said. "Do you want it or not?"

"Claire, if anything, that chip just supports the case theory: she drowned, her chip came loose and her body washed out to sea."

"So you don't want it?"

"I didn't say that."

"So you'll send someone for it? Along with the note? I was hoping you would run the prints on it and the chip for me."

"What am I, your assistant now?" I heard the amusement in her voice. "Oh, fine. I'll write the note up as a threat, and send it to the lab."

"Send Vic for it," I said, relishing the idea of the expression on his face when the stink hit him. "I'll leave these with Shirley, down the hall."

"Screws up the evidence chain," Suzette said. "But what the hell. You just want the prints from the note and chip? Not the ink, paper, and so forth?"

"Whatever your budget can afford. Thanks."

"Budget?" Suzette laughed. She hung up laughing.

There was no other mail requiring my attention. I opened the door to my office, and found Mr. Rhodes on his knees, scrubbing at the stain on my doorstep. A most aromatic garbage bag sat against the wall opposite.

"Whatever you did to piss someone off," he snarled. "Don't do it again, okay?"

I stepped past him, closed my door and locked it. "I'll do my best," I said mildly. "From now on, I'm giving out your office address as my own."

He sputtered angrily at me as I walked down the corridor. I pushed open Shirley's door; she waved me to silence, speaking into her headset. "Yes, sir. I will set that up for you right away. Yes, sir. Thank you. Have a good day."

She disconnected and made a face at me. "I think I'm going downstairs and buy some perfume. Or room spray. Something. Ew, that's awful," she said.

"I hope you're referring to the smell," I said.

She smiled. "Of course. How are you? What was that?"

I told her. Her eyes got round when I told her about the note. When I laid it on her desk, she stared at it as if it were a live thing. "You want me to keep this?"

"Until Inspector Delorey shows up," I said. "And you'll have to sign for it here, and date it. Same thing with this timing chip in its bag. Don't open them, or you'll break the chain of custody."

She drew back from it. "I don't want to touch them."

"You don't have to," I said. "Just let them sit on your desk here."

She twisted her head around to read the writing. "Oh, my! Who's dead?"

I shook my head. "I don't know, but I have my suspicions." At her scared expression, I hastened to add, "There's no danger to you, Shirley. I don't even know if it's connected to any of my cases."

She eyed the plastic envelopes. "Well. If you say so."

"Thanks. I owe you,"

She smiled at me, her cheeks dimpling. "You bet you do. A decaf caramel soy latte, next time you're on your way up."

I shuddered. What some people call coffee.

CHAPTER 20

I took the elevator down, thinking about the note. *She's dead. Let it go.* Why? Why would anyone not want me to look for Allison's body? The obvious answer was that there was no body to find, that either it had been disposed of or that there had never been one to start with.

Allison Farley had disappeared off a dock, in the middle of two thousand witnesses. Her chip had washed ashore at Alcatraz, probably off her corpse. No one thought she was still alive but Marty. So why warn me away? What else was going on?

I stepped off the elevator and nearly ran into Wyatt. I don't think you call what I uttered a squeak, exactly. But there is no question that I hopped to one side, drawing a stare from a woman getting a drink at the water fountain. I smiled innocently at her and pulled out my phone. Turning away from her to face Wyatt, I hissed, "What?"

"Rafferty got a phone call ten minutes ago," he growled. "He said, 'I'll have the money, I swear to God. Just don't do anything stupid.' Then he hung up and called someone else, I think it was his partner. He said, 'Meet me at the bank. We have to liquidate everything. Right now!'"

"Which bank?"

"Could be one of two. He banks at Wells Fargo and at California Merchants Trust. I can take one of them and you take the other."

"You think this is related to the case?"

"I think something is eating at Wayne Rafferty, and he's taking action. And you already told me his partner is selling everything he can. This case ain't just about a missing woman, Claire, it's about money. Big money."

I thought of what I had just heard from Suzette and from Leesa Kern. Could this really be tied to drug dealing? Could Allison have fallen foul of a deal gone wrong? Or had she been killed as a message from dealers to Wayne? "I'll take California Merchants Trust," I said. "It's down the street."

"If they don't show up at Wells Fargo in half an hour, I'll meet you there," Wyatt said.

"Same goes," I said.

He stalked through the water fountain and the woman drinking from it. I hurried through the front doors. Outside, the day was bright but cool, with a gray shadow in the west where the fog was already forming. Foot traffic was light and taxis were scarce, so I hoofed it five blocks east, nearly to the Ferry Building.

California Merchants Trust of San Francisco lived in a modest five story glass and steel construction from the Sixties, fronted by big tubs of lavender and petunias. I tossed a couple of quarters in the cup of a street beggar who was sleeping on a bench, and pushed through the doors. The lobby was spare, modern, mostly chrome and glass. A guard caught my eye and I walked over, pulling out my ID.

"Turnbull Investigations," I said crisply. "I'm showing you my ID and my carry permit so you don't get nervous if you spot the gun at the middle of my back waist."

He was black, beefy and fortyish. "I already spotted it," he said acidly. "If you have business with the bank, I can hold it for you."

"I don't expect to be here that long," I said. Out of the corner of my eye, I saw the glass door open. Wayne Rafferty walked in, carrying a briefcase and looking harassed. "I'm just following a guy. I plan to be discreet."

"It's against bank policy," the guard said.

I moseyed over to a very large display of pamphlets and brochures. I opened one to hide my face while I watched Rafferty. He marched right up to a desk and spoke to the woman behind it. She looked a little startled, then spread an artificial smile across her face. She gestured him to a seat and I looked around for cover closer to the desk.

I had almost decided to risk standing at the window next to the woman's desk, when the door opened and Jackson Harrington strode in. He glanced around; I deliberately dropped the brochure and bent over to pick it up as he walked by. As I rose with the brochure in my hand, the two men greeted one another. Even from halfway across the lobby, I could feel the tension. They sat down and spoke urgently to the bank officer.

In a far corner near the windows, Wyatt Earp materialized out of thin air, like fog coalescing. It was a jarring sight. Wyatt glanced around, saw Rafferty and Harrington, and sauntered over to listen to them. Then he suddenly straightened, looked around, and spotted me. He nodded solemnly and turned back to the conversation.

The guard was standing behind me. "You know, I can't let you stay in here armed. My boss would have my head."

I could have made a stink, could have insisted on staying. But when I thought about it, there was no real point. Wyatt could see and hear everything, he could follow the two anywhere they went in the building, and I could not. And the longer I stayed in the lobby, the greater the chance one of them would spot me, especially with the guard looming over me. "Okay," I said. "Any problem with me hanging around front, tailing them when they leave?"

He looked relieved. "What you do on the sidewalk is none of my business," he said.

I gave him a friendly smile, even though I didn't bank there, and left quietly. There was a bus shelter ten steps down the sidewalk, and I settled in to watch the front door.

The early afternoon sunlight held little warmth. I sat in the bus shelter through the arrival and departure of four buses, two taxis and a bike messenger. Two panhandlers shuffled over and I gave each a dollar to get lost. A street musician set up a makeshift drum kit consisting of boxes and plastic buckets, and proceeded to hammer and thump until a cop came along and made him move. A street peddler with a large cardboard box shuffled along, trying to sell yellow Alcatraz Triathlon T-shirts at half price. A dog tried to pee on the corner of the bus shelter and his owner towed him away.

I enjoyed people-watching for awhile. But time was getting on and I was getting hungry, until finally Rafferty and Harrington walked out the front door. Rafferty was still carrying the briefcase, but now he held it closer to his body. That told me there was something valuable in it, probably money. The two men huddled together, speaking quietly. Wyatt Earp stepped through the stone wall of the bank and stood behind Rafferty, listening. He caught sight of me but continued listening.

Harrington shook hands with Rafferty and strode off around a corner quickly. Wayne Rafferty stood a moment, blinking and looking around. I raised my newspaper to shield my lower face. Finally he walked my way, passed me, and headed for the parking garage. Wyatt wandered over, hands in his pockets.

"What's up?" I said. "Where are they going? Should we follow them?"

"Harrington said he's going to the worksite out on Alcatraz to straighten out some argument with the Park Service; he kept hurrying Rafferty along 'cause he says he's late. Rafferty said he was going home to wait for the phone call."

"The phone call? A specific phone call?"

Wyatt's blue eyes met mine. "Yep. I reckon we got a few minutes while he drives home, then I'll show up there. Or I can go out to the Rock if you want me to follow Harrington."

"So they were liquidating assets, like he said?"

"Yup." Wyatt adjusted his hat. I wondered if the sun bothered a ghost's eyes. "There were some partnership papers, and they had to call in a bank officer to countersign. Not sure I understand all the details, but apparently they were cashing some certificates in. The bank officer took them into an interior office and called in a guard with a cash box. He counted out several hundred thousand dollars. And what's more, that briefcase was already half full of cash when Rafferty first opened it."

I thought about what Wyatt had overheard. "He said he would get the money. It's got to be either a ransom or a drug deal."

"That banker fellow looked mighty pained. It wasn't just handin' over the cash, which hurts them awful. I think he was real suspicious but didn't know any way to stop them."

"He'll have to report a disbursement that large."

Wyatt nodded. "That part I understood. The banker fellow tried to explain it to Rafferty, who kept saying he didn't care, to get on with things."

I thought about it. "And Harrington didn't object? I mean, half that money is his."

Wyatt shrugged. "Hardly said a word, kept looking at his watch and tapping his fingers on the desk."

"How much of the money did Harrington take?"

"None of it. And there's something else. I got a look at one of them papers. It was a deed for some real estate. It had Allison Farley's name on it."

I stared at him. "Allison? Hmm."

"He's selling off land he bought from her, or with her." He rocked forward and back on his bootheels. "Looks familiar."

"Like what?"

"Real estate fraud." He shifted from one foot to the other, his gaze going past me. "Happens I know a little about land fraud. Back in Tombstone, we had to deal with a bunch of smooth boys called themselves the Tombstone Townsite Company. They got in ahead of the official survey of the town, got their own patent application in to the Territorial Governor while the Town Council was still organizing itself. By the time everything got sorted out, the Townsite Company held title to land that people had already built on. Took a long time to get everything settled, and in the meantime folks were mad enough to bite the heads off rattlers. Tied up the courts for years. I heard some folks were faking up deeds and titles in the dark of night, signing every name from President Hayes on down to Governor Fremont."

I cocked my head. "How deep in it were you?" I had few

illusions about my ethereal partner's shady past.

The hint of a smile came and went. "Me? Not much. But my brother Virgil was deputy under Sheriff Shibell; they had their hands full with people claiming land, jumping claims, or claiming claims that had already been jumped. At one point, the mayor handed over the entire town, lock, stock and barrel, to the speculators. He got run out of town in less than two weeks."

"Probably moved to San Francisco," I said dryly.

Again the hint of smile. "Possible. Possible. But my point is that these land speculators got a jump on the law, partly because they had the mayor in their pocket. And the 'signatures' of a lot of folks who apparently had come into town at midnight, signed deeds, and left before dawn."

"Phony signatures? Are you saying they're faking Allison's signature?"

Wyatt fingered his mustache. "Don't have to fake it at all, if Rafferty's her heir. Remember, she's dead."

I lifted an eyebrow. "Of course. If Wayne is her heir, his signature is all that's needed to sell joint property."

Wyatt's mouth was a grim line under the walrus mustache. "You know what this adds up to, Claire."

I felt something in my stomach go tight and hard. "I can't decide if it adds up to murder or kidnaping. But either way, it looks like someone liquidated Allison Farley and is cashing in all her assets."

Wyatt shifted impatiently. "So they'll be leaving town very soon. I should keep tabs on Rafferty. He may be driving home, but he could take a phone call on his mobile any moment."

"But that leaves me with Harrington," I objected. "And I can't easily follow him to Alcatraz. Can you?"

Wyatt squinted at me. "Reckon so. But you'd better get moving on Rafferty, then." He adjusted his hat, took two steps and vanished.

The bus would be a lot slower, so I hailed a cab.

CHAPTER 21

I was halfway to Rafferty's house when my cell phone rang. I told it my name and Suzette Melton's voice came back at me. "Get down to Illinois Street," she said. She sounded grim.

"Why am I going to the waterfront?" I asked.

"Crab fisherman brought up a woman's body outside the Golden Gate. Coast Guard is bringing it in now."

"You think it's Allison." I felt disappointment sweep over me.

"Don't know yet," Suzette said. "But Vic's betting it is."

I closed my eyes. "Which pier?"

She named it and hung up. I redirected the cabbie and wished, once again, that I had a way to get in touch with Wyatt. He was now on his way to Alcatraz Island, or already there, and I had no way to tell him what had happened. I let myself think about this all the way to the southern piers along Illinois Street. We passed JackWay Holdings' yard on the way; I noticed that the chain link gate was closed.

The cabbie pulled up at the pier. "Cop convention," he said. "Anyone you know?"

"I hope not." I swiped my debit card through the meter.

A lanky cop in uniform stopped me as I approached, but a shout from Suzette earned me entry.

Suzette stood in a tan trench coat, her hair tossed artistically by the wind. I had more or less thrown clothing at myself this morning until something stuck: I wound up in a San Francisco Giants T-shirt in black, worn stylishly outside my belt to hide the gun at the middle of my back, over distressed jeans and half-boots. I flung a black windbreaker on top and called myself ready for the day. But I was jealous of Suzette's trench coat. She looked like Philippa Marlowe; I looked like a felon.

Out on the dock, a ninety-foot Coast Guard cutter was nosed in to the pier, with uniformed men moving briskly on and off. Two uniformed women carried a body bag on stretcher.

Suzette nodded a greeting as I walked up. "Onboard medic says it looks like she's been in the water about a week."

"That corresponds to the time Allison disappeared." My hands were cold and I stuck them in my pocket. "ID?"

"It'll be tricky. The sharks have been at her." She turned, putting her back to the wind. "You know the chances are high this is her."

I nodded unhappily. "Even though there are two major rivers that empty into the Bay, and hundreds of miles of shore. Not to mention four different bridges to jump off of, three major port facilities, and more swamps than any state but Florida. But yeah, it couldn't be anyone but her."

Suzette cocked her head to one side. "Why so cheerful?"

I sighed. "I've spent a lot of time on this case. And yesterday afternoon I got a notion that this might be a murder case after all. So yeah, I'm in a grumpy mood."

She narrowed her eyes at me. "Murder? Are you talking about that RFID chip? That doesn't prove anything."

"Not that. I may have uncovered a motive." And even as I said it, I wanted to kick myself. How was I supposed to tell Suzette what Rafferty had said on the phone or in a bank where I was not present?

Suzette stepped close. "Tell me."

An ambulance with the words MEDICAL EXAMINER on its side pulled up beside us. A slender Asian woman in a muffler and jacket got out of the passenger's side. Seeing Suzette, she walked over. "Inspector."

"Anna." Suzette jerked her head at me. "You know Claire, right?"

"Sure do." Anna Shinn was neutral, not unfriendly, but didn't offer to shake hands. She's been an assistant ME as long as I can remember, yet never seems to age a day. "So what do we have here, a sinker or a floater?"

"Sinker. Crab fisherman brought the body up with some pots. I think it got tangled in the shot rope." Suzette clutched her coat together as the breeze off the water picked up.

"Okay, I'll take a look," she said.

Suzette hesitated. "Claire? You want to see?"

Anna stopped. "She's a civilian now."

"I'll take responsibility," Suzette said. Anna shrugged and walked off towards the end of the pier.

I wasn't crazy about looking at something that had been in the water over a week, but I felt I owed it to Marty. He was paying for closure, and if I could give it to him, I had to. So I braced myself and followed the other two to the end of the pier. Five steps from the body, the breeze shifted and the stench hit me. It was all I could do to keep from retching, but I was damned if I was going to lose it in front of all these cops.

Suzette had been right: the sharks had been at her. So had the crabs; there wasn't much face left. She had one arm and one leg remaining, on opposite sides. The body was naked, but that was not unusual in something that the tides and rocks had tossed for days. I covered my nose with my hand automatically, knowing it would not make a difference. Suzette stood stoically over the body, looking down. The wind tossed her coat around, but she was immovable. Her eyes met mine across the corpse and I saw the same pity there I had always seen in her eyes, when looking at the dead.

"Well, she's female, that's for sure." The voice was raspy, the tone salacious. "Nice tits, or at least they were."

I didn't even need to turn around to know who it was. "Classy, Vic," I said. "As usual."

Vic came around the body and stared at me. "What is she doing here?" he demanded. "She's a civilian."

"Vic, can you start the documentation, please?" Suzette sounded weary. Not for the first time, I wondered why she put up with a jerk like Delorey.

"Sure thing," he said, and pulled out a notebook.

"You pick up that evidence I left at my office?" I asked Vic. He sneered but didn't reply.

Anna Shinn squatted down by the body, pulling on gloves. She spoke into a smart phone, making notes. "Body is that of a Caucasian or mixed-race female. Evidence of extensive scavenging. No visible GSW, ligatures, or stab wounds. Age undetermined. Height approximately five-ten, weight estimated at one-sixty."

"She don't weigh that now," Vic said.

"Knock it off," Suzette said.

Unperturbed, Anna continued. "Body is missing right leg, severed at the iliofemoral ligament. Also missing is left arm, severed at the humerus approximately two inches distal to the shoulder joint. The head has been severely damaged; scalp, eyes and left ear are missing." She touched the screen to turn off the recording and stood. "I'll have to do the rest at the lab," she told Suzette.

"No right leg," I muttered. "Damn."

Vic glared at me. "What?"

"Allison Farley had a dolphin tattoo on her right ankle," Suzette told him. "It would have been a positive ID. Anna, you got fingerprints?"

Anna shook her head. "Not in this condition. Water damage. I'll take her back to the shop and let you know."

"Was Allison ever fingerprinted?" I asked Suzette.

"Not that we know of."

"She was an athlete," I said. "She would have worked out. I know my gym logs members in and out with a fingerprint scan. You might try asking around in the fitness centers."

"I know how to do my job," Vic snarled. "This is my case. Butt out."

Suzette turned her back to me and faced Vic. "She's a civilian consultant on this, Vic. I expect you to be a professional. Now how about talking to the Coasties, getting a couple of statements?"

Vic's narrow face turned red, but he said nothing. He stalked away.

I turned to Anna Shinn. "Marty told me that Allison usually dieted down to around one-forty when she was training. She'd have trained like crazy for the triathlon. You said this body looks like it was around one-sixty?"

Anna tugged at her gloves. "Yeah. Assuming, of course, the other leg and arm were present. I'll weigh her back in the lab, but I'd say this one was nothing less than one-fifty-five. More, probably."

"So maybe it's not her." I searched Anna's face, but she wasn't giving anything away.

"Maybe. Maybe not." Anna tossed her gloves into a red medical waste sack. "Look, if I can get prints off of her, we'll have her ID within a day. If not…" She shrugged. "Unless it's a priority, the DNA goes into the queue. And they're so backed up they're processing cases from the twentieth century."

Suzette asked, "How long?"

"You'll have to ask down at 606," Anna said. "I gotta get this lady indoors now." Building 606 was the forensics lab at Hunter's Point.

I pulled out my smart phone. "I need a picture," I said, looking at Suzette.

She frowned, and held up a hand as Anna started to protest. "I know you'll be … discreet."

"Yeah," I said. I held my breath, leaned close, and got a couple of shots. I wished I didn't have to.

We watched as she accompanied the body to the waiting ambulance. As it was loaded, Suzette stuck her hands in her coat pockets, turned her back to the wind and said, "You said something about murder evidence?"

I no longer had the appetite for a coffee, but I wanted to get out of the wind. "You got a car?"

She led me to her police issue sedan and we got in. "I can't believe the department is still using Crown Vics," I said. "It's not like anyone but cops ever drive these things any more."

Suzette turned down her radio. "Not true. My neighbor drives one."

"Your neighbor is ninety years old and only drives it to Burning Man once a year," I said.

"Quit stalling," Suzette said. "What's this new motive."

I'd had some time to think about it. I took a deep breath. "Okay. You know Wayne Rafferty and Jackson Harrington are partners, right?" I told her about my visit to JackWay Holdings, including my unauthorized search of the premises.

Suzette interrupted only once. "You say the door wasn't locked?"

"Yeah," I said. I swallowed. "Which means I was technically not trespassing, since it's a commercial building and I had already visit—"

"Don't split hairs with me, Claire," she said. "Unless they press charges, I don't care."

I told her about JackWay's debts, about Harrington selling off equipment. "And today, they met at California Merchants Trust. I saw them talking to a banker, and then Rafferty walked out with a briefcase."

"So?"

"So I think they're cashing in everything they have, either in a drug deal or money laundering."

"And you think that's motive?" She patted her pockets, then got an annoyed look. Suzette had recently quit smoking for the eleventh time, and still reached for a cigarette by habit. "All I see is you interfering with the legitimate business concerns of citizens who have been known to contribute to the Mayor's re-election campaigns. And you haven't tied Allison to any of this."

This would be delicate, so I chose my words carefully. "My financial research showed that Wayne Rafferty and Allison Farley were joint owners on several instruments, like deeds and mortgages. He was cashing them in today, and he could only do that because the coroner ruled her dead."

"Claire, they just took her body off to the lab," Suzette said. Her fingers twitched. "That would make her even deader, and make it perfectly legal for her heir to cash in the property. If you think this is some kind of tax evasion scheme, I can refer you to—"

"But what if Wayne Rafferty killed her so he could liquidate all that property?" I said impatiently.

"In order to make a buy?"

"Yeah."

She stared off into the distance, looking thoughtful. "I dunno. It's thin, Claire. Real thin. I may have a body, but I still don't have evidence of a crime. You heard Anna: no gunshot wounds, no ligature marks, no wounds except for scavengers."

"Which I would expect, if someone deliberately drowned her." I felt myself going cold and still deep inside myself, in the place where rage lived. It didn't often come out, but the sight of that pitiful, chewed-up woman, and the idea that someone had casually killed her for a drug buy or for her silence, scraped some raw nerve in me. I had to concentrate to uncurl my fists. "You going to go see Rafferty about this body?"

Vic Delorey was walking towards us, holding his hand on his head. I wondered (not for the first time) if he wore a hairpiece. Suzette sighed. "Look, I have to wait until Anna gets back to me with an ID. Until I know who that body was, and what happened to her, I can't move against Rafferty or Harrington."

"Okay." I'd already decided Suzette couldn't help much. The cold anger inside me was reminding me that I wasn't bound by her rules. "I'll go now. Thanks for calling me."

"Yeah. I'll let you know when I hear something." Suzette was reaching for the cigarette lighter before she stopped herself.

Vic was surprised to see me climb out of the car. Then he scowled. "You're trespassing on my crime scene," he snarled.

"No, I'm leaving it," I said, and walked off.

CHAPTER 22

I had been on my way to Rafferty's house before my little detour to the docks, and now I was in an even greater hurry. Two things were driving me: anger, and the fear that Rafferty was already gone.

Miraculously, I found a cab on Third and made it crosstown in record time. I fought to remain calm, but now that I'd seen the body I was haunted by the image of her falling through cold water, struggling, maybe struggling with someone who was drowning her. She'd fight a long time but in the end, the cold and water and tides would have her, and her body would drift helplessly out to sea…

I had the cabbie drop me at the end of the block. The late afternoon sun was warm on my face as I climbed the hill to Wayne's house. I was walking up to the front steps when Wyatt Earp stepped through a window to meet me.

"Why are you here?"

"Harrington got a call from Rafferty. He didn't say much, except once he said, 'Where's the meeting?'"

"What meeting?"

"I don't know. That's why I came back here. But why are you just now getting here?"

"Wayne's home?" I asked.

"Yes," Wyatt said. I leaped up the steps, and he stepped back quickly to avoid me. "He's in the upstairs bedroom. What—"

I banged on the door and rang the bell. "Come on," I muttered.

"What happened?" Wyatt asked.

"Cops found a body in the Bay," I said in a low voice.

"Damn. Allison Farley?" Wyatt said.

Feet pounded down the stairs, and then the door was flung open. Wayne Rafferty stood there barefoot, in trousers and a dress shirt hanging out over jeans. "What the—?" Wayne scowled at me. "Who are you?"

"Claire Turnbull. I was here the other day, asking about Allison. I have news."

"I'm busy," he said, and nearly shut the door in my face. I shoved against it and he stumbled back, surprised. "Hey!"

"Did Allison have any marks or tattoos other than the dolphin?" I asked.

"What? You're trespassing. Get ou—"

"Tattoos. Marks. Scars." I made my voice as hard as I could. I thought of Marty, nearly weeping in my office. I thought of a young woman tossed to the sharks like so much garbage. "Tell me now. Right now."

"I don't understand."

I yanked out my cell phone and punched up the shot of the corpse I'd made an hour ago. "They pulled this body out of the water just outside the Golden Gate," I said, and turned the screen so he could see it. He went white as a sheet. "The right leg is missing, so I can't identify Allison by the dolphin tattoo, but if she had others—"

I stopped because my audience was retching, doubled over and clutching his middle.

"Pretty raw of you," Wyatt said. I heard disapproval in his voice.

I didn't care. "Did you put her in the water, Wayne?" I demanded. "Did you have someone pull her under? Did she know something she wasn't supposed to?"

"Get out of here," Rafferty said, his voice raw. He pushed himself upright, hanging on to the door jamb with one hand and wiping his mouth with the other. "Damn you, go to hell!"

He tried to shut the door on me again and once again I shoved him back with it. I put my face close to his. "This woman drowned a week ago, the same time as Allison. I don't think it's a coincidence. Why are you cashing out your bank accounts, converting all your assets to cash? Why are you selling all your equipment?"

He stared at me. "What? How do you—Get out! You'll ruin everything!"

"Ruin what?" I pressed, and he backed up.

"Claire, what are you doing?" Wyatt said. He was standing in the living room now, frowning at me.

"What am I ruining, Wayne?" I said. "Did Allison get in the way of a drug deal? Or is it money laundering? Why haven't you held a funeral for her? Guilty conscience? Or did you just not give a damn that your girlfriend, the woman you said you were going to marry, is dead?"

"Stop!" Wayne flailed backwards, almost tripping over a stuffed armchair.

"Why were you and Jackson Harrington at the bank today, cashing out your—"

I stopped because he was pointing a gun at me. He'd pulled it from his back waistband before I saw it. He aimed the gun (a Smith & Wesson SD40, I noted) at my forehead. "Get. Out."

"Look out, Claire!" Wyatt stepped forward, reaching for Wayne's arm. His hand passed right through the arm, and Wayne showed no reaction. "Damn it, get out!" Wyatt said fiercely.

"You got no business butting into my affairs," Wayne snarled. But his eyes told me he wouldn't pull the trigger. "Get out. I'm calling the police."

"Sure," I said. "Be sure to tell them about the briefcase full of cash you've got upstairs."

His eye got big and round. "How do you know about that? Did Jack tell you about it?"

"Claire, shut up!" Wyatt yelled. "He'll fire, for sure!"

I kept my eyes on Wayne. "What is it, two million? Three? Is that all Allison Farley was worth to you?"

Wayne's eyes blazed, the skin tightening around his mouth. I wondered if I'd misjudged him after all. "You don't know anything. You got everything wrong. And you're going to get somebody killed if you don't butt out." He stepped forward, leading with the gun, and marched me backwards out the door. Wyatt followed him closely, his face tense.

"Don't come back." Wayne slammed the door.

Wyatt stepped through it and stood facing me. "What the hell, Claire?"

I turned and trotted down the steps. The spot between my shoulder blades itched. My hands were clenched in fists.

Suddenly Wyatt appeared in front of me, blocking my way. Rather than risk a trip to the hospital, I stopped.

"That was the stupidest thing I've ever seen you do," Wyatt said angrily. "Damn fool female. Don't you know no better than to run hot on a man like that?"

"Your grammar goes to hell when you get mad," I said.

"Dammit, Claire! What if he'd pulled the trigger? Why didn't you pull on him? Or get backup? What were you thinking?" His blue eyes blazed.

"I was thinking that it's a good idea to spring surprises on a suspect, in an attempt to elicit an inadvertent confession," I said. "I was thinking that if Wayne Rafferty had killed his girlfriend, or had her killed, he might be shocked into an inadvertent confession if he saw the result. Most civilians have never seen a dead body, let alone the body of someone they know."

"It was a damn fool move," Wyatt said. "You should have told me what you were going to do."

"And what difference would that have made?" I snapped. I remembered his hand passing through Wayne's arm. "It's not like you could have done anything about it."

His face went dead white. His eyes looked like chips of glass. "I could have warned you," he said in a flat voice. "I saw him upstairs. And I saw his gun. If you'd waited, I could have told you he was armed. But no, you got to bull ahead—" He stopped, and his lips made a thin line. "I got half a mind to drop this whole partner thing," he said in a low voice. "If you ain't got no more use for me than just running errands, I got other things I can do."

I cocked my head to one side. "Like what? You play pool in the afterlife? You got a book club to get to?" I put my hands on my hips. On the sidewalk, a woman jogged by, wearing headphones and paying no attention to me talking to thin air. "Wyatt, I'm the one with the client, the case and the responsibility. I'm running this case. I decide what tactics to use."

"Then use better ones!" he fumed. "If you get yourself killed—"

"Then I'll wind up on your side of the aisle, won't I? And then you can smack me if you want. Until then, I run this case."

His fingers worked, closing and opening his fists. Finally, he stepped to one side to let me pass. "I ain't giving up on this case just because you've turned into a mule. But we ain't done here."

"I am," I said. I walked past him into the twilight.

CHAPTER 23

I could hear the annoyance in Suzette's voice. "Claire, I can't just call for a stakeout based on your gut."

"You would if I was still a cop." I was standing behind the orange tree next door to Wayne Rafferty's house, talking to her on my phone.

"Yeah, but you're not a cop, are you?" She sounded annoyed. "That's more than a techhicality, Claire. You aren't even officially on this case. What the hell, it isn't even officially a case."

"You have a body."

"Which may be suicide, accident or homicide," she said firmly.

"Wayne Rafferty has money, a gun, and a reason to run," I said.

"Poetic, but beside the point," she said. I heard the ding of an elevator in the background as she talked. "It's not yet illegal to own a gun in San Francisco, or to use it to evict a trespasser. And we don't even know if we've found Allison. Look, I'm at the morgue. I'll call you back."

"Someone should be watching Wayne," I said, and then realized I was talking to a dial tone.

Wyatt had stomped back into the house after our argument and had not come out. For all I knew, he'd walked right out the back wall and was brooding somewhere. To hell with him, I thought. My temper had cooled somewhat, but I didn't regret pushing Wayne. It was past time someone started pushing on Allison's behalf.

I didn't know where Jackson Harrington was. I didn't

know what Wayne was planning. So I hung back behind the neighbors' orange tree, waiting. The sun had set half an hour ago. Clouds scudded in, hiding the stars, and the temperature dropped. I was glad I had worn my jacket, but could have used another layer.

The front door opened and Rafferty emerged, carrying a gym bag. He locked the front door behind him, then walked over to the garage door and raised it. Wyatt sauntered through the front wall, looking around. As soon as Rafferty entered the garage, I stepped out of the shelter of the tree and raised my hand. He walked over, even as I heard a car start.

"He got a phone call. He's going to Golden Gate Park," Wyatt said. "The Horseshoe Pits. I'll follow."

And just like that, we were back. Partners again, working smoothly in tandem. I felt a little lighter again.

"See you there," I said, and then ducked back behind the tree as Rafferty barrelled backwards out of his garage. In the dark I could not be sure, but it looked like he was driving a late-model dark blue BMW. He squealed into the street, made a three point turn, and hurtled away. Wyatt touched the brim of his hat to me and vanished. I imagined him coalescing in the front seat of the BMW, unseen by Rafferty. In any case, it was up to me to get myself to Golden Gate Park in a hurry.

And there's no faster transport in any city than a police squad car with the sirens going. I punched my cell phone. Suzette answered after five rings.

"Claire, I—"

"No time for chit-chat," I said, walking fast down the street. "Wayne Rafferty is carrying several million dollars in cash in a gym bag, on his way to Golden Gate Park."

"How do you know this?" I love it that Suzette didn't even ask me if I knew it was true.

"I saw the cash," I lied. "He's meeting someone at the Horseshoe Pits in Golden Gate Park. I'm on my way there."

"Claire, hold on. You don't—"

"Whether he's making a buy or paying blackmail, you need to talk to him. You know it. And even if you don't get there in time, you'll want a witness who can testify in court," I said tersely. "But I need a ride. Is there a squad car near Jackson Street?"

"Where are you?"

"Washington and Taylor, but I'm on a one-way street that goes the wrong way. I'll go north and get on Jackson, walking west."

"I'm sending a squad car. Agent Kern and I will meet you at the corner of Fulton and Stanyan in twenty minutes."

"Don't linger," I said.

I walked all the way down Jackson to Polk Street, and then there was a patrol car screeching to a stop in front of me. The driver opened her door and stuck her head out.

"Your name Turnbull?" she called.

"That's me." I hurried around to the passenger side. As I slammed the door, the officer punched the sirens and the car leaped forward.

The driver was a mixed-race woman in her mid-thirties, with short black hair and a no-nonsense demeanor. "Gutierrez, Officer Amelia. Inspector Melton told me to get you to the Park," she said, glancing to her left as she whizzed through an intersection. "She didn't say why."

"Drug buy going down," I told her. "So maybe you can kill the sirens after we cross Divisadero."

"Gotcha." She drove competently, quickly. The radio squawked its usual chatter from Dispatch, but I paid no attention. I sat halfway forward on the seat, peering through the windshield. Gutierrez expertly dodged two bike messengers, an old lady pushing a shopping cart slowly across the street, and three skateboarders trying to get themselves killed. We caught a break at Divisadero, the big north-south artery, and slammed through on a green light.

Gutierrez swung into the southbound lane, sirens howling, and we made it to the Fulton intersection at the speed of cop. She cut the sirens but not the lights as she turned onto Fulton, and after that it was all a blur of cars and people and houses going by.

This part of San Francisco was middle class, mostly three and four story apartment buildings interspersed with churches and schools. When we were a block away, Gutierrez cut the lights and slowed down. When she reached the corner of Stanyan Street and Fulton, she pulled to the curb.

"Thanks," I said, opening the door.

"Mention me to the Inspector," she said laconically. As I shut the door, she drove away.

In the daytime, the upper northwest corner of Golden Gate Park is a pretty, sunny spot. A waist-high stone wall ran west and south, marking the boundary of the park, and a small circle edged in stone held flowers. A picnic table sat against one wall. Ten or fifteen feet from the corner, the ground gave way to thick woods. Two dirt footpaths split off into the woods; at night, they looked like they were entering tunnels. I jumped when a pale figure floated out of one of them.

"Claire?" Suzette whispered loudly. Her beige trench coat flapped in the breeze.

I hurried over. "Any sign of Rafferty?"

A stir in the bushes, and Leesa Kern emerged, wearing dark clothing with "DEA" in large letters on the front. She carried a Heckler & Koch UMP45. Two men in dark SWAT uniforms, carrying the same, flanked her.

"Holy moly," I said. "Did you bring the tank, too?"

Kern frowned and glanced over at Suzette. "Is she trying to be funny?"

Suzette tilted her hand and touched her ear. "Forward post reports a single individual entering the Pits. Carrying a bag."

"That's him," I said. I started forward.

Kern put her hand out to stop me. "No civilians."

"But I—"

She glared at me. "You heard me. Stay here, or I cuff you to that picnic table."

I appealed to Suzette. "Come on, you know I won't get in the way."

Suzette opened her mouth to reply, but Kern shook her head. "This is a DEA op. My jurisdiction. This is my call."

Suzette shrugged. "Sorry, Claire."

Kern stuck out her hand. "And I want your weapon."

"What weapon?" I said.

Suzette maintained a carefully neutral expression. "Is that really necessary, Agent Kern?"

Kern addressed Suzette, as if I weren't there at all. "It's my op. She either goes, right now, or she stays here, on this bench, without a weapon."

I would have argued further, but decided it wasn't worth wasting time. I pulled my Colt out of my holster and handed it over. Kern handed it to an aide, with some muttered instructions.

"You wouldn't by any chance be related to a Vic Delorey, would you?" I asked her.

Suzette shot me a shut-up look, but Kern paid no attention to me. Standing, she gestured to her men. "Let's move."

I sat down on the picnic table bench with a loud sigh, and watched as everyone disappeared into the woods down the left-hand path, heading south and west. I counted to thirty, then thirty again. Then I got up and followed them quietly.

This corner of the great park was an anomaly; a pocket of hilly forest in the middle of an urban canyon. The path soon ramped up into a steep climb, made all the more difficult by the utter lack of lighting. I passed a lamp post whose bulb had long since been smashed. I knew this was one of the most dangerous corners of the park, precisely because of the undergrowth.

The path climbed higher, and here and there a root or bush tried to trip me up. I heard something rustling in the darkness off to my left.

The hill got steeper and I slowed down, hoping not to run into Leesa Kern in the darkness. The path wound around, still climbing, and then I was at the brink of a cut. I stopped, wobbling before I stepped back. I found a bush and crouched.

The horseshoe pits had been dug in the 1930s as part of the Works Progress Administration. The hillside below was cut sharply downward, and the concrete lined pits lay about thirty feet below my location. At first glance, it looked like a large, empty swimming pool. As my sight adjusted, I saw that there were about sixteen pits ranged in a long row, bordered by steel rails and a raised viewing platform. A solitary lamp cast a feeble light over the open area.

I heard voices and slunk back; at the far edge of the pits I saw Wayne Rafferty speaking to someone in shadow. I could not see Wyatt anywhere.

To my right, whispers: I recognized Suzette's voice as she spoke into a walkie-talkie. I knew DEA agents and cops were probably quietly surrounding the two men down below. I wished I could get closer, but just as I eased to my right I heard the click-click of a safety being released. At least one agent was in the brush to my right. If I moved, I stood a good chance of getting arrested at best and shot at worst. I stayed put, straining to see what was going on below.

Raised voices; and then a shout. The dark man tugged the gym bag out of Rafferty's grasp, holding it out of reach as the other man lunged at him. It sounded to me as though Rafferty was pleading. I didn't see the dark man hand anything to Rafferty, but he did unzip the bag and peer in. Apparently, he was satisfied. He turned abruptly and headed into the courts, straight towards me.

"Wait!" Rafferty called, trotting after the dark man.

The man stopped, reached into his jacket, and pulled out a handgun. He pointed it at Rafferty and said something in a low voice. Rafferty stopped short, then raised his hands again, pleading in a low voice.

The dark man moved into the light, and at that moment I saw the back of his jacket: he wore Washout colors. He turned, and the light caught his face. It was Dan "Hog" Shaeffer, from Nicky's bar. What the hell?

Rafferty stepped forward and caught his arm. "Where is she? Tell me! Please!"

Shaeffer growled something and raised the gun.

"I don't care!" Rafferty said, his voice rising to a desperate shout. "Tell me where she is! Have you hurt her? You have to tell me!"

I thought Shaeffer was going to fire, but he surprised me. He backhanded Rafferty across the face with the gun. Rafferty gave a grunt and fell backwards, striking his head on a concrete curb.

"Federal agents!" Agent Kern shouted from the far end of the pitch. "Put your weapon on the ground and put both hands on your head—"

"Shit!" Shaeffer fired at her voice.

I ducked down below the lip of the cliff edge just as the return fire opened up. I heard the zip of bullets overhead and the smack as at least one bullet hit a tree.

Suddenly Wyatt was beside me. "Get down!" he yelled. "Claire, he's heading this way!"

I kept my chin flat on the dirt and briefly wondered how Wyatt had found me in the dark. "What's going on?"

Wyatt moved away, to stand on the edge of the slope, hands on his hips, gazing down with complete disregard for the bullets whizzing past. Or maybe through. "It wasn't a drug buy," he said. "Rafferty is paying ransom for Allison. Shaeffer took the money and ran."

"Ransom! Then she's alive!" Even as I said it, I knew I was probably wrong. Many a ransom had been paid for a victim long dead, unknown to the relatives desperate to buy their lives. "Where is she?"

"Shaeffer didn't say. Here he comes—wait. He's angling off to the left. Damn. He's headed your way!"

The firing had stopped and I heard the tromp of SWAT boots on pavement. Shouts below: "Stop! Drop your weapon!" But apparently Dan Shaeffer was not inclined to obey, and I soon heard panting and scrabbling as he clawed his way up the dirt wall. I wriggled to my left.

"Don't do it, Claire," Wyatt said.

"I can surprise him," I hissed.

"And get shot for it," Wyatt warned. "If he don't shoot you, them agents down there will. They don't know you're up here."

He was right. I stood a better chance of getting shot by Suzette than of taking down an armed and desperate man twice my size. "Shit." I scrabbled left, belly down, hoping Shaeffer wouldn't see me. Then his head appeared over the edge, and as I scuttled backwards he heaved himself over. Below, I heard shouts and more running, but no one was shooting. I jumped to my feet and raised my hands.

"Claire!" Wyatt yelled. "Stop!" He took a half-step towards me.

"Stop where you are!" I yelled.

Shaeffer stopped, all right. He skidded to a stop, an arm's length away. He was wearing a black T-shirt, black leather Washouts jacket and jeans. In one hand he held the gym bag. In the other he held a gun that looked roughly the size of a cannon. I had a half a breath to see his eyes, hard and staring.

"For God's sake, Claire!" Wyatt dove towards Shaeffer, but his arm passed right through the man.

"Bitch," Shaeffer snarled. "Get out of my way."

Then he raised his gun and aimed it at my face.

CHAPTER 24

The only thing that saved me was long years of training. I dropped and rolled forward in a classic *mae ukemi*: I dropped my left shoulder, put my foot behind me, and curved my left arm into a circle. Even as the shot exploded over my head, I flung myself into a forward roll, spinning around my own axis, and landed in the three-point position: left knee raised, foot planted, right leg supporting me from behind. I was almost on Shaeffer's foot.

He swung his gun downward, aiming at me. I leaned to one side, grabbed his gun arm, and drew it towards me. This meant I was pulling him along the path he had already chosen, with his entire body weight behind him. He grunted, off balance, and fell forward. I grabbed the back of his neck as he fell, and pulled. Shaeffer rotated around his own center of gravity and slammed to the ground on his back, arms outflung. A perfect *kaiten nage*; I wished my sensei had seen it.

I pivoted on my right knee, planted my weight on Shaeffer's forearm, and reached across him for his gun. I knew even as I did it that it was a mistake. He brought his gun hand up and slammed the weapon into my face. Pain exploded through my head and I saw stars. *He'll shoot me now,* I thought. I waited for the gunshot, knowing it would be the last thing I heard.

Then there were shots and loud voices and the sound of people crashing through underbrush. Feet pounded away.

"Claire! Claire? Can you hear me?" I heard Wyatt beside me, near my head. "Claire!"

I blinked. His face swam into view above me, an anxious expression on his face. "W-wyatt?"

"Are you hurt?"

"Where is he?"

"Ran east, towards Fulton. Inspector Melton and some officers are chasing him."

"Rafferty?"

"In custody," Wyatt said. His gaze searched my face. "You're going to have a hell of a shiner in the morning."

"Serves me right," I said. I pulled myself to a sitting position, then painfully to my feet. "We have to go after Shaeffer."

"You're in no shape to go anywhere," Wyatt said. He stretched out a hand, then snatched it back before he could touch me. "Dammit, stay here and I'll follow him."

"Nothing doing. Which way?"

Wyatt silently pointed into the woods, back the way I'd come. "Let me go first," he growled. "I can see better'n you even in daylight."

I doubted it, but he was clearly in no mood for arguments. I plunged into the woods behind him.

Under the trees it was pitch black. "I can't see you," I hissed.

A whisper of cloth, and then I saw Wyatt's white shirt. He had stripped off his waistcoat and long frock coat. He flung them away, gestured for me to follow, and turned back to the trail. I followed the white shirt down the twisty path. I wondered which would happen first: I would run into an armed and dangerous felon who would shoot me, or collide in the dark with my partner who could kill me with a single touch. I really wished Agent Kern had not taken my gun.

Suddenly, Wyatt stopped and bent forward at the waist.

"What is it?"

Shouts from the woods ahead, moving away. Suzette and her minions were probably at Fulton Street by now. But Wyatt swung his head from side to side, almost like a dog casting for scent. Then he stepped off the path, circling around. "He left the path and doubled back. Come on."

I followed him, but it was tough going. Wyatt Earp passed like mist through the underbrush, but I had to push through thorns and bushes. One low hanging branch nearly put my eye out when I walked into it. "Ow!"

"Shh." Wyatt stopped, turned, started up again. He kept his gaze on the ground in front of him. "He dodged the police line," Wyatt muttered. "This boy's been in the woods before."

"Probably at his pot patch," I said. "I'll concede your Boy Scout skills, but where is he going?"

The ground changed, now sloping down instead of up. We were rounding the edge of the horseshoe pits.

"Heading for Conservatory Drive, I reckon," Wyatt said. He darted left, then came back to his former heading. We emerged into a clear patch of dirt, probably some homeless person's campsite. Wyatt halted, knelt, pointed at the dirt. "Footprint."

We were only a few yards from the lights of Fulton Street, but the woods were so dense that little of it filtered through. "Can I risk a light?"

Wyatt shrugged. I pulled out my cell phone and turned it on. The screen lit up and I pointed it towards the ground. It wasn't a flashlight, but it was better than nothing. A boot print stood out in the ashy remains of a campfire. Another half-print beyond it showed Shaeffer's direction.

"Definitely the drive," I said. "Damn."

"I'll go right, you go left. If you haven't found him in a hundred paces, come back this way. I'll do the same. We'll find him in the middle."

I cut south through the brush. It was thinner near the road, and in a moment I broke through to a grassy bank that ran along Conservatory Drive, the road that looped through the eastern end of Golden Gate Park. Two leaps took me to the paved surface of the road. There were more lamps here, and most of them worked. I tried to listen for running steps, but heard nothing over the pounding of my own boots. A hundred feet from where I'd entered the road, it curved right and then I stopped, panting.

At this point, Conservatory Drive East met up with the extension from Hayes Street, as well as two footpaths that wound down through the park, for a total of six different directions my quarry could have gone.

I stopped and bent over, hands on my knees, panting. I heard shouting behind me, distantly, as the SWAT and DEA teams tried to find Shaeffer. Approaching sirens wailed, but the intervening woods and hills surrounding me muffled everything. It was very quiet and very dark under the trees. Had Shaeffer doubled back? Was he lying in wait for someone chasing him?

Wyatt caught up with me, no more than a shadow in moonlight. "No sign of him all the way to Fulton," he growled. "You see anything?"

I shook my head. Wyatt glanced around. "Five ways he could have gone, not counting the road we're standin' in. If he's on pavement he'll be harder to track." He turned to look at me. "How lucky you feelin', partner?"

I shrugged.

"Then we take the footpaths, because they're dirt. If he left sign, we can follow him."

I nodded my agreement, pointed to the left hand path, and took off. Wyatt headed down the right hand trail. I hadn't gone more than fifteen feet down the pathway before Wyatt was back.

"Found his tracks," he said. "Come on."

CHAPTER 25

I followed him as he cut through the brush separating the paths. We came out on another dirt path curving into another woody thicket. Wyatt pointed to some blurs on the ground that I supposed were footprints; in these matters, I deferred to his expertise. He bent over, walking quickly, then straightened as we came to a bend.

He looked over his shoulder. "You heeled?"

"Feds took my gun," I said.

He shot me a disgusted look but went around the bend, scouted out the path, and waved me forward. Sure enough, the path divided here, and then divided again a few yards further on. I heard muted conversation in the trees to my right and turned that way, but Wyatt shook his head. "Homeless fellows," he said. "Got a campsite there. Our man is ahead of us. Looks like he's bearing left, headed for Peacock Meadows."

As I trotted onward, my cell phone buzzed in my pocket. I hauled it out. "Yes?"

"Claire, where the hell are you?" Suzette's voice was nearly drowned out by the sound of shouts in the background.

Panting, I told her, "In pursuit of armed suspect, Caucasian male, six feet one, one seventy, wearing motorcycle leathers. He's got the bag and he's headed for Peacock Meadows. Shut down the Park and get a team to JFK Drive! Make sure the exits are blocked."

"Claire, stay where you are! Do not attempt to apprehend—"

I shut off the phone and jogged onward, following Wyatt. Just as we emerged from the trees onto the grassy lawn of the meadows, a motorcycle roared to life ahead of us.

"Damn!" I yelled, and broke into a run. Ahead of me on John F. Kennedy Drive, a big Harley Davidson thundered to life. Dan Shaeffer, his back to me, gunned the engine and then took off, headed west. In moments he was out of sight. "Wyatt! Follow him!"

Wyatt blinked out of sight. I heard sirens and tires squealing behind me, and a black-and-white with lights going full pulled up behind me. Before it came to a stop, Suzette was out of the car and running. I ran to meet her.

"Claire, what the hell—"

"He's on a bike," I said. "Harley two-tone, black and blue with tooled leather saddlebags, going west on JFK." She turned and headed back to the car. I followed, and just as she reached the car I jumped in between her and the door. "I'm going, too."

"The hell you are!"

I glared at her. "And I know who he is!"

"Get in the back," she said, and shoved past me. The lock popped on the rear door and I jumped. The door wasn't even completely shut when we took off. The driver, a beefy guy I didn't know, plowed up the middle of JFK, disregarding the possibility of oncoming traffic. Suzette twisted to talk to me through the wire mesh that divided the perp seat from the front. "We've got all the exits blocked, but you say he's on a Harley?"

"Yeah. He can cut through to the bike path or through the landscaping, and there's no walls along Fulton," I said.

Suzette picked up the mike and sent out a BOLO with the description I gave her of the Harley. All the time we were barrelling up the long curve of Kennedy Drive, then jolting right onto Eighth Avenue. A few feet ahead, two squad cars had the exit to Fulton blocked, roller bars going. A patrol officer jogged over as we pulled up and spoke to Suzette. "Saw him just now, coming out of the trees onto Fulton. He bumped between two cars and headed up Seventh." As he spoke, one of the squad cars was backing away to open a space, and our unit shot through onto Fulton. Careening on two tires, we cut across the traffic lanes (thankfully empty at this time of night) onto Seventh.

"All units, all units, converge on Seventh Avenue between Fulton and Balboa. Subject is armed and dangerous, riding a late model Harley—"

The radio crackled. "This is Unit 21. Subject just passed us on Balboa, now heading east at approximately ninety miles an hour."

"Damn!" Suzette keyed the mike and relayed new orders. I wondered where Shaeffer was heading with that bag of cash.

The driver screamed up Seventh and then right onto Balboa. This was a larger street, with shops and stores still open. A delivery van was double parked in our lane, and there was an oncoming bus in the other lane. We screeched to a halt behind the van, and Suzette keyed the bullhorn built into the unit. "Get this van out of our way or someone is going to spend the night in jail!"

A skinny guy in a ball cap dropped the laden dolly he was pushing and ran around to the cab. In a minute, the van rumbled away, we swerved around him, but by now reports were coming in from all over the Inner Richmond district: they'd spotted the Harley, they'd lost the Harley, or the Harley they were chasing was the wrong one.

"Cut the flashers," Suzette said wearily. The car slowed to street speeds and fell silent. "Take me back to the rally point."

CHAPTER 26

W e got back to Fulton Street, where they'd dropped me off seeming hours ago. Men in SWAT outfits were packing cases and boxes into a black van. Several squad cars rolled away as we parked. Leesa Kern, still wearing her DEA vest, was sitting on the bench she'd threatened to chain me to.

"No sign of him," she said as Suzette walked up. She glared at me. "You were supposed to stay put."

"If I had, you'd never have known that he's on a motorcycle right now," I said. "So you're welcome, Agent Kern."

She twisted the top off a bottle of water and drank half of it in four gulps. Ignoring me, she spoke to Suzette. "I put your BOLO on the Federal wires. Rafferty gave me some bullshit story about ransom. Personally, I think he knew the guy."

"His name is Dan Shaeffer, and he used to work for Rafferty." The two law officers stared at me. I told them what I knew about Shaeffer. "And I guess I don't have to tell you that the Washouts worked security for the race," I finished. "So whatever happened to Allison Farley, he knows about it. This was a ransom drop."

Leesa Kern looked at me skeptically. "Yeah, that's Rafferty's story. You believe it?"

"I heard his voice when he was begging Shaeffer to tell him where Allison is. I believe him." I turned to Suzette. "You know the clock is ticking. They've got the money and the victim. She may have no more than an hour left."

"If she's not already dead." Suzette's mouth was a grim line. "I want to talk to Rafferty."

We followed Agent Kern over to a black Crown Vic.

Wayne Rafferty was handcuffed in the back, his head sunk on his chest. He looked ten years older than he had this afternoon at the bank. As soon as he saw us, he started shouting. "Where is she? Did you catch him? You've got to find him! He knows where Allison is!"

Kern opened the door but held out a hand to stop him when he tried to get out. "Mr. Rafferty, are you waiving your right to counsel?"

"Screw that," Wayne said. His face was red and his eyes were puffy. There was a huge blue-black bruise forming on one side of his face where Shaeffer had pistol-whipped him. "I'll waive anything if you'll just listen to me! Don't stand around here arguing, go after him!"

"Mr. Rafferty, we have units searching the city for Dan Shaeffer," Suzette said. "But we can't help you unless you tell us what's going on."

I reached into the front of the unit and found a half-empty water bottle. I handed it to him. He held it in his handcuffed hands and chugged it down. "Thanks." He looked from me to Suzette to Agent Kern. "The day of the race, as we were looking for Allison, I got a call on my cell. A guy said he had Allison. He made her talk into the phone. She was crying. She—Oh, God." He hiccupped and shuddered.

"Steady," I said, and put a hand on his shoulder. I squatted down so I was closer to his eye level. "Just relax and tell us what happened. We'll find her."

He kept his gaze on me, desperate. "She said, 'Wayne, they're going to kill me if you don't give them money'. I believed her. She was crying. Allison never cries. She sounded so scared." Tears rolled down his cheeks. "When the guy came back on, I told him I'd pay anything if he just didn't hurt her. He said, 'That's the plan'. And then he said I had six days to put together three million dollars in small bills."

"Six days?" Kern sounded skeptical. "Mighty generous of him."

"Maybe he knew I didn't have that much cash," Wayne said. "I sold everything. Everything. When the guy called back, I didn't have all of the three million. He put Allison on and she was, she was." He squeezed his eyes shut. "She said they had hurt her. She said if I didn't get the money they would, oh God, they would rape her…" He was panting now, his hands making fists on his knees, cuffed together.

I put a hand on his cuffed wrist. "Wayne, take a deep breath. Come on, slow now. Another. You have to focus on Allison now. She needs you to tell us everything you can."

He took a couple of deep breaths. Again he stared into my eyes, ignoring Suzette and Kern ranged behind me. "I told the guy I would get the money, but I had to wait until the bank was open so I could get to my safe deposit box. And the bank wanted forty-eight hours on two of my big CDs before they would pay them out. The guy said if I didn't have the money the day after that, he would send Allison home one piece at a time. God, why aren't you out there chasing him?"

Kern spoke for the first time, disbelief in every syllable. "Did he warn you not to contact the police?"

"Yeah, and he said they were watching me, so they'd know if I went to the cops."

So that was why he had been so hostile when I showed up asking questions about Allison. "Did you recognize the voice on the phone? Either of them?"

"He sounded a little familiar, but there was a lot of background music. Someone was playing AC/DC really loud. And well, I didn't recognize his voice at first. But tonight when I heard the guy, I knew it was him."

"Dan Shaeffer was the voice on the phone?" Suzette said quickly.

"Yeah." Rafferty frowned. "Shaeffer? Is that his name. Wait a minute. I think he used to work with Jack and me, on a couple of projects two, three years ago."

"He doesn't work for you now?" Agent Kern asked.

"No. I think he quit. No, I remember now. He flunked a drug test on a work site and we fired him." He looked at me with horror in his eyes. "Is that what this is? Revenge? Oh, Jesus. Jesus. What will he do to Allison?" He trembled all over.

"That's enough, Claire." Suzette touched my shoulder. I rose and backed away as a paramedic moved in with a blanket and a medikit. "We'll get him downtown, and then we'll question him some more."

Special Agent Kern walked up. "No trace of drugs on him, or on his hands. No sighting of drugs at the scene."

"You don't have probable cause to be involved in this case any longer," Suzette said. Her voice was firm.

Agent Kern's expression soured. "I still think we've got money laundering going on, and we can—"

"I'll be taking over this crime scene," Suzette said. "Appreciate the help from the DEA."

Agent Kern was not happy. "I really thought we had the guy. I can stay on, in an unofficial capacity, if you need me."

"The department will keep you informed." Suzette's expression was neutral to the point of immobility.

Agent Kern nodded and turned to go, beginning to shed her DEA assault jacket.

"Hey?" I said.

Kern turned back to me. "What do you want?" Her tone told me she blamed me for the entire botched mission.

"Pick it up from Inspector Melton in the morning." Kern stalked away. She barked an order to her aide, who trotted behind her carrying an evidence bag with my gun in it. Well, hell.

Suzette had been talking to one of the uniformed cops, and now turned back to me. "I'm going downtown with Rafferty. This is now an open homicide case, and I can't let you in on it." Her tone was not apologetic, but I took no offense. Kidnapping fell under the jurisdiction of the Homicide department, and she had a job to do. Suzette took her job seriously, which was one of the reasons we are friends.

"I'll catch a cab," I told her.

I wanted a shower and food and a nap, if I could persuade my body to actually sleep. Buses were out of the question at this time of night, so I caught a cab. Going home, I thought of the two fast rides I'd had in cop cars tonight, and allowed myself to miss, for just a moment, the thrill of being an actual police officer. Then I remembered mountains of paperwork and jerkwad lieutenants, and congratulated myself for being out of that bureaucratic cesspool.

Benetto's was long since closed when the cab dropped me off, but I could still smell the wonderful scent of garlic. My stomach growled. I climbed the stairs, trying to decide between ramen and a peanut butter sandwich. I opened the door to my apartment.

Wyatt Earp was striding back and forth across the living room floor, still dressed in the white shirt and black pants I'd last seen him in. He whirled when I came in. "Where have you been?"

CHAPTER 27

I was tired. I snapped, "Did you lose him, too?"

"No, I followed him 'til he went to ground," Wyatt said tersely. "I waited and waited, but you never showed up. I went back to the park but everyone was gone. I was hoping you found a way to tail him."

I told him about my wild ride with Suzette in the squad car. "We lost him on Balboa," I concluded. "Where did he end up?"

"I left him in the Tenderloin Club on Leavenworth," Wyatt said. "He's waitin' for someone."

"Has he made any phone calls?" I turned to leave, closing and locking the door behind me.

Wyatt answered me as he stepped through my wall. "Not before I left him," he said. "You going there?"

"Yes," I said.

"You better be armed," Wyatt said.

I was already trotting down the stairs. "I am," I said. "Meet me there." Wyatt nodded and vanished.

I caught a cab on Columbus and gave him the address of the Tenderloin Club. The cabbie stared at me in the rear view mirror. "Lady, that's a boxing club. You know that, right?"

"Yeah," I said. "I'm working on my uppercut."

"At three in the morning?" The cab pulled away from the curb.

"I'm training for a professional bout. Drop me off a block away, will you?"

The streets were almost deserted at that hour, and after I paid off the cabbie I strolled up Leavenworth. At this time of night, the Tenderloin was alive with activity: panhandlers, homeless people wandering and pushing shopping carts, hookers and dealers, drag queens, gangsters and gangster-wannabes lounging a little too casually on corners and lampposts.

Most of the buildings were cheap hotels, pawn shops, and boarded up shops. I kept my head up and my stride firm and authoritative. I studiously ignored the catcalls as I walked by a knot of teenage males with nothing better to do on a week night than hold down the sidewalks.

Wyatt Earp stood on the sidewalk in front of an old three story building in an advanced state of disrepair. He had re-acquired his long frock coat but dispensed with the vest. "He's still inside," he said.

"I should call Suzette," I said.

"Hey, who you talkin' to, sistah?" yelled a dilapidated man sitting with his back to the building.

I ignored him. Wyatt shook his head. "Not yet," he said. "We don't want to spook him."

"But he knows where Allison is," I said.

"And that's why we don't want to spook him," Wyatt repeated patiently. "This fellow has already outrun the police once. I'll go in, keep an eye on him. You stay out here and follow him if he leaves. If he calls anyone, I'll listen in." Without waiting for my reply, he stepped through the brick wall and disappeared.

I didn't like this plan, mainly because it involved me standing on a sidewalk in a bad part of town at four in the morning. I hoped Suzette would get my message soon. I tugged my jacket close around me, wished I'd brought a muffler, and prepared for a long wait.

I spent my time scoping out the site. The Tenderloin Club was the oldest boxing gym in San Francisco, and its exterior showed it. Peeling and faded boxing posters overlaid one another in layers. I suspected if you dug down deep enough, you'd find posters of George Foreman or Sonny Liston underneath. Or even Gentleman Jim Corbett, from Wyatt's day.

The entrance was a stairway that slanted down; apparently

the gym was in the basement. One light burned over the entrance, and when the door opened the musty smell of lockers and old sweat floated out. This was definitely not a place people went to work out to Pilates instructors in leotards. The door only opened twice, both to emit large men in warm-up suits carrying gym bags and smelling of liniment. The locals gave the men a wide berth.

I eyed the street carefully, but didn't see Shaeffer's motorcycle. However, there was an underground garage half a block up Leavenworth, and it was possible he'd stashed his ride there.

"Hey, honey, you lookin' for a date?" The hooker was tall, black, and dressed in flaming red. Two women behind her, dressed in as little as possible to show off as much as possible, giggled.

"Sure," I said. "But I'm broke. You work for free?"

All three of them thought this was hilarious. I saw movement down the street; a tall white man was approaching with a scowl on his face.

"For a sistah, maybe," the hooker continued.

"Better clear it with your boss," I said, nodding towards the approaching pimp.

All three women turned, looked, and then walked away in three different directions.

The pimp came up to me. He wore a thousand dollar warm-up suit on a fifty-dollar body, showing a gravy stain on the front. From ten feet away, I could smell the tobacco smoke. "You workin' my street, baby?" he said.

"Baby? Seriously?" I straightened, swept my jacket back and turned so he could see my holster. "You need better radar, buddy. I'm on the job. Stakeout."

He took a step back. "I ain't seen you here before."

"I've never been here before, so we're even."

"I don't want no trouble, but you can't be hasslin' my girls." He tried to look menacing, and it would probably have worked if he hadn't kept glancing nervously at my holster.

"I'm not hassling them, and you need to move on," I said

in my harshest cop-voice. "Or we can continue this conversation downtown…"

He stuck his hands in his pockets and tried to look nonchalant. "That's cool. No hassles here, lady. Just keepin' an eye on my corner."

"Funny," I said coldly. "I was under the impression this corner belonged to the City of San Francisco."

He blinked, shrugged, and then turned and walked back the way he had come, with a deliberate swagger to show any onlookers that I hadn't fazed him at all.

The result of this confrontation was predictable: nobody bothered me. The panhandlers moved away, the prostitutes crossed to the other side of the street, and the dealers simply vanished. The gangsters remained, but the remarks stopped.

In a situation like this, where a newcomer unbalances the delicate balance of street society, gang members usually either stay quiet or get belligerent in defense of their turf. No cop can predict which way it will go, but I got lucky tonight. Nobody seemed inclined to challenge me, so I leaned back against the cold brick of the building and waited.

Hours crept by. Ice ages came and went. The galaxies rotated. Or so it felt like it; actually, when I checked my watch I saw that only about thirty minutes had passed before the door opened and Shaeffer stepped out. I stepped behind a newspaper kiosk, cupping my hands as if lighting a cigarette, but he never even glanced my way. He turned south on Leavenworth, passed me without a glance and kept on going. I turned to follow, and then Wyatt was beside me.

"He left the bag in one of the men's room lockers," Wyatt said. "I can stay and keep an eye on it, see if anyone shows up to claim it. You follow Shaeffer?"

I nodded and set off after my quarry.

He walked fast, and I nearly had to trot to keep up. I was afraid he would turn and make me—it was too late and I was too tired to do much in the way of fancy dodging. It was my good luck that he didn't turn, but barged right on, across Golden Gate Avenue, across McAllister, finally slowing as he entered the UN Plaza.

This was a large area set aside to commemorate the founding of the United Nations in San Francisco in 1945; it consisted of a paved brick plaza marked with marble inserts, several marble pillars listing the names of the member nations, and a big fountain that looked like a giant's collection of toy blocks tossed in a haphazard heap. In short, a terrible place to have to tail someone even in the daytime. At least the farmer's market wasn't up, so I had a few clear spaces. But once Shaeffer got into the shadows and murk in and around the monuments, I would lose him.

Fortunately, he slowed even more, so I closed up the distance between us. Just as I began to worry that my footsteps might echo in this brick canyon and alert him, Shaeffer pulled out a cell phone. I closed up the gap even more, anxious to catch his conversation.

"Yeah…yeah…right. I'll be there." He stuck the phone back in his pocket and I dropped back, disappointed.

The fountain was on, and the splash of the falling water masked the sound of my footsteps a bit. I dared to get even closer to Shaeffer, but then he strode out into the open space in front of it and stopped, looking around. I stuck to the shadows and watched.

At this point the UN Plaza fronted Market Street, the main artery of downtown San Francisco. Even at this hour traffic was medium heavy. To my right was the big blue UN flag on its flagpole, and beneath it the entrance to the underground BART station. To my left was an area with a few anemic trees planted in holes in the sidewalk, and another entrance to BART. I was sure Shaeffer was poised to enter the transit system, and was trying to figure out how to follow him down without being seen.

Shaeffer stood looking uptown. Was he waiting for a car? I cursed myself for not insisting on Wyatt accompanying me; if Shaeffer caught a cab here I would never be able to follow him. It's only in the movies or Manhattan that a detective can hope to hop into a taxi and say, "Follow that cab."

Shaeffer stepped to the curb, lifted a hand to wave. I saw a big black Mercedes Benz sedan swerve towards the curb. I took two steps forward; at least I could get the license number of the car.

The engine of the Mercedes suddenly accelerated. The big car leaped forward and jumped the curb. There was a shout of surprise from Dan Shaeffer, the sickening thud of impact, and Shaeffer flew through the air. He came down on one of the concrete blocks of the fountain, one with an edge turned upward, and from fifteen feet away I heard the crack of his spine. The Mercedes screeched tires, bounced back onto the street and roared away. I strained to see a license plate, but my view was blocked by a trash can on the curb side.

I scrambled down the slippery steps leading into the fountain and reached Shaeffer. Blood welled from his mouth and his eyes were unfocused, but he was still alive. To reach him, I had to climb up a slippery rock face chiseled with names I didn't recognize, and balance on a ledge with water flowing over it. As I stepped into it, it changed color; Dan Shaeffer was bleeding down the slab.

"Shaeffer! Can you hear me?" I called. His face was about six feet away from me, but his eyes could not meet mine. I wasn't sure he could see anything. "Where is Allison? Tell me where she is!"

His mouth moved, but no sound came out. He suddenly slipped sideways; he lay on a very steeply tilted block, and from the position of his legs and spine it was clear he could not move himself.

"Dan! Where is Allison!"

I suppose I should have been more compassionate, maybe I should have tried to help him, or should have called for help sooner. But my concern was for Allison Farley, and the sound of Wayne Rafferty's voice full of horror and fear for her. I tried to find some way to get closer to him, so I could hear any reply. Water sheeted down the block, mixed with his blood. The surface was slick and wet, and there was no purchase for my hands.

"Dan! Can you hear me?" I shouted. The splash of water

drowned out my voice. "Dan!"

His mouth moved again. I tried to read his lips in the illumination from the street lights. But it was no use.

His eyes moved, fixed, and then he died.

CHAPTER 28

To my dismay, it was Vic Delorey, not Suzette, who answered my 9-1-1 call. As soon as he saw me, his face turned as sour as pickle juice. "You're like a goddam cockroach," he hissed at me. His long black trench coat was open, showing a gray shirt and navy tie and a coffee stain. "Always messing up whatever case I'm on."

"Just doing my job, Vic," I said steadily.

Behind us, paramedics were getting wet tugging Dan's body off the tilted slabs of the fountain. He flopped like a broken doll. Which, when I thought about it, was pretty much what he was now. I turned my back on the sight.

"You ain't on 'the job'," Vic sneered. "We kicked your ass off the force ages ago."

"I resigned, if you remember," I said. I had to work on keeping my voice level. It wouldn't do to piss him off, not now anyway. "Did you send a team to the Tenderloin Club, like I asked?"

"Yeah, and there's nobody there. It's locked up. You do know it's nearly dawn, right? No, that's right. You're a vampire or something."

This was an oblique reference to my insomnia, which Vic knew about but didn't really believe in. I remembered that during the investigation that ended in my resignation, he had stated loudly and often his opinion that I had a drug habit. I didn't, and could prove it, but there are always those who will believe anything negative. Vic's prejudice had cost me a few friends. I tightened my grip on my temper.

"There's evidence in a locker in there," I said. I'd already told him this once, but he hadn't been listening then either. "You might not even need a warrant."

"How do you know there's anything in there? Did you see Shaeffer go in there? And why didn't you call us right away?"

"I had it from a reliable informant," I said. If I couldn't tell Suzette about Wyatt, I for damn sure couldn't tell Vic Delorey. "Are you getting a BOLO out on the car, at least? You know this is tied to the kidnapping, right?"

"I don't know any such thing. There's no kidnapping, there's just that jerk Rafferty lying about a drug deal gone wrong."

"Fine, it's not ransom. Call it drug money, if it makes you feel any better. But go after it. You can call the owner—"

"You're trying to tell me how to do my job now?"

My temper snapped. "Someone needs to! You have evidence of a major crime and you're blowing it off? Just because you have your panties in a permanent twist over me? Christ, Vic, even you're not that stupid."

His narrow face went white. "God damn. I mean, God damn. I don't have to take that from you!"

I was almost yelling now. "Damn it to hell, Delorey, are you going to send a squad car to the Tenderloin Club?"

"Hell, no," he said. "I got no probable cause. You can't even tell me why you think the money's there. You got no witnesses, you didn't see anything, but you got, what, intuition or some junkie telling you the money's there?"

As usual, he was worse than useless. "Vic, you have my—"

"*Inspector* Delorey," he said.

There are limits. I'd known this jerk when he was a rookie. "Vic, you have my word on it. I promise you, just go and look—"

He snapped his notebook shut and stuck it in his jacket pocket. "I got work to do. I got an accident to clear."

"Accident? You think this was a traffic accident? Hell, even you can see this has to be murder! The only witness to the ransom exchange, the only person who can tell us where Allison Farley is, gets taken out just as he's leading me to her, and you think it's an accident?"

His face got closed and hard. "Yeah. I got no reason to think otherwise. Just an unreliable witness who'll say anything to worm her way into a real case."

Clearly, I was wasting my time with this moron. "You have my statement, *Inspector*. Can I go?"

He hesitated, and I could see he was just looking for an excuse to haul me downtown. While he was cogitating, I shrugged and walked away.

It was only a few blocks back to the Tenderloin Club. When I arrived, the lights were out and the door was locked. I was wondering whether I should wait around for Wyatt or put in another call to Suzette, when Wyatt stepped through the windows of the closed gym.

"There you are," he said. "So where did the fellow get to? Did you find out where Allison Farley is?"

I told him about the foot chase, about the car that hit Dan Shaeffer. By the time I finished, he was wearing his poker face: steel blue eyes, hardened jaw.

"If he's dead, how do we find Allison Farley? Still assuming this is, in fact, a kidnapping."

"And assuming that it wasn't her body Suzette found," I said. "They put out a BOLO on the car."

He tipped his head to one side, and I said, "A BOLO means 'Be On the Look Out'," I said.

"I know. But is that all they're doing? Are they looking for the ransom money?"

"Suzette may be. But I can't get hold of her."

"Probably interrogating Wayne Rafferty. Do you know if anyone's searching his house?"

"I don't know."

He shrugged, adjusting his coat. "If you'll wait here, I can go take a look."

I wanted coffee. I wanted breakfast. I wanted a hot shower. But six years as a cop had taught me to put those thoughts away. "Okay," I said. "Be quick."

He vanished as I pronounced the last syllable.

I hugged myself for warmth as the last of the night faded

around me. Cars began to drift down the street; commuters arriving at work. The pimps, whores, gang bangers and dealers disappeared, leaving only the eternal homeless, now bunking down for the day on their cardboard squares and filthy quilts. I watched as a van pulled up, and a young Asian man got out to load up the newspaper dispenser.

I bought a copy of the morning edition and found the story of the Golden Gate Park shoot-em-up on Page Two. There was a shot of the Horseshoe Pits taken in daylight, with the enormous Depression-era bas-reliefs picked out on the slopes above the courts. The official PD press release stated that an aborted drug deal had been interrupted by "elements of law enforcement". Not a word about the intrepid PI who had tracked an armed man through a dark woods to his motorcycle. And not one syllable about Allison Farley or Wayne Rafferty or Dan Shaeffer. I swear I don't know why anyone reads the papers for anything but the comics any more.

After about an hour and a half of this, my cell phone rang; it was Suzette. "Where are you?" she demanded.

"Holding down the sidewalk in front of the Tenderloin Club," I said. "Did Vic tell you about Dan Shaeffer?"

"Yeah. He says you were trying to distract him with something about the Club. What's the deal?"

I'd had a little time to cook up a story that might convince Suzette to trust me, without revealing Wyatt's presence. "You know I identified Shaeffer at the Park, right?"

"Yeah."

"I asked around among some folks I know. One of them called me back and said he'd seen Shaeffer entering the Club last night, about the time we lost him in the chase."

"And you didn't tell me?"

"Check your messages, Suzette! I left three, telling you to meet me here. Since you didn't show up, I had to surveil the place all by myself, and let me tell you I am damned cold!"

"Skipped your morning coffee, Claire?" Suzette sounded sarcastic.

"No, I'm just getting tired of the San Francisco Police Department ignoring my input on an important case," I snapped. "I've never steered you wrong, Suze, but ever since I brought you this case, you've dismissed all my attempts to help."

"It wasn't a case when you brought it to me," she said reasonably. "It still may not be."

"Dammit, we caught the kidnapper in the middle of a ransom drop! You have Allison's body in your morgue—"

"Actually, we don't," Suzette said. "That's one reason I didn't call you back; I was talking to Anna Shinn. The woman in the Bay was a jumper."

I grimaced. I hated the fact that the beautiful Golden Gate Bridge was a prime target for suicides, who took their last dive from 450 feet above the water. "You're sure?"

"She was identified through dental records. Sheila Thompson of Vallejo. No relation to Allison Farley. Reported missing ten days ago by her husband after she walked out during a fight."

"Damn. That was fast."

"Her ID was on file already, some accident ten years ago. Anyway, Anna confirmed cause of death as multiple fractures."

I felt very tired. "So Allison Farley is still missing."

"And presumed drowned," Suzette said. "Accidentally drowned."

"Still no body, Suzette," I reminded her. "And in any case, someone tried to extort millions out of her grieving fiance. And the millions are here in a gym locker. Do you want to come get it?"

A black Crown Vic rolled to a stop at the curb in front of me. The driver's door opened and Suzette climbed out, holding her phone to her ear. "Yeah, I do," she said. I heard it in person and over the phone.

Shutting off my call, I nodded to Suzette. "How do you do it? You look like you were dressed by professionals." She wore a camel hair coat over a blue silk blouse and navy trousers. She held a cup of takeout coffee in one hand, her cell in the other.

"I went home to change after I saw the judge." She slipped the cell phone in a pocket and took out a folded paper. "Search warrant," she said. "Unlike Vic, I believed you."

That almost made up for being up all night, chasing bad guys and watching them get killed by hit-and-run drivers. It didn't quite make up for being cold and hungry, but I could live with it.

"By the way," she said. "Rafferty made bail. His lawyer came and took him home."

"You don't see him as a flight risk?"

"Since nearly every dime he had was in that bag, no," Suzette said, sipping coffee. The smell was driving me nuts. "Anyway, the DEA impounded his car and cell to search for evidence."

"Kern still thinks this is a drug buy gone wrong?"

"I don't know what she thinks."

"Do you think this was a drug buy gone wrong?"

Suzette hesitated, then said. "Claire, we checked the numbers on Wayne's cell, the ones he said were ransom calls. Every one of them was from a burner phone."

"Which is exactly what I'd use if I was a kidnapper," I said.

"And if I was a drug dealer, I would use a burner phone. Better, if I wanted to establish a fake call from an imaginary kidnapper, I'd buy a burner phone and call my own number."

"You cops are such cynics," I said.

CHAPTER 29

A very large black man in a warm-up suit rounded the corner and stopped when he reached us. "You the cops?" he said in a deep voice.

Suzette held up her badge. "You're Sam Cornwell, the owner of this gym?"

He nodded. He stood well over six feet and looked about thirty-five. The seams of his warm-up suit bulged over muscle; I estimated his weight at around one-seventy, none of it fat. "Middleweight?" I asked him.

He looked at me, and I saw the typical busted nose and cauliflower ears of the professional boxer. "Used to be light heavy, but I lost a few pounds. You say there's something in my gym you need to fetch?"

"We need to search the men's locker room," Suzette said. "I have a warrant here."

"Don't need no warrant. All you got to do is ask." He glanced around. "Ain't no men cops you could send?"

"What's the point?" I asked. "There isn't anyone in the gym, right?"

He shrugged, his shoulders moving like small mountains, and pulled a ring of keys out of his pockets. "Guess not," he said.

"We'll be as quick as we can," Suzette said.

I followed them down the stairs, smelling old socks, arnica and liniment and aging canvas. The gym opened up into a big room that took most of the basement. Speed bags, heavy bags, sets of barbells and weight machines lined the walls, but the center was dominated by the ring. The mat was dingy and showed a couple of patches, but it was smartly put together and showed signs of care.

Sam Cornwell led us past it and through a door in the middle of the rear wall. This opened into a short passageway, with doors on either side and a set of stairs leading up to a rear door. He stopped and gestured.

"My office on the left, bathrooms and locker rooms here." The door had once been painted black, but now showed scars and nicks. Suzette and I pushed through and found ourselves in a large locker room smelling of disinfectant and sports creme. Rows of lockers lined the walls.

Suzette turned to Cornwell. "Do you have master keys to the locks?"

Cornwell frowned. "What do you mean? They ain't supposed to be locked."

I walked over and opened one locker. The smell of mildew wafted out at me, but it was empty. I opened the next, and the next. None of them were locked.

"I don't 'llow nobody to keep stuff overnight," Cornwell was explaining.

I opened the entire first row of lockers. Apart from the odd jock strap, I didn't find a thing in any of them, certainly no bags of money. I began to sweat.

"You're certain no one has stored any bags with you?" Suzette was asking. "Did anyone ask you to keep something in your office, or an equipment locker?"

Cornwell shook his head. "You lookin' for drugs? You go on ahead and look all you want, ma'am. I don't allow drugs in here. There's no doping in my gym, all my customers know I'll kick 'em out on their asses if they bring that shit in here."

I started on the second row. Still nothing.

"Claire, I'm going to check the offices," Suzette said. I nodded and she left.

Finished with the lockers, I sat down on a bench, rubbing my eyes. There were no bags in the lockers. Wyatt had specifically said that Shaeffer had stashed the ransom money in one of the lockers. Had he been mistaken? Had he left for a period of time, allowing Shaeffer to return and get the money? My stomach growled and I told it to be quiet.

I was midway through my second search of the lockers when Suzette returned. "No sign of a bag anywhere," she said. "No sign of the money."

"Could he have taken it out of the bag, maybe stashed it here in a hiding place?" I looked around.

"If he had a hiding place here I haven't found, it's damn well concealed." Suzette shrugged. "Most likely he took it away again. Or someone else did. You did say you left to follow him. Maybe he had an accomplice to pick it up while you were gone."

I almost blurted out that Wyatt had been here the whole time, watching the money. It had been under his eye from the time Shaeffer left it here. Could he have pulled a switch, with Wyatt watching him the whole time? And why would he, since Shaeffer couldn't even see Wyatt, couldn't know he was being followed?

"Look, Claire, I hate to say this, but I am really going to have to talk to your client," Suzette said.

I looked at her with astonishment. "Marty? He's in Canada."

"Are you sure?" Suzette shifted her feet. "He told you that, but maybe he's been hanging around, working a kidnapping scam with Shaeffer. If Marty was into drugs, and Shaeffer was part of a distribution network, and then Allison found a link between them…"

"Fine," I said angrily. "I'll give you his number. In Canada. And if it turns out he lied, that he's behind all of this, I'll take him down myself."

"Claire—"

"Forget it," I said, and stormed past her.

"Didn't find what you was lookin' for, huh?" Sam Cornwell stood in the hallway, making no attempt to conceal his interest in our argument.

"Sorry to waste your time," I said bitterly.

"No problem," he said. "Can I get my keys back now? I need to open up."

I backed up as Suzette came out of the locker room, and bumped up against the bottom step of the rear staircase. I turned, looked up, and saw the door. "Is this door open during the day?" I asked. "Could someone come in through the front door and leave by this exit?"

"Not any more," Cornwell said. "Used to be they could, but I had guys sneakin' in here to use the equipment without paying. So I got it reinforced when I had this here office remodeled." He indicated the office behind him. "Now it only opens with a key, and I got the only key right here." He held up the keys that Suzette had returned to him.

Suzette's eyes met mine in perfect understanding. "Can you make sure it's locked now?"

"Why, sure it's locked," Cornwell said. He mounted the stairs, each step creaking under his weight. "I lock it up every—"

He pulled on the door to demonstrate, and it swung open. Cornwell goggled. "I'll be damned! I swear I locked this last night."

Suzette turned to me. "Well, that explains what happened to the bag. He forgot to lock—"

"No, I'm telling you!" Cornwell was vehement. "I locked it last night!"

"Does anyone else have a key?" I asked.

"No," Cornwell said strongly. "I have the only one. I'm gonna have a talk with that contractor, I tell you!"

"Contractor?" I turned to him at the same time Suzette did.

"Yeah, the guy what put this door and in and did my remodel. He come recommended to me. Now this crappy work."

"Who did your remodel?" I asked.

Cornwell shrugged. "Some guy from Hunter's Point. I got his card—"

Suzette pulled a mug shot out of her pocket. "Would it be this man?" She handed him a picture of Dan Shaeffer.

"No," Cornwell said. "Not even close. My guy was dark haired, like this one, but he looked younger. And he didn't have no mustache."

I pulled out my phone and brought up my photo of Wayne Rafferty. "Could it be him?"

Cornwell shook his head. "Not him neither. Why? You think someone broke in here last night?"

"I'm thinking someone used a key to get in here this morning, after you closed," I said. I did not add *while I was standing at your front door.* I showed him pictures of Marty Hancock and Kenneth Mannheim.

"Ain't neither of them guys," Cornwell said.

Suzette had been watching silently, curious. "What are you thinking, Claire? You got a hunch?"

"An itch, maybe," I said. My intuition was telling me this unlocked back door had more than a minor role to play. "I don't believe in coincidences, and the fact that this door was found unlocked in the same place a bag full of cash went missing should be ringing your alarms as well."

Cornwell was looking from one to the other of us. "This important, then?"

"Yes," we said together.

He turned and entered his office. Like the locker room, it had been sectioned off from the main basement room. It was tiny but well made, neatly arranged. The wall next to the gym contained a large picture window which allowed Cornwell to keep an eye on his gym. He opened the middle drawer of a gray metal desk and rummaged around. He brought out a stack of business cards held together with a rubber band and thumbed slowly through them. "Here." He held out a card.

Suzette and I nearly bumped heads as we leaned over to read it:

Jackson Harrington
Harrington Construction

Suzette straightened. "Harrington? Wayne Rafferty's partner?"

"What the hell does Jackson Harrington have to do with Allison's disappearance?" I met Suzette's stare with my own.

Wyatt Earp appeared on the other side of Cornwell's

office window. He spotted me and stepped through, which meant his torso intersected a low filing cabinet. He looked at me with some fierce emotion in his eyes.

"Wayne Rafferty's house is afire," he said. "And the firemen say they've found a body."

CHAPTER 30

I opened my mouth to tell Suzette about the fire, hesitated while I tried to explain how I'd learned it, and then shut up when her cell phone buzzed. As she pulled it from her belt I pulled mine and held it up as if answering a call.

"What is it, Vic?" Suzette's eyes got wide and she turned to meet my gaze as she spoke. "You're sure? The whole house? I'll be there."

I 'hung up' as she did. "Wayne Rafferty's house is on fire," I told her.

She peered at me. "I don't know who your mole is, but he's good." She turned to Sam Cornwell. "Thanks for your time. Here are your keys. You can open up now. Claire, you coming?"

I didn't need any second invitation. The top half of Wyatt nodded as I left the room. "I'll meet you there," he said, and vanished.

Suzette hit the lights and siren, so for the third time in two days I was roaring through the streets of San Francisco in emergency response mode. By the time we passed Jones Street I could see the smoke spiralling into the sky. We screeched to a stop at a barricade and piled out.

Suzette's badge got us past the uniforms and a couple of firefighters. Fire trucks were slewed across the street, even up onto sidewalks. The air smelled of soot, ash, and burnt oranges; the neighbor's orange tree was nothing but a charred stick now. Suzette ran to speak to the scene commander and I stood on the sidewalk, staring.

Fire had engulfed not only Wayne Rafferty's house, but the ones on either side. The heat forced me back; I heard glass

breaking as the inferno raged. From a ladder truck, one fire-
fighter sprayed water on the roof; men directed other streams
into the fire from below. Firefighters in turnout rigs milled
and shouted; hoses snaked across the lawns of neighbors. An
elderly couple stood huddled nearby, soaking wet, watching
their roof burn. Their house was the one with the crisped orange tree.

Then I saw the gurney and the body bag and my stomach
did a slow roll. I walked over to where a paramedic was writing on a clip board. "That Wayne Rafferty?" I asked.

He was short, Hispanic, thirtyish, wearing rimless glasses.
A stethoscope stuck out of a coverall pocket. "And you are?"
he said.

"I'm with Inspector Melton," I said. "Rafferty was a mate-
rial witness in a case."

He shrugged. "Identification will have to wait for the coroner, but I'd say odds are pretty good this is Rafferty."

Wyatt stepped out of the burning house and walked down
to me. I blinked. I knew most physical objects couldn't touch
him, but walking through fire? Literally? Yet he looked exactly
the same as he had fifteen minutes ago.

"Nobody else in there," Wyatt said. "His office safe was
open and empty when I first went in. It's full of ash now."

Behind him, something inside the burning house crashed,
sending a fountain of sparks skyward. I flinched, but Wyatt
didn't even react.

"Not to be obvious, but do you have a cause of death?" I
asked the paramedic.

He looked at me quizzically. "Funny you should ask.
When the firemen brought him out, his skull was dented. Of
course it's for the ME to say, but if this guy hadn't burned, I'd
say he was bashed on the head."

"Blunt force trauma?" I said.

"Don't quote me," he said cautiously.

"Any assessment of the origin of the fire?"

"Ask the captain. He's over there by Engine 30." He
shrugged and put his clipboard down on top of the body bag.

There was a whispery sound, like breaking embers, and the contents of the bag settled slightly. The paramedic bent to push the gurney towards the open back of an ambulance. He was in no hurry.

Wyatt walked over to stand by me and watch the fire. "Can't believe this is a coincidence," he said. "Got to be related. You know that. Did you find the money?"

"No." I described our search of the gym. Wyatt scowled more and more grimly as my tale unfolded.

"So he got past you," he said. "I watched Shaeffer put that bag in Locker 81. He locked it with a combination lock."

"None of the lockers were locked when Suzette and I searched them. And all of them were empty. Did you know there was a back door to the place?"

"Yes," he said. "But it didn't signify. I was standing right next to the bag. I was ready to follow whoever picked it up, whatever door he went through. But nobody came for it."

"Could Sam Cornwell have found it?"

"Who?"

"The owner."

"I tell you, I waited until everyone was gone. That big fellow who owned the place, he went out the back door and locked it. I heard the lock go. The whole place was dark and empty when I came up to meet you on the sidewalk."

"Obviously, Jackson Harrington came back for it, with a key," I said. "And I stood there, like a dummy, in front of the place for hours while he went in the back."

There was a short, angry silence. "So he's got the money," Wyatt said. "And I'll wager a dime to a dollar he killed Rafferty and set the fire."

I nodded slowly. "And now we have no idea where to find Allison."

"Assuming she's still alive," Wyatt said. He met my look with a solemn expression. "You know the odds on kidnap victims turning up alive."

Suzette walked up, hands in the pockets of her trench coat. She stared at the dying house. "Captain says it started in the garage."

"Pretty easy access," I said. "Doesn't take much to get into a garage."

"He also said he suspects accelerants. Like gasoline, diesel, paint thinner by the smell. Maybe some turpentine."

I looked at her. "Those are all used in construction work."

"Right." She turned to me, absently patting a pocket before she remembered she didn't smoke any more. "Scene commander said it's a problem, 'cause he can't determine if this is a suspicious fire or an accident. Since Rafferty was a contractor, he could have stored flammables in the garage. It's possible it's an accidental fire and not arson. We'll have to wait and see what the fire investigator finds out."

"You really think this is an accident, Suze? Just an amazing coincidence?"

She gnawed the inside of her cheek a moment, staring at the fire. "No," she said quietly.

"Paramedic said Wayne's head had been bashed in."

She blinked at me. "Have you been questioning witnesses on my crime scene, Claire?"

"Until just now, it wasn't a crime scene." I shrugged. "Just a little shop talk. Anyway, the ME will say one way or the other. Are you calling it murder?"

She met my eyes with a challenge in hers. "Like you said, the ME will say."

"She don't give nothing away, that one," Wyatt murmured.

"Are you even looking for Jackson Harrington?"

"I've put out an APB on him. Although there's a good chance his body is in there right now."

"Probably half way to Mexico by now," Wyatt said. "There was only one body in that house."

I figured telling Suzette that bit of information would do more harm than good, so I said nothing.

The three of us stood in the darkness and watched Wayne Rafferty's house burn to the ground, despite the efforts of thirty firemen and five trucks.

CHAPTER 31

B y the time the house was reduced to hissing embers, my
stomach was giving notice to quit. "There's a coffee shop
one block over," I told Suzette. "Buy you a large?"

"Later," she said, sighing. "I have to stay until we're sure
there are no more bodies."

"Good hunting," I said. I waved good-bye and hiked on
down the street, turned east on the cross-street, and found
Madeleine's Coffee Heaven still open. Several firefighters
emerged with paper cups and cartons as I walked up. Inside, I
ordered and found a tiny table to sit at. Wyatt walked through
the plate glass window and sat down on the inner ledge.

"So where do we look for Allison Farley?" he asked.

I pulled out my cell phone and held it to my ear. "More to
the point, perhaps, where do we look for Jackson Harrington?"

"I can take a look at his place," Wyatt offered.

"You have his home address?"

"Yes. I'll be back directly." He stepped through the plate
glass window, disappearing as he went. As I put down my
phone, it rang. I answered it and told it my name.

"Have you found Allison yet?" It was my very anxious
client.

"Hi, Marty. Where are you?"

"I'm in the Montreal airport. My plane leaves in an hour.
Have you found her?"

"No, but there have been developments." I filled in my
client, while listening to the background noises: crowd noises, the echo of large spaces, and boarding announcements in
English and French. By the time I finished catching him up, I

was certain that Marty Hancock was, indeed, in Canada.

"Rafferty's dead?" Marty sounded stunned.

"Burned to death," I said. "No sign of his partner."

"I don't know anything about his partner. But God, if she was kidnapped, she's alive! Right? The cops, they said that body in the water wasn't Allison's, right?"

He sounded so hopeful it hurt to disillusion him. But I owed him the truth. "Marty, don't get your hopes up. I'll do the best I can, but we only had one lead to her—if she's alive at all—and he's dead. We're looking for Harrington, but so far no one has spotted him. And he's got three million dollars to help make sure nobody does."

"Why would Rafferty kidnap his own girlfriend?"

"You're not listening," I said. "I don't think Wayne did it. I think his partner did."

"This Harrington guy?" Marty clearly was having trouble with this new theory of the crime.

"Yes."

"But he knows Allison! That means he wouldn't hurt her, right?"

"Maybe not," I said. I was afraid that meant exactly the opposite, but there was no point in adding to my client's anxiety.

There was a short silence, and I clearly heard an announcement for a London flight. Then Marty spoke in a very subdued voice. "You don't sound real hopeful. Are you quitting, then?"

"No," I said. "Jackson Harrington is still out there with three million dollars, and if we find him maybe he can tell us where Allison is."

Relief flooded his voice. "Then you think there's still hope! Oh, thank you! I've been so worried!"

"How was the race?" I asked.

"The race? Oh, I placed second. Made good money," he said carelessly. "And I qualified for the Canada Open in the spring, so that's good. Allison would be proud." He stopped abruptly. "Guess I should stop thinking of what I'll tell her," he said.

"Decide that when you see her," I told him. We rang off.

I wondered about Agent Kern's suspicions of Marty, but just could not see him as a drug dealer. He wasn't smart enough, for one thing.

I had finished my second latte and two croissants, and was eyeing a cinnamon roll when Wyatt popped through the back wall of the cafe. He strode over and leaned against the wall across from me. "No sign of Harrington at his place," he said. "Couple of detectives searching it right now. They ain't got to the attic, though. I took a peek. The gym bag is in there."

"Is the money in it?"

Wyatt shrugged. "It was open. And empty."

"So he could have put the money in something else. A briefcase? Backpack? Could you tell if a suitcase or anything was missing?"

"Takes a pretty good sized case to carry three million dollars," Wyatt said.

I hadn't ever seen Harrington's home, and in my mind's eye I was thinking of the construction offices. "You check Dogpatch?"

"I can do that now," he said, straightening.

"Even if he's not there, or the money's not there, we should take a look at his office," I said. "I'll meet you there."

Wyatt vanished.

I left my coffee half-drunk and dashed out of the cafe. It took me a good twenty minutes to find a cab, though. We were smack in the middle of rush hour, and nobody wanted to go out to Dogpatch after sundown. I finally persuaded a cabbie to take me, and he dropped me off forty five minutes later in front of JackWay Holdings.

The sun was down behind Potrero Hill, and the evening was coming in chilly. The chain link fence was locked and I saw no sign of anyone. I waited for a moment, to see if there were any guard dogs lying in wait for me. After five minutes I decided that if there had been guard dogs, Harrington had probably sold them. The lock would have been easy, but it would also have been easy for someone to spot me while I was picking it, so I opted for time over finesse. I climbed over the fence, tore the hem of my trousers on the top, and jumped down. No lights or sirens went off. The parking lot was nearly empty; probably most of the trucks were now in used vehicle lots across the San Francisco Peninsula.

I trotted across the deserted lot, keeping my ears and eyes open. Wyatt stepped out from behind a corner of the building as I approached. "Nobody here," he assured me. "But I think the door is locked."

"Not a problem. Keep a lookout, will you?" I reached into a jacket pocket and took out my emergency-entry kit, which consisted of a nail file, a paper clip and a tiny screwdriver used to repair eyeglasses, all tucked inside a small plastic envelope. Wyatt watched, fascinated, as I straightened the hairpin, bent the end into a 90-degree corner, and got to work.

When the lock clicked and the door swung open, Wyatt whistled in admiration. "Three minutes." He put away his large pocket watch.

"I'm out of practice," I said. "Used to be, I could have picked that lock with boiled spaghetti. I'll leave the lights off."

A small stack of mail lay on the floor just inside the door. The place smelled of paint and glue and dust and neglect. On a hunch, I stepped to the copy machine and lifted the lid; the same Allied Machinery Resellers invoice lay on the glass that I had seen last time I was here. Maybe that had been the last time Jackson Harrington had been to the office. Nevertheless, I swiftly went through the invoices on his desk, as well as the latest mail. I was starting to search the middle drawer, when Wyatt said, "What's this?"

He pointed to the ashtray I'd seen on my earlier visit, with a collection of keys. I met Wyatt's look. "You think there's a key to the back door of the Tenderloin Club in that?" I asked.

"One way to find out."

I took them out, one by one. Most were unlabeled, and could have been to anything. One of them had Rafferty's address on a key tag. "Most of these are padlocks," I said. "No labels. Just numbers written on each one with permanent marker."

"Is there a list?" Wyatt strode over to examine the many pages stapled or taped to the walls.

12 - Turk St.

13 - Highland View Master

14 - Light

15 - 10th St Cafe

16 - Abihu Tennis

17 - Tenderloin

18 - Dogpatch Shipworks

19 - Wm Water Cove Toolshd

20 - Warden

21 - Main Block

I sorted through keys, comparing them to the list. "Four are missing," I said. "Numbers 14, 17, 18 and 21."

"We know what happened to the Tenderloin one," Wyatt said, musing. He stroked his mustache thoughtfully. "That has to be the gymnasium."

"And 'light' could be the electrical junction box on any of these job sites," I said.

"Like he abbreviated 'toolshed' on number 19." Wyatt shifted from foot to foot. "But that doesn't help us."

"Number 21." I stared past him, thinking. "Main Block? Main block of what? There's no 'Main Street' in San Francisco."

Wyatt shrugged. "We're wasting time. We need to find out where Harrington went, not where he worked."

I thought about the remaining missing key. "Dogpatch Shipworks," I said. "It's two blocks east of here."

"Good place to hide a getaway boat." He straightened. "Meet me there." He didn't wait for an answer, but vanished.

"Some day I'll leave before you do," I muttered. There was a big 9-volt battery powered flashlight on a shelf next to the desk. I took it, in case the shipworks was shut down for the night. I made sure the door locked behind me when I left.

Fifteen minutes of brisk walking brought me to the waterfront. I heard gulls squalling as they settled in for the night, and the slap of waves against concrete and wood. Giant cranes on Pier 70 stood out against the darkening sky like alien invaders stopped in their tracks. Rusting warehouses with broken windows scowled at the deserted streets. A car passed slowly, stopped briefly, then prowled away. Extravagant graffiti overlaid decades of corrosion on wall and street. The street dead-ended abruptly at a NO EXIT sign, and the rocky shore began six feet in front of me. The murky waters of San Francisco Bay slopped and tossed. Rows of rotting wooden piers jutted from the water, supporting nothing.

"Over here," Wyatt called. I turned to see him standing in front of a corrugated iron shed built out over the water. He waved me over.

The building was secured with a rusty lock that took me all of two minutes to pick. I must be getting better. The door groaned when I pushed it, and I stepped inside. The sounds of water echoed inside the metal shell, showing me two empty berths. One of them bore a plate: JackWay Holdings.

"He took the boat," Wyatt said.

I looked around, measuring the boat shed. "Couldn't have been a very big boat."

Wyatt bent over some red cans. "Must have fueled up. Could be half way to Monterey by now."

"Maybe," I said. "This shed can't hold a boat large enough to take into the open sea, unless Harrington is part seal. More likely he's sticking to the Bay."

"Which gives us a couple hundred miles of shoreline to choose from," Wyatt growled. "Not to mention marinas, islands, marshes, inlets—"

"Islands." I stared at him. "Alcatraz."

I turned and headed for the door.

"Where are you going?" Wyatt called.

"To steal a boat."

Wyatt caught up with me as I walked slowly along the decrepit waterfront, searching. "You got some kind of hunch?" He squinted at me.

"Yes," I said. I straightened my shoulders. "Call it woman's intuition, if it makes you feel better."

"I like 'hunch' better," he said.

"Why would he go to Alcatraz? That makes no sense."

"Remember our tour of the island? Remember the construction sites? The generators that halted you in your tracks."

"Yes," Wyatt said, frowning at the memory. "But what does that have to do with—"

"They had signs listing the contractors working on the site. One of those names was JackWay Holdings. Think about it. If you wanted to hide a few days until the search for you quieted down, the Rock is ideal," I said. "What if he's stocked up over there? He could have brought in enough food and water for months with construction supplies."

"That's true of any of his construction sites," Wyatt said.

"But they don't have tunnels, and caves, and deserted buildings where people can't go. It's also the only construction site for JackWay Holdings that requires a boat for access."

Wyatt stared off into the distance, thinking. "He wouldn't even have to take her there." He looked back at me. "She went there of her own free will."

I thought of the video of Allison Farley marching off the boat. No one could confirm seeing her after she reached the jump-off point. "He could have taken her right there," I said. "And the Rock is, as we know, the perfect place to keep someone prisoner."

"Claire, he's more likely at the airport."

"Fine," I said. "Go look for him there. I don't give a damn about Harrington, I want to find Allison. I'm going to the island."

"It would be a lot easier to hide out on a mainland site."

"Right," I said. "And from the point of view of a man hiding out, that's bad. If it's easy for him to reach, it's easy for the cops to find. But hiding on Alcatraz—"

"Would be like that Hamilton fellow, breaking back into prison. Last place they would have looked for him." Wyatt met my gaze, blue eyes thoughtful.

"Help me find a boat."

Wyatt placed himself in my path, forcing me to stop. "Even if you find a boat and get to the island, they're shutting down this time of night. You can't dock that boat, not without being seen and maybe arrested."

"So I'll tie up at that cave we found. I climbed the slope above it once, I can do it again."

I started to go around Wyatt and he put himself in front of me again. "At least call Inspector Melton. Tell her where you're going."

"She'll have the Coast Guard out in fifteen minutes to stop me," I said.

"Then tell the Park Rangers. Tell them to search the island."

I thought about it. "Very well, once I'm in the boat and headed for the island, I'll call them." I stepped around Wyatt.

"Dammit Claire, this ain't the way!"

He stepped into my path again, and I stopped, furious. "Get out of my way, or so help me, I *will* walk right through you!"

"You can't," he said. "You'll—"

I stepped forward, and he vanished. I walked on, and he appeared to my right, pacing me. "Dammit! You nearly walked into me! You could have been hurt!"

"So get out of my way. And help me find a boat."

I searched the shoreline, but all I saw were rocks and empty piers. This part of the waterfront was long deserted since San Francisco's main ship traffic had moved to Oakland. Mostly I found pieces of plastic bobbing in the dirty water along the shoreline. Most piers were rotting, deserted.

One was not. A rooster tail of sparks fountained out of the back of a corrugated tin shed built close to the shoreline. A sign in fading white paint read DRAGER SHIP WELD-ERS. The dock below it looked neat and well kept. A dinghy was tied to the end of it. "Check it out," I whispered to Wyatt.

"Claire, this is not smart," he said.

I looked at him coldly. "Harrington already has the ransom money. How much time do you think Allison has left?"

"Let me go over to the lighthouse and look," Wyatt said. "If she's there, you can call Inspector Melton."

"Good idea," I said. "If you find her, come tell me. I'll be in the Bay, heading for the island in that boat."

"Claire!"

I ignored him. Bending low, hiding in the shadows, I came up on the shack. A radio inside blared hip-hop music, and someone banged loudly on metal. More sparks. Whoever was inside wouldn't have heard the outbreak of World War Three.

I tiptoed past the open door, saw two men with their backs turned to me, and raced down the dock. No one shouted. Wyatt kept pace grimly beside me.

At the end of the dock, I jumped into the boat. It was a ten foot fiberglass dinghy with a V-shaped hull and an outboard motor. Wyatt stepped down into the bow as I knelt in the stern next to the motor. "Why are you here?" I said. "You should go to the island and start looking."

Wyatt harrumphed. "I'm going to stick right by you. Maybe you'll need some help."

"At least go see if she's there," I said. "You'll save me a trip."

He frowned. "The weather is picking up. If you drown out there—"

"Then you'll have all the time in the world to nag at me in the afterlife. Go find Allison."

Wyatt disappeared.

It was cold as hell, with a freezing wind off the Pacific. Outside the Golden Gate, fog gathered and curled. I opened the tank vent on the motor, checked the fuel level, shifted the gearshift into neutral, and set the choke to half. I set the throttle and then primed the fuel, my fingers clumsy in the cold.

Finally I pulled the starter cord. Nothing happened. I prayed the guys in the shack wouldn't step out for a cigarette; in the growing light they could plainly see me. I blew on my fingers to warm them, grabbed the starter cord, and yanked again.

The engine coughed to life, and I hoped like hell the owner had fueled up recently. I throttled it back and clipped the motor's kill switch cable to my belt.

I cast off, put the boat in gear and eased away from the

dock, alert to any shouts from shore. I heard nothing but the engine as it putted out onto the Bay. Fifty feet out, I revved the engine and roared away.

CHAPTER 32

S an Francisco Bay is either a joy or a menace to boaters. Once away from the shallow waters near the shore, the wind picked up and the ride got a lot rougher. Much as I wanted to get the boat up on a plane, for speed, the whitecaps slapping at the hull made it impossible. I lowered the bow and resigned myself to creeping through chop for an hour or more. I've sailed in open water before, but I was younger, stupider, and had my mother's companion, Angus, at the wheel. He'd made it look easy. It wasn't.

If it had been nighttime, I'd have surely been swamped and drowned. As it was, after twenty minutes Alcatraz Island didn't look any closer. I was fighting the incoming tide, and the currents near Alcatraz are all they're rumored to be: fast and deadly. Worse, I had to stop and wait while a huge tanker lumbered past. It was like watching a mountain go by.

When it finally rumbled away, I shoved the throttle wide open, gritted my teeth, and headed for the Rock. I kept an eye out for Coast Guard boats, tankers, recreational sailors and windsurfers. A sea lion popped his head out of the water a dozen yards away and watched me; I swear he was laughing.

The current was trying to carry me past the island and out towards the Golden Gate and out to sea. Waves dashed themselves over the gunwale and slapped me in the face. I fought the launch and babied the engine, turning right, right, right. It looked as if I'd be swept out to sea no matter how hard I struggled against the current.

The darkness was almost complete; my only guide was the lighthouse on Alcatraz, with its light flashing every few seconds. Inch by inch I drew closer to the island, heading west. I didn't want to come close to the eastern side, where the public loading dock was manned by Rangers.

I was exhausted, and my face and hands were numb with cold, and I was soaked through by the time I came up on the tide cave. I ran the dinghy aground on the gravel shore, and nearly fell out of the boat into the icy water. I was in a race with the incoming fog, quickly covering the moon. There was just enough moonlight left to show me that the tidal cave I'd explored earlier was half under water, and the tide wasn't even all the way in.

I tethered the boat as best I could to a rock outcropping, forcing my tired and chilled fingers to tie a knot. I shoved the big flashlight into a pocket of my jacket; it would only go in halfway and kept threatening to fall out so I had to watch it constantly. Finally I turned to the hillside and started up.

It had been easier in full daylight, with Wyatt there to cheer me on and point out loose rocks and handy roots to grab. I slipped once and slid all the way down to the waterline. My shivering didn't help, and I mightily wished for a hot cup of coffee or five. By the time I made it all the way to the top of the slope, my hands were scraped raw and I had split a fingernail on my left hand. But I made it to the top, soaked to the bone and feeling as cold as a marble slab. This late in the year, the vegetation hadn't yet thinned out, so there was plenty of cover. I ran quickly up the same road I'd come down a couple of days before, hoping the rangers didn't have motion detectors or radar. I gained the top of the slope and crouched down behind some bushes. I ducked when the beam from the lighthouse swept over me, like a spotlight aimed by prison guards.

I had come out a few dozen yards to the left of where I intended. Directly ahead of me was a small white shack, in need of paint and new front porch. It was tiny, no larger than my living room, and sported a tall white scaffold arrangement at the back. Behind it stood a monolithic four story building in ruins; rows of empty windows gaped like the eye sockets in a skull.

As I peeked over the top of a bush, I heard a quiet cough

behind me. My heart thudded violently as I swung around, but it was only Wyatt, standing behind me on the slope.

"Y-you startled m-me," I said, trying not to let my teeth chatter. "And you're dry and warm, damn you."

Ignoring my comment, Wyatt waved at the white shack. "Used to house a fog bell," he said. "Back in the 1890s, the island had one at each end. Big old bell weighed several tons. You could hear it as far as Butchertown, when the fog was in."

"F-fascinating," I said. "Is Harrington in there? Or Allison?"

He shook his head. "Already looked. She's not in there. Nothing but dust and old burlap sacks and mice."

"W-where else have you s-searched?" The wind cut to the bone; I hugged myself for warmth.

He sighed. "Just about everywhere. But I'm working in the dark."

I was still getting used to the idea that even a ghost has his limitations. Wyatt could no more see in pitch darkness than I could. "So you d-didn't look in the tunnels?" I knew Alcatraz was honeycombed with tunnels, some built during the Civil War, most of them forgotten and abandoned. Men had been building, digging, renovating, rebuilding and recon-figuring this island for over a hundred and fifty years; it didn't even have the same profile it had when the Spaniards sailed in. "M-maybe part of the prison not on the tours?"

"I looked in some of the ruins and storerooms," he said. "But the ones below ground I had to pass on. Black as the mind of a sinner down there, and most of them blocked or bricked up so's you can't reach it anyhow. Not unless you can walk through stone."

I eyed him. "Are you bragging, Wyatt?"

"Not a bit." That might have been a smile at the corner of his mouth. Maybe not.

"Then I g-guess we can eliminate those t-tunnels."

He was quiet a moment. "I'm real glad to see you, Claire. I worried about you, on that water. You should go back on the ferry, first light."

"I'll g-go back on anything that has hot coffee on it," I

said, trying not to shiver. "But not 'til we've s-searched this island for Harrington or Allison or both."

He shrugged. "I've looked in the offices, the prison, and the bookstore. I looked in the sally port and everywhere else the public can go."

"You d-didn't really expect to f-find her there," I said crossly.

"No, but I had to eliminate them," he said calmly. "And I looked in the old morgue, the laundry and the power house. I also looked into the old chapel, the bachelor's officer's quarters and the old officer's club."

"You got a l-lot done," I admitted.

"Most of those buildings don't even have a roof." He sounded as crabby as I felt. "I only covered the obvious ground. Now we got to look where most folks don't go, or where it's dark. But I think we need to get one thing straight, Claire. Are we looking for an escaped felon or a kidnap victim?"

"B-both."

"You armed?"

I reached around and patted the holster at the back of my waist. My Colt Defender was still there. "Yes. Where sh-should we start?"

Wyatt looked up. Towering above us was the four stories of the old model industries building, where the Feds had once attempted to teach the likes of Al Capone and Machine Gun Kelly an honest trade. Weeds and brush grew up to its base. "Start at the prison workshop and work our way east," he said.

At least the exercise would keep me warm. I followed Wyatt as best I could up the decaying gravel path to the building. One doorway yawned black as the mouth of Hell, and I hesitated before I went in. "Keep an eye out," I told him. "Someone might see the light and come looking."

He stayed at the door, looking up the slope of the island. The lighthouse flared high above us, flared again. I shielded the flashlight and switched it on. The beam was pretty feeble, the battery nearly dead, but it was enough to show me the floor, holes where the weather had rotted the beams, and a decade's worth of dead leaves piled into corners. I stayed close to the walls, hoping the floor was stronger there, and made my way through the echoing, empty rooms. At the far end I found a staircase and climbed it; one of the treads was missing and others shook under my feet. Rats scuttled away as I drew near; some merely halted and stared at me out of red beady eyes. I refused to think about how they outnumbered me.

Most of the rooms were large industrial spaces now filled with decaying machinery. On the second floor I found several rusted hunks of metal that might have once have been a machine shop. One room held a row of ancient, rusted sewing machines. Another held a shallow lake from where the ceiling had leaked during a rain. It took me over an hour to go through all three floors, opening the occasional closet door. At the end of it, I emerged into the cold night no wiser than when I had gone in. I switched off the flashlight to save the battery.

"Find anything?" Wyatt said. He stepped out of a shadow, tilting his hat back on his head.

"No," I said. "This must have been a busy place back in the day, though. Machines everywhere."

"Busy." He chuckled. "More escape attempts happened here at the shops than any other place on Alcatraz," he said.

"Will this be on the final exam?" I stepped forward, ran into a half-fallen chain-link fence, and climbed over it awkwardly. "What's the next building?"

"Laundry. Watch your step there."

Wyatt strolled ahead, watching for Rangers, although it was unlikely we'd find any this late at night. I counted on my fingers and decided it was probably close to four in the morning. We crossed the open plaza between the prison workshops and the laundry. Here there were rows of rusting washers and dryers, even a bunch of dilapidated ironing boards. "Hard to think of Big Al wielding a steam press," I said.

"He didn't," Wyatt said laconically. "He shined shoes, though. Here, this is the main door."

The only difference between this search and the last one

was that this building was twice as large, so it took twice as long. And at the end of it I still didn't have a suspect or a victim. I sat down to catch my breath and shiver a bit. I rubbed my hands together, trying to get some feeling back into them. I looked up at Wyatt, who stood with his back to me, staring out a window at the dark Bay. "Thanks for not rubbing it in," I said.

He didn't turn around. "Rubbing what in?"

"The fact that we haven't found Allison or Harrington," I said. "I guess you think he's halfway to China and she's dead."

"I'm hoping you're right," he said. "And hopin' I'm wrong on both counts. But we should get on. From this building, we got two ways to go. If we go right, we'll be heading into the parts of the island where Rangers and tourists go."

"Not likely Harrington would hide anyone in a public area," I said.

"So we go left," Wyatt said. He pointed out the window. "That way takes us past the old quarry, then the incinerator. Not many hiding places there, 'less Harrington found some old barbette still open."

"Barbette?" It sounded like a stripper name to me.

He turned and smiled a little. "Gun emplacement," he said. "Guess cannon weren't much in your line."

I pushed to my feet. My stomach growled with hunger. "Lead on," I said.

I followed Wyatt out onto a gravelled walkway. It wound around, following the line of the shore, along the top of the cliffs that plunge straight down to rock below. At one point, the cliffs receded and a small beach appeared below. "Barker's Beach," Wyatt said. "Named after an escapee they shot there."

I said nothing; life on the Rock had been harsh, but then its inmates weren't Boy Scouts, either. I climbed over a barrier, tore my trousers, and examined a gardening shed that held nothing but tools and fertilizer. Fatigue crept into my bones. Soon I was stumbling along, weaving a bit, until finally I ran smack into another chain link fence and sat down suddenly.

"This was a mistake," I mumbled to myself. Another kind

of weariness settled on me, the kind of exhaustion you get when you know you've failed. Allison was probably dead. Harrington had killed his partner, stolen the ransom money, and was gone. And I was probably going to wake up with pneumonia in the morning.

Wyatt stood on the edge of the cliff with his back to the ocean. He turned slowly, scanning the buildings. The lighthouse beam flared, but didn't seem to hit him at all. I was trying to figure out if it passed through him or skipped over him, when he turned to me with a strange look on his face. "You remember them keys, the ones in that office?"

"Yeah."

"What were the missing ones? There was one for the Tenderloin club, and another was for the boathouse. But what were the others?"

I blinked. "One was labeled 'light'. There was one that said 'Main Block'."

"The cellhouse used to be called the Main Block," he said.

I got to my feet and stared up at the bulk of the cellhouse, crowning the island like the Parthenon. "You think he had keys to the cellhouse? But hundreds of people go through there every day."

"Not everywhere," Wyatt said. "There's lots of locked doors, off-limits in there. In D Block, the isolation ward, there's a door in the floor no one ever opens. It leads down to the tunnels."

"You think the 'Main Block' key is to the cellhouse?"

"Good chance of it."

"It would be stupid to put Allison in the biggest tourist attraction on Alcatraz," I said.

He looked at me with a stony expression. "Not if she was dead."

He was right. Maybe I had been repressing that possibility, but the truth was that statistics were on Wyatt's side. If Harrington had the money, if he had gotten here before us, things didn't look good for Allison Farley. I swallowed. "You're right. We need to look. I've got the key, but you'll have to watch for the Park Rangers."

He shook his head. "Too much security. They got motion detectors, cameras, everything."

I pondered it. "I can't get in without setting them off."

"I can," Wyatt said. "Meet me in front of the cellhouse."

"Wait!" I cried, but he had already disappeared.

CHAPTER 33

I felt very exposed as I reached the end of the gravel path and entered the open area in front of the cellhouse. To my right, a waist-high concrete wall circled the top of the dropoff; below that was the wide expanse of the Parade Ground. Two feeble lights merely defined its edges; from where I stood at the wall I had an unbroken view all the way across the Bay to the shining city of San Francisco. It looked like it belonged on some other planet.

To my left, the cellhouse was a forbidding bulk against the stars. Two powerful spotlights shone on the door and the eagle carved over the lintel, its faded paint barely visible in the glare. Directly ahead of me was a burnt-out ruin of a multi-story house. Wyatt waited for me in front of it, hands in his pockets.

"Well?" I said.

"Pretty dark down in the tunnels," Wyatt said. "Could hardly see a thing. But one thing is for sure, nothing down there is breathing. I listened, and never heard a thing. So if Allison is down in the tunnels, she's dead."

I felt numb when he said that, as if someone had shot me with Novocaine. My knees suddenly felt soft and I sat down on a pile of concrete blocks. He walked over and stood in front of me.

"This is a hard business," he said quietly. "You been workin' hard to find this gal. I know you been hopin' she's alive. But you got to face the truth. Likely she's dead. If you can't take that, maybe you got no business in this business."

I made a fist, looked at it, opened it slowly. "Not fair," I said. "I'm tired. I'm cold. But I'm not ready to quit yet. Don't go jumping to conclusions." I nodded at the ruins behind him. "Did you look in there? Even if it's only a body, I need to know. What is that place, anyway?"

"Warden's House," Wyatt said. "Burned down in 1970. Roof is gone, so I already looked inside. They're renovating it, so there are tarps and other hiding places all over it."

"One of Harrington's keys was labeled 'Warden'," I said.

"Can't be for this place," Wyatt said. "There's no door, no key."

"Maybe the fence is padlocked?"

He shrugged. "Didn't notice if it was." He shifted from foot to foot restlessly. "I was thinking about those keys," he said. "One says 'Warden' and one says 'Main Block'. What was the other one?"

"The one that says 'Light'? But that was for a junction box or—" And then it came to me, as quick as a flash of light from a rotating searchlight. "Damn! The lighthouse!" I spun around to stare at it. "The lighthouse!"

It soared above me. The first twenty feet or so was a square base of masonry; after that the octagonal column of concrete rose another sixty-four feet into the air. At the top I could make out the railing which circled the lantern room. I had to lean back so far to see it that I nearly fell over backwards. A brief flare of light made me blink.

"Perfect hiding place," I said. "If she was alive, even if she yelled, no one would hear her."

"Or would think it was seagulls," Wyatt said, his voice a low growl. "Or a tourist prank. We got to get up there."

"You first," I said. "Can you—" But he was already gone.

My clothes had dried and my teeth were no longer chattering, but I was still shivering with cold. That's why it took me all of five minutes to get through the padlock on the chain link fencing that surrounded the lighthouse. I slipped through the rollaway gate and detoured around a spool of cable half as tall as I am.

The doorway faced east and appeared to be bronze, about twelve feet tall. The doors themselves were double doors, locked tight. A faded sign on one door read "Closed for repairs. No public access." Scratches in the weathered bronze around the lock that told me someone had used a key recently. Probably the missing key labeled "Light".

Picking this old lock would take a while, and at any moment a Ranger could walk past on patrol. The spotlight on the tower lit me up like a bug under a sunlamp. I had no time to lose. I knelt, hoping the stacks of lumber and cement sacks would shield me from view, and went to work. I dropped the nail file twice. On my fifth try, I heard a squeak, knew I had it, and was reaching for the knob when Wyatt stepped through the wall next to me. I yelped and fell back on my ass.

"What the hell! Give me a little warn—"

"She's up there," he said abruptly. "But she's unconscious."

"Alive?" I felt relief sweep over me. "Are you sure?"

"She's breathing," Wyatt said. "I listened for a while, and it sounded normal. But I can't wake her up, of course."

Since Wyatt was invisible and soundless to the rest of humanity, unable to affect the living (except for me), it stood to reason that all he could do was stand and watch. "Where is she?" I went to work on the lock again with renewed energy.

"Top of the stairs," he said. "Room below the light. Under a blanket, asleep. Looks like he's got her drugged."

The lock clicked and the door opened. I almost fell across the threshold. My big flashlight fell out of my jacket and smashed on the floor. "Damn!" I picked it up, but the bulb was gone and I didn't have a replacement.

The air smelled cold and damp and musty. The darkness was complete; it took my eyes a few moments to adjust, and then the only light available was the remnants of starlight or moonlight filtering down from the tiny slit windows halfway up the tower. My footsteps echoed as I carefully closed the door behind me.

"Better go quiet," Wyatt said. He spoke in a normal voice, but I kept mine low.

"Why?"

"Echoes," he said. "Sound may carry outside."

"What's wrong with that?" I kept my voice low. "Maybe the rangers will hear us. We *want* them to come find her!"

"What if they're not the ones who hear you?" Wyatt said. "We still don't know if Harrington is on his way. We'd better get her out of here before he gets here."

"Right." I hesitated. "I can't see you. I don't want to run into you. Stand out of the way, okay?"

I heard a chuckle, then a muffled voice. "I'm inside the wall on your left."

I drew a deep breath. "Okay, that's creepy." I felt my way across the narrow room, touched cold iron, and smacked my ankle against the bottom stair of a spiral staircase. I grasped the rail and looked up; the dizzying spiral above me seemed to go on forever. "Oh, boy." I stepped up the first stair.

"Do you need any help?" Wyatt asked.

"Like what?" I panted.

A short silence. "I'll meet you at the top," he said, and then there was no sound but my harsh breathing as I climbed.

I'd been up all day, crossed the Bay in a tiny boat, and climbed up a steep cliff to get on the island. Then I'd spent the last three hours looking in every corner of Alcatraz' abandoned buildings. Now I faced an 84-foot climb on steep, rusted stairs. Good thing I was getting paid a fortune for this job. Oh, right. I wasn't.

Step up. Again. Again. My calves ached; my thigh muscles wanted to cramp. I stopped at about the halfway point, when I arrived at the slit windows. They were smeared and fogged with dirt and age, but I could see the flash of the light beam reflecting briefly off the facade of the cellhouse. Something moved at the corner of the Warden's House: a shadow. A park ranger? A tree or bush shaken by the wind? Jackson Harrington, carrying a gun? Or maybe just fatigue and an overactive imagination. I turned back to the climb, thinking of Allison. I'd been looking for her for five days, and she'd been missing longer. I should be elated at finding her, against all odds, but I was tired and cold and something was bothering me about this.

Step up, step up, step up. Stop to breathe, but not too long or the muscles will freeze up. Sometimes the whole structure shook; often, it groaned or squealed or wobbled. I thought about aging steel, rusting rivets, bolts pulling free of hundred-year-old cement, the same crumbling cement that prisoners had dug through with spoons fifty years ago. Don't think about it. Step up, step up, step up. Allison is alive, and she's up there, and you'll rescue her.

A voice in the darkness: "Stop there." It was Wyatt. I couldn't see him, it was too dark, but he sounded near. I sagged against the rail, heard it creak, thought about the straight eight-story drop and leaned forward, resting my hands on my knees. "What?" I panted.

"She's right above you," Wyatt said. "This stair goes through the room with the gears and such below the light, then on up onto the railing outside. Allison Farley is asleep against the north wall."

Below me, creaks and groans. It sounded as if the stair was complaining about my intrusion. I shook my head to clear it. "Okay," I said. I took a deep breath, put my hand on the rail and hauled myself the last couple of steps. The spiral stair climbed through a square opening; as soon as my head cleared it I could see better.

And there she was.

Allison Farley lay on her side, sleeping. A folded blanket lay across her. She looked healthy, if perhaps a little thinner than I expected. After looking for her for so long, after fending off so many people who "knew" she was dead, it felt a little surreal to see her alive, in the flesh, as ordinary as daylight.

Wyatt lounged against the concrete wall of the round room. "Like I said, I couldn't wake her." He suddenly straightened and cocked his head as if listening. "Be right back," he said, and vanished.

I climbed all the way into the room. It was cold, but at the top of the room an opening about six feet wide let in the light from the lantern. It flashed rhythmically across Allison's face. I noted a wadded up lump of black I assumed was her wetsuit, a plastic five gallon jug of water, a cardboard shoebox half full of energy bars.

Not wanting to startle her, I knelt beside Allison and gently shook her shoulder. "Allison?"

Her eyes opened, she blinked, then gasped. "Who are you?" She scrambled up and away from me, pressing herself against the wall clutching the blanket up to her neck protectively. "How did you get here?"

"It's all right, don't be scared," I said, my voice as calm as I could make it. "My name is Claire Turnbull, and I'm a private investigator. Your boyfriend hired me to find you."

"Wayne hired you? But he wasn't supposed—um." She scooted farther from me, hugging herself. "They said not to contact the police. They told him."

"Wayne didn't hire me," I said. "Marty Hancock did. He's very worried about you."

She frowned slightly. "Marty? What's he buttin' in for? He'll just cause trouble. They told Wayne not to call the cops. Now they'll think Wayne did. They'll—they'll kill me!"

"So you don't know who kidnapped you?" Actually, it would be good news if Harrington hadn't revealed himself to her. A victim who knew her kidnapper, or could identify him, often did not survive. I told myself it was good news, but something about this situation bothered me.

"Not a clue," she said.

"Good. Now tell me, are you all right? Are you hurt?"

"No, I'm okay." She nodded at the supplies. "He, I mean they brought me food and stuff. They didn't, um, touch me."

"But they threatened to, right? Wayne told me about your call, when they threatened to rape you."

She looked away. "They made me do that. Is Wayne mad? Did he get the money?"

I didn't think it was the right time to tell her that Wayne was dead and the money was in the hands of the kidnapper. "The important thing is that you're all right. Now we have to get you out of here."

She looked behind me. "Look, no offense, but are you

all by yourself? I mean, are the cops coming too? You called them, right?"

"No," I admitted. "I was working on a hunch, so I came up here alone. I didn't want to call them until I knew I'd found you." I fished in my jacket pocket for my cell phone. "Now I know you're okay, I'll go ahead and—damn."

My cell phone didn't boot up. I thought about the waves that had been splashing over the gunwales of the little boat. I snapped the battery cover off and yanked out the battery. Sure enough, the indicator dot in the corner of the battery compartment had changed from white to red. "Dammit!"

"What's the matter?" Allison said. She looked from me to the phone in my hand.

"Water damage," I said. "My phone won't work. That's all right, though. We can get down the stairs, if you're good to walk. We'll go to the administration office, or if we're lucky we'll run into a park ranger on patrol. From there we can—"

Three things happened at once: Wyatt shouted my name from somewhere below, Allison suddenly lunged towards me, and Jackson Harrington charged out of the stairwell to my left.

CHAPTER 34

Wyatt's warning came fast enough to kick my reflexes, so I ducked when Harrington jumped me. I was kneeling next to Allison, and his lunge knocked her back against the wall.

He had been aiming for a body hold, but only managed to grab my forearms. I immediately raised them towards my face, keeping my thumbs towards me; he had to either let go of me or raise his elbows. As I had hoped, he raised his elbows; I pivoted from my hips and threw him. He fell sideways, cursing. It wasn't the best *suwari waza kokyu ho* throw ever made, but it worked.

"Jack!" Allison yelled. "She's by herself!"

"Watch his eyes," Wyatt said. He was half-emerged from the wall behind Harrington. "You'll know which way he's going before he moves. Get your guard up!"

Harrington scrambled to his feet, but I had leaped to mine. He dodged sideways, trying to drive me towards Allison, who had gotten to her feet with her back to the wall. Her eyes were shining. The blanked fell to her feet; her hands were not bound.

I fell into *hanmi* stance, arms raised, weight balanced as I drew one foot back to present the smallest profile. Harrington threw a right punch at me and I swung my head to one side and slapped at his arm. He stumbled forward, a surprised look on his face, and tried a left jab at the last minute.

I pivoted again, brought my arm up inside his guard and caught him under the chin with my forearm. His own momentum forced him forward, which raised his chin until he was looking at the ceiling. I stepped past him, winding up behind him with my arm around his neck. This was dangerous, because he was too tall for me to choke and strong enough to throw me over his shoulder. So I kicked his right knee from behind. He slumped to the floor, twisting around to clutch at me as he fell. But I was already backing away and he missed.

"Damn you," he panted. "Stupid interfering bitch."

"Watch out!" Allison squealed. She was huddled against the wall, sidling around to be out of our way.

The room was too small for a real fight.

"Get down the stairs!" Wyatt said tensely.

"I'm trying," I said.

"What?" Harrington replied, as he stood up. He glanced over at Allison. "You okay?"

"Yeah," Allison said. "Get her, Jack! She'll ruin everything!"

I raised my arms, back in *hanmi*.

"Keep him circling," Wyatt advised.

Harrington was trying to keep me away from the stairwell. I moved left, then right, evading a jab. "I should have known," I said. "You're not tied up, Allison." I ducked away from another jab and kept just out of Harrington's reach. "No shackles, no ropes. You weren't kidnapped at all, were you?"

"Shut up!" she said loudly. "Jack, come on! Finish her!"

"Get lower!" Wyatt yelled. "Get under his guard!"

"Bloodthirsty little bitch, aren't you?" I said. Harrington swung and I ducked. "Was it your idea to kill Wayne, once you had his money?"

She goggled at me. "Kill Wayne?" She stared at Harrington. "Jack? What is she talking about?"

"Shut up!" he snarled. He lunged at me, and I reacted too slowly. He slammed into me and we hit the wall next to the staircase. His fist plowed into my head and I saw stars.

Harrington was big and strong and fast, and I was smaller and very tired. I knew I couldn't hold out, and my *aikido* needed more room than I had. Harrington tried to crush me in a bear hug, but I stomped on his instep. He yelped and let me go, and I squirmed free. Allison threw the blanket at me, and

I tangled with it. Harrington kicked me in the ribs. All the air went out of me and I saw red. He picked me up and shoved me towards the stairwell.

"Claire!" Wyatt sprang forward, as if tackling Harrington, and passed right through him.

The railing of the spiral staircase slammed into my midsection. The spiral stairs flashed into view, and the long drop yawned below me. I felt my balance going, couldn't grab any air. But my hand struck the railing and out of sheer reflex I caught it. I swung over and past the opening to the stairwell below, and Harrington stumbled to his knees, avoiding the fall at the last minute. Now he was at the landing opening and I couldn't go down.

So I went up.

The rust was thick on the railing as I dashed up the few remaining steps to the landing. I pushed open the trap door at the top and cold wind hit my face. Even as I was thinking stupid move, I felt Harrington grasp my ankle, yanking. I pulled hard on my leg and he released me. I fell back onto my ass as the wind whipped around the bulk of the glass housing behind me. I struggled up, found myself facing the glass wall surrounding the light just as it flashed in my face.

Blinded, I blinked and grabbed onto a rung, and realized there was a set of rungs climbing the lantern room exterior, leading to the top of the lighthouse. Should I climb it? There would be nowhere to go. There was nowhere to go now.

Noise below, and then Harrington's head stuck out of the opening to the stairwell. I kicked at his head and missed, but he ducked down again. I heard machinery humming behind me—the turning light.

Wyatt popped into view. "Claire, he's got a gun!"

My vision cleared enough for me to see again, and I realized I was standing on the edge of a narrow circular platform nearly ninety feet above the ground. Across a mile and a half of open water, I saw the lights of San Francisco twinkling in the darkness. It was a hell of a view. I hoped it would not be my last one.

Shouts from below told me park rangers had spotted me, but my more immediate worry was Jackson Harrington. I circled the lantern room, keeping low, hugging the exterior walls. I didn't trust the rusted railing. Noises, and the echo of boots on metal; Harrington was climbing up to my level. Wyatt stepped backwards, and now was standing nonchalantly on the very rim of the platform, half on air. "He's coming around the other side," he said urgently. "Wait until he's on the opposite side of the stair, and then you can get down."

That might be true, but there was still Allison to contend with. Still, she didn't have a gun. I hoped. I edged further around the platform, wind stinging my eyes. A bird swooped in, as if to land, then suddenly veered away. I heard a scuffling noise from the other side of the platform.

Two more steps to the stairwell. One more step…

Allison Farley stuck her head out of the stairwell and saw me. "Jack! She's over here!"

"*Damn* the woman!" Wyatt said.

Jackson Harrington came around the opposite side of the platform with a gun in his hand. "Get down, Ally," he snarled. Her head disappeared below the platform. He raised the gun and aimed it at me.

And the lantern in the lighthouse rotated, the beam striking Harrington full in the face. He cried out, blinded, and flung up a hand to shield himself from the glare. I barrelled forward, knowing it was my only chance, and struck him in the middle of his body with my shoulder. He grunted, fell backwards against the railing.

With a crack the railing disintegrated in a shower of red flakes, and Jackson Harrington screamed all the way down to the pavement eight stories below.

Chapter 35

S uzette Melton was not happy. "Hell of a thing."
I was in the visitor's chair. She was behind her desk. Agent Leesa Kern had pulled a chair in from the bullpen. Wyatt Earp stood with one booted foot crossed over the other in the corner of Suzette's office, hands in pockets, looking bored.

"The DA won't press any charges against Allison Farley?" Agent Kern said.

"She's partly responsible for the death of Wayne Rafferty," I said. "Somebody ought to pay for that."

Suzette drank some coffee out of her cup. The doughnuts I'd brought were gone, leaving only memory and sugar dust. "Allison denies it. There's no proof to support it, other than what she said to you during your fight with Harrington. And of course she claims she was terrified, afraid Harrington would kill you and then blame her. Or something like that. Boils down to hearsay, or so the DA wants to believe."

"What about Dan Schaeffer?" I said. "Do you think Allison was in on that?"

"Probably," Wyatt said.

"Probably," Suzette said. "But we'll never know. We found a black Mercedes Benz sedan in Hunter's Point, burnt out. No license plates. The VIN matched one that was stolen last week, and the grill was bashed in, but we can't positively identify it as the car that hit Schaeffer."

"Harrington killed him?"

"Almost certainly," I said. "I think Allison is a plotter and a manipulator, but I don't think she's a killer." I thought about the ugly expression on Jackson Harrington's face when he was trying his damndest to kill me. "He was. She wasn't."

"She played him like a piano," Wyatt said. He shifted from one foot to another. "She's gonna get away with it."

"This is bullshit," Agent Kern said. She was in another classy suit, dark gray this time, with a white shirt and a quiet gold necklace. Very conservative, very tasteful, very government. Suzette was in black trousers, dark gray hip length sweater with a leather belt. I was stylishly laid back in my jeans and sweatshirt with the San Francisco Giants logo across the front. We were a fashion triumph. "I'll talk to the US Attorney. Maybe she'll file."

Suzette shrugged. "Knock yourselves out. But my money says that the judge will throw the case out if she does. There just isn't enough to prove that she wasn't kidnapped. We subpoenaed Wayne Rafferty's phone records, and got both recordings of Allison appealing to him. They'd look pretty convincing to a jury."

"Quite the little actress," Wyatt growled.

"So she walks?" Agent Kern said. "Three guys are dead, and she walks?"

"And what about the money?" Wyatt said.

"What about the money?" I said.

Suzette and Agent Kern looked at me. "You didn't hear?" Suzette said.

"I've been recovering for the last 24 hours." At her look, I felt my face get hot. "Yes, I slept. I actually slept, thank you."

"Congratulations," Suzette said. "I think I'll mark this day down in my diary."

Agent Kern looked from her to me. "What's the deal?"

"Claire doesn't sleep much," Suzette said to her. She looked back at me. "The park rangers found the money in a tool locker below the lighthouse. The key was on what was left of Jackson Harrington."

"All of it?"

"Three million and change." Suzette sipped coffee again, made a face. "I really need to get new filters for that coffee pot."

Agent Kern rubbed her eyes. "This has been a hell of a case. And now we get nothing out of it—no prosecution, no reward. And the drug connection goes under again."

Suzette peered at her. "I don't think there ever was a drug connection, Agent Kern."

"Sure there was," Agent Kern said bitterly.

"Look at it," Suzette said quietly. "All we had on Rafferty was rumor and speculation."

"Ron Stedman said Marty was dealing," she said.

"No," I answered for Suzette. "All he said was that Marty was present when drugs were being used."

"Marty Hancock tested clean in the Canada race," Suzette said. "I got the results from Montreal this morning."

"You found Marty's name in a couple of address books," I said. "That doesn't make him a user or a dealer. Just a guy who picks the wrong friends." I leaned forward and picked up my mug. The coffee was, indeed, memorably awful. "Marty may not be the brightest bulb in the chandelier, but he's clean."

"And I've personally confirmed with Narcotics that we have no suspicion, no probable cause to investigate Kenneth Mannheim, the race director."

"He's in import and export," Agent Kern said.

"That's not illegal." Suzette spoke calmly, but there was a hint of steel in her voice.

"She don't like that," Wyatt chuckled.

He was right. Agent Kern was frowning. She set her cup down. "I don't like your attitude."

"Ruins my day to hear that," Suzette said. "I'm all for co-operation with the Federals, Agent Kern, but I think you're way off base on this drug chase. And in any case, there is no reason for you to be pursuing a case which is solely in the jurisdiction of the Park Service and the San Francisco Police Department."

Sourly, Agent Kern pushed up out of her chair. "Sorry to see you take this position," she said. "I'll be filing a report with my superiors, recommending action against Allison Farley, and noting your non-cooperation."

She didn't even look at me as she left. I don't think she remembered I was there.

"Testy," Wyatt said. He looked longingly at the coffee cup Agent Kern had left behind.

"I hate when that happens," Suzette murmured.

"Being written up for non-cooperation? Used to happen to me all the time, and I survived." I leaned back in the chair. It squeaked. Maybe it was a law of the universe that any chair used by an investigator squeaked. Maybe I was too cheap to buy oil. Maybe the SFPD was, too.

Suzette opened her desk drawer, brought out my gun, and pushed it across to me. "I hate it when I get crossways with the Feds. Crazy as it may sound to an iconoclast like you, I like being on good terms with other law enforcement officers."

"Iconoclast? Are you doing the Sunday crosswords again? No one in the bullpen is going to take you seriously if you use words like that."

"I only use them with you."

"I'm flattered." I yawned. "My client is back in town. I've got a mid-afternoon appointment with him, but I'm free for lunch."

"Your turn to buy," Suzette said.

"Like hell," I said. "I haven't even been paid yet."

CHAPTER 36

I met my client the next morning. I had the windows open, but it was probably too late in the year for that. It didn't seem to matter to Marty Hancock, who sat red-eyed in my client chair.

"She won't see me," he said. "Won't answer her phone or email. When I went to that hotel she's staying at, she wouldn't open the door. She called security."

"Maybe she doesn't want to see you," I said. "It's probably for the best."

He frowned. "I don't believe you. I don't believe she staged her own kidnapping."

I sighed. I'd explained things to him twice. This would make it three times.

"It's hard to explain things any other way," I said. "She and Jackson Harrington probably had this planned from the day she met Wayne Rafferty. Harrington got greedy, started borrowing against the assets of the partnership. Rafferty was getting suspicious, and Harrington figured out a way to get all the money. He and Allison staged the kidnapping; she simply walked away from the crowd at the jump-off dock. In fact, Suzette Melton and I think the guy who 'accidentally' fell into the water got paid to do that, probably by Dan Schaeffer."

"He's the motorcycle guy? I'm confused." He was wearing khaki trousers, tasselled loafers with no socks and a very tight red sports shirt with a bike manufacturer's logo; it showed off his shoulders and pecs very nicely. When he rubbed his forehead in confusion, his well-defined forearms flexed pleasingly. It was all pleasing, until I saw the expression in his eyes. He really did not understand how he had been betrayed. It almost hurt to tell him. But knowing is better than not knowing, and he wasn't paying me to lie to him.

"Dan used to work for JackWay until Wayne caught him doing drugs. He had a mad on at Rafferty, and it wasn't hard for Harrington to convince him to join in the scheme. Harrington talked Rafferty into signing Dan's gang up as security, and that put Schaeffer in a position to squirrel Allison away."

I didn't tell him, but strongly suspected that it would have been part of Dan's job to kill Allison if she showed signs of wanting out of the deal. Or maybe even if she didn't.

"Dan made the ransom calls to Wayne," I continued. "With Allison joining in to plead with him if Harrington reported that he was dragging his feet. Meanwhile, Harrington sold off everything he could get his hands on. He pressured Rafferty to get the coroner to declare Allison dead so they could cash in the deeds in her name. Basically, they cleaned Wayne Rafferty out and planned to split the money three ways. Or maybe only two ways."

"This Harrington guy killed his own man?"

"Yeah." I remembered the sound of the car hitting Schaeffer, the sound of him hitting a slab of rock. I remembered his eyes changing when he died.

"But Allison, maybe she didn't know about all this," Marty said. "Maybe he talked her into the idea, but then didn't tell her about killing this Dan guy, or Wayne Rafferty. She didn't… didn't actually commit murder or anything."

"Maybe," I conceded. I wouldn't personally put anything past Allison Farley. "Legally speaking, a person who is part of a conspiracy is just as guilty of murder as the killer, even if they didn't personally kill anyone. If the DA was able to prove Allison was guilty of conspiracy to extort, she could also be charged with the murders of Dan Schaeffer and Wayne Rafferty."

At that point Wyatt entered the room in his usual manner, through a wall. I glanced at him and he nodded curtly at me. He walked around so he could see Marty's face, keeping his usual distance from me. It was safer that way.

"But she hasn't been charged," Marty said. He leaned forward, his body tense. "So maybe you're wrong. Maybe the DA is not charging her because she's innocent." The hope in his voice, in his eyes, was as pathetic as it was useless.

I felt a pain starting behind my eyes. I was tired, and my ribs still hurt from my fight with Jackson Harrington. "No, she's not, Marty. But nobody will ever prove it."

"You're wrong," Marty said stubbornly. "I know you are. Everyone was wrong about her being dead. Now they're wrong about her involvement. She's innocent. I'll tell her that. I'll tell her I believe in her. She'll talk to me again. We can be together again."

"He's a fool," Wyatt said quietly. "I guess love makes fools of us all."

I nodded, not caring what Marty made of it. "Suit yourself," I said glumly. "But you might have a hard time getting close to her now."

"Why now? Why wouldn't she talk to me?" Marty's fists clenched on his knees.

"This idiot is never going to pay you," Wyatt said, with disgust in his voice.

He was probably right.

"She won't talk to you because she's through with you," I said. "She was through with you the minute she found a millionaire she could charm. And now that she's got his money, she's really through with you."

"The money?" Marty said blankly.

I leaned back in my chair. It squeaked.

"That's the fun part of all this. In order to cash in the real estate deeds, Jackson Harrington turned over his share of the partnership to Wayne, to 'raise the ransom money'. Of course he knew he'd be getting the cash, so he didn't care about the partnership any more. Rafferty, thinking he was about to marry Allison, had made a will giving her everything. So when Jackson Harrington killed his partner, the money went to Allison. When the ransom money was recovered, and no charges were filed, the cops released it. And the only person left to release it to was Allison Farley, who has not been charged with anything."

There was a long silence as Marty digested this. "So... she's got three million now." He swallowed.

"Pretty clever gal," Wyatt commented. It didn't sound like a compliment. "Makes a black widow spider look innocent."

I agreed, silently. I watched as Marty wrestled with the facts as presented to him. "I know it's hard to hear," I said as gently as I could. "But the truth is always better, don't you think?"

He looked at me, despair in his eyes. Then he got up and walked out without a word. His step was slow, like a man with arthritis or a burden too heavy to bear.

"Well, damn," Wyatt said regretfully. "There goes your fee."

"Maybe I can bill Allison for rescuing her," I said. I sounded only a little bitter. I thought about the boat I'd used to get to the Rock, and the money I owed the owners. Where would I get that? But then, compared to what Rafferty and Shaeffer had lost, maybe it didn't matter.

Wyatt turned to look out of the window. The wind blew through him, affecting him not at all. "Marty didn't get what he wanted."

I thought about love and hope and greed, and the tendency of people to believe what they wanted.

"Who does?" I said.

THE END

When and how did Wyatt and Claire meet? Read
the first chapter of *Deadfall*, the first novel in the
Phantom Partner series from Sarah Stegall.

DEADFALL

CHAPTER 1

I wasn't supposed to be in that room, but then neither was the
corpse. He lay face up, arms flung wide, brown eyes open and
staring. Out of habit, I dropped to one knee (glad I hadn't worn
a skirt today) and felt for a pulse—nothing. I smelled burned
gunpowder and expensive aftershave—an interesting combination. No question this was my quarry, though; I recognized him
from the pictures. Thick, wavy brown hair, cleft chin, sculpted
cheekbones, sensual mouth; it was easy to see why so many
women found him attractive. His three wives had hired me to
find him and bring back the stuff he'd stolen.

Right now, though, I wanted to make sure this wasn't a party
of three. I stood and pulled my Colt Defender out of my purse
and checked the load. This very pricey suite of the St. Francis
hotel was designed to make anyone with an income of less
than six figures feel out of place. Large enough to play tennis
in, furnished in fake Victorian antiques—camel-back sofas, a
leather wingback chair, a rosewood secretary. Huge windows
on the left hand wall framed the view out over San Francisco's
Union Square, twelve stories down.

It took me only a moment to see that no one was hiding
behind the wet bar, and then I stepped to the open door to my
right. A little light spilled from the door behind me. As I groped
for the light switch with my left hand, I felt the hairs rise on my
neck. It felt as if someone in the darkness was watching me. I
froze, barely breathing, for a long moment. Hearing nothing, I
snapped on the light. I saw no one.

The master bedroom was a blue and gold confection almost
as large as the suite's living room. I knelt to check under the

bed—nothing but dust bunnies. I held my gun in both hands when I kicked open the closet doors—no bad guys jumped out. The bathroom would have impressed a Roman emperor, but it was empty. Nevertheless, I could not shake this jumpy feeling.

I pulled a tissue out of a box in the bathroom to guard against leaving prints, and searched the bedroom. I used my cell phone camera to take pictures from every angle. No papers, no missing jewelry, no large amounts of cash. Returning to the main room, I knelt by the corpse again. A quick pat-down confirmed that he didn't have the stuff on him. Damn.

I'd delayed the inevitable long enough. Although my instincts were still ringing alarms in my head, I speed-dialed a number I knew well.

"Homicide," said a clear voice. "Inspector Melton speaking." Suzette Melton was my oldest friend.

"Hi, Suzette," I said. "It's me, Claire Turnbull."

"Oh, hi, hon. Listen, can I call you back? Not to be rude, but I'm busy, busy."

"You're about to be busier. I'm standing in the most expensive suite at the St. Francis Hotel. Just thought you guys in Homicide would like to know that there's a dead man—"

Maybe it was reflex, maybe it was instinct, but I glanced up and saw a man standing fifteen feet from me, next to the windows. Tall and broad-shouldered, he wore a wide-brimmed black hat, a black suit and white shirt set off with a black waistcoat. A knee-length coat and coal-black polished boots added to the Amish undertaker look. His eyes were an icy blue, and he was staring at me.

I sprang to my feet, pulling out my gun. "Freeze!"

He looked at me blankly. I pointed the gun at him.

On the phone, Suzette said, "Claire?"

"Can you...can you see me?" the guy rumbled. He ignored my gun, looking at me with an expression between puzzlement and shock. "Who are you?"

"Never mind who I am. Put your hands where I can see them."

"Claire, what's going on?" Suzette's voice on the cell was sharp.

I cradled the cell phone against my shoulder, holding the gun out straight with both arms, as the Police Academy had taught me long ago. "Suzette, I'm at the St. Francis on Union Square, in the State Suite. There's a dead man on the floor, looks like he's been shot once in the chest. Bring backup."

"I'll be there in ten." She hung up.

I pointed the camera at the man in the black hat and clicked off a couple of pictures. He paid no attention. "Put your hands on your head," I said.

He didn't move, staring at me intensely. "Good God." It sounded like a prayer, not an oath. "You can hear me, too?"

Nut job. Great. I tightened my grip on the gun. The only thing worse than a frightened perp was a calm one. "Hands on your head," I said. I tried to sound firm and authoritative, but something about him sent shudders through me. Was it the eyes? The stillness about him? Something in the way he was standing, hands at his sides, focused. It felt like someone had aimed a spotlight at me.

"I hear you fine," I said. "Now put your hands up."

He slowly lifted his hands about shoulder high.

"Now I want to know who you are and what you're doing here," I said. "And what you know about this." I jerked my head at the dead man.

"That's a lot of questions," the tall man said laconically. "Reckon I better come back later. You stay here. I have to go find someone."

"The hell you do! Stay right—hey!"

He turned to his right and walked through the wall.

Astonishment paralyzed me for a moment. Then I ran to the bank of windows and looked down on Union Square, thronged with cars and tourists. There was no body sprawled on the sidewalk. There was no ledge, no fire escape, just a straight twelve-story drop. I looked up and saw only blue sky. The window was locked from the inside. My stomach tensed.

Where had he gone? And more importantly, how?

I heard the ding of the elevator down the hallway and figured my time was up. I put the Colt in my purse just as two uniformed members of San Francisco's finest halted in the doorway. One of them was Jimmy Gilbert. I knew him from my days on the Force.

I didn't know his partner, a woman. They advanced with their hands on their guns.

"Hi, Jimmy," I said.

"Claire Turnbull? Uh, hi." He looked from me to the dead guy and back. "What's going on?"

"Came in and found him like this," I said. "The rest had better wait for Inspector Melton."

"Yeah, okay," he said uneasily. I had heard that tone before—something between camaraderie with a (former) fellow officer, and wariness with a possible suspect. It wasn't a tone you forget easily.

I held out my purse. "You'll want to hold this until she gets here," I said. "My gun's in it. Where do you want me to wait?"

He jerked his head and I went to stand against a wall. I heard more elevator dings, and the sound of voices. The circus was arriving.

Author's Note

The Alcatraz Triathlon is fictional, but it is based on the many race meets, swim meets, bicycle races and triathlons that are run in the San Francisco Bay Area every year. For information about triathlons and races in the Bay Area, I am indebted to Keith Maness, who has worked in race coordination for many years. He was generous with his time, advice and information; any inaccuracies in this book regarding racing are entirely my own. Thanks, Keith.

Contrary to FBI lore, it is very possible to swim from Alcatraz Island to either the San Francisco shore or to Angel Island; in fact, thousands of people a year do just that. Most of them wear wetsuits, but even without a wetsuit, it is possible to swim in the cold waters of the Bay. If you can persuade them to come in out of the water on a sunny afternoon, any member of the Dolphin Club can tell you that people have been swimming in the Bay since 1877.

Anyone interested in the history of Alcatraz before it became the home of Big Al and all the rest, can do no better than to consult *Fortress Alcatraz: Guardian of the Golden Gate*, by John Arturo Martini. Written by a former park ranger and noted historian, this meticulously researched history of the Rock details the many building projects, extant and abandoned, that honeycomb the island. He also describes the boxing matches staged on the island in the 1920s, with guests ferried over from San Francisco. Given Wyatt Earp's history as a referee and boxing aficionado, it's easy to imagine him at ringside on a Friday night, watching the "barely restrained mayhem".

Credit must also go to *A History of Alcatraz Island,* by Greg L. Wellman, which is a gold mine of old photographs of the prison and military fortress.

The lighthouses of California have a long and varied history, none of them as well-established as Alcatraz, the first lighthouse on the West Coast. I am indebted to Aileen Weintraub's *Alcatraz Island Light* and to Ray Jones' *California Lighthouses* for information on this venerable light station, still doing its job after nearly 160 years.

Wyatt's tale of Floyd Hamilton and three other men escaping from Alcatraz to the water on April 14, 1943 is true. Hamilton and his brother Raymond had robbed banks with Clyde Barrow and Bonnie Parker for awhile, and in fact Raymond had been executed in 1935. Two of the escapees in 1943 were recaptured, and Hamilton hid out in the cave for three days before climbing back up the Rock, where he was found. But one of the runaways, James Boarman, was never seen again, and no body was found. The FBI presumed that he drowned.

But then, the cops also presumed that Allison Farley drowned...

ABOUT THE AUTHOR

Sarah Stegall is the author of *Deadfall*, *Farside*, *Chimera* and other novels. She researched and co-wrote the first three *Official Guides to The X-Files*, which spent fourteen weeks on the New York Times bestseller list. She has written for TOPPS, TVGuide Online, and SFScope.com. She has been reviewing science fiction and fantasy movies, books and television since 1994, and her critiques are widely cited in academic works.

After earning a BA in honors liberal arts from the University of Texas, where she majored in drama, philosophy and English literature, she was a stage manager, video editor and technical writer.

Sarah lives in northern California. Visit her at www. munchkyn.com.

COLOPHON

The text for this book was set in Adobe Caslon Pro, a variation of the typeface designed by William Caslon (1692 – 1766). Caslon is one of the world's most popular and readable fonts. Benjamin Franklin was fond of it and employed it extensively in his printing press. The United States Declaration of Independence and the Constitution were set in Caslon type for their first printings. Adobe Caslon was designed by Carol Twombly.